A WYATT BOOK *for*

W

— ST. —
MARTIN'S
PRESS

Saudade

$(\text{SOW} \cdot \text{DAHD}')$

A Portuguese word

considered untranslatable.

One definition: Yearning so intense

for those who are missing, or for

vanished times or places,

that their absence is the most

profound presence in one's life.

A state of being, rather than

merely a sentiment.

SAUDADE

Katherine Vaz

A Wyatt Book for St. Martin's Press
New York

Portions of this book have appeared as:

"Original Sin" (*Black Ice*, 4, 1988, Belmont, Massachusetts); "Fado" (*Triquarterly*, 76, Fall 1989, Evanston, Illinois); and "Add Blue to Make White Whiter" (*Other Voices*, 12, Summer/Fall 1990, Highland Park, Illinois).

Design by Sara Stemen

Library of Congress Cataloging-in-Publication Data

Vaz, Katherine.
Saudade / Katherine Vaz.
p. cm.
ISBN 0-312-11055-3
1. Portuguese Americans—California, Northern—Fiction.   2. Women, Deaf—California, Northern—Fiction.   I. Title.
PS3572.A79S28   1994   94-2042
813'.54—dc20   CIP

First Edition: June 1994
10 9 8 7 6 5 4 3 2 1

*for José Francisco de Carvalho
and Ana Clementina Vaz*

BOOK I

ONE

The mermaid who fell in love with a mortal man asked for feet so she could hurry to him from the sea. She wanted her green tail split into legs to wrap around him. The water-gods warned that if she ventured into another world, her new body would constantly tremble, and each step would cut like a sword.

Despite this she said, "I must go." As she ran toward the man's arms, her scales littered the ground like mother-of-pearl monocles and enclosed, as if in skins, the blood that dropped from her freshly carved feet. Many water-children arose from this trail, all doomed to sharp pains on land.

They made their homes in the islands of the Azores, which float like the shells of enormous ashy turtles in the Atlantic. Many of the men spent long months away on fishing voyages. Some women, while running to the incoming fleets to discover which fishermen had survived, removed their shoes in the hope that stones would lacerate their feet. A sacrifice of slicing the body might forfend a slicing of the heart. They bled on the sand like the first ocean beauty and waited for the men to sail in on the tenders sent ahead from the ships. No one but the water-gods could distinguish the night howls of making love from the keening of the newly widowed, and they wound their sentences like lassos of kelp around the women who crouched alone: "Come to us; come back—the ocean is your steadfast groom."

"Water is a rich drink, but it pours through our fingers, and with the fish we could have many affairs, but they slip instantly away," the women moaned. "Flesh we can hold, if only for a while."

"Good luck, then," the water-gods concluded, "for here is the mark on your brow: The feeling of Absence will become your truest Presence. Your longing will wax until it becomes the giant looming at your side."

DURING THE FAREWELL party in his honor, José Francisco Cruz became desperate for an answer to his nagging question about the sea. In his nervousness he checked the contents of his sailor's knapsack often enough for the guests to tease him.

"Forget to pack your head, Zé?" said Henrique Cerqueira, laughing. He was his closest friend, who milked cows for such interminable hours hoping to save money for America that his hands were swollen into bleached sacs, each with five teats. At night his wife had to bathe them in cold camomile water because they were too heavy for him to lift over the side of the bed.

"No," said José Francisco, "I'm making room in case your hands want to go along as stowaways."

Everyone, including his pregnant wife, Conceição, figured that he was distracted because this would be his first trip to the mainland and his first long fishing voyage. He was leaving his island of Terceira in the Azores, out in the Atlantic, to sail to Nazaré on the coast of Portugal, where he would join a five-month cod expedition to Newfoundland. He preferred that everyone think he was green about such a large undertaking; his real quandry was too embarrassing.

"Have some wine," said Conceição as she carted plates out to their old stone mill wheels used as picnic tables. She gave him her look that made it clear she was wondering about his oddness.

He smiled. Should he chance sounding like a fool by asking her? He was not certain that she could explain the secret of the ocean that was troubling him, but she might offer some words of comfort.

"Ah . . . Conceição?" he began.

She turned but then had to abandon him to greet Maria

4

Josefa Magalhães, who had left her husband snoring in his chair at home and arrived with *nógado*, made with the leaves of an orange tree, ten eggs, olive oil, and a liter of honey. (Maria Josefa incessantly tidied and cleaned everything. She was a relentless hunter of stains, and José Francisco suspected that she would be no help in solving his messy and mysterious puzzle.)

The sky was turning forged-iron gray and iris-purple. At a loss for what to do, uneasy at being a host, he stuffed a glove with dried lima beans to make an udder and hid it at Henrique's seat, marked by a name card, at one of the tables. Henrique brought green, white, and red wines and crabs, lobsters, and coins stuck in apples for good luck. He came bearing *abrotea* fish for grilling, black *morcela* sausages, salted tomatoes, pork with clams and red peppers, and eels killed with tobacco in the water to remove their slime. Instantly he was swept into an argument with Maria Josefa about the right way to cook pork. If only José Francisco could have a private moment to speak with him!

The arrival of Senhor and Senhora Dutra was a further interruption, and it took all his reserves of strength not to run to the opposite end of the garden. He hated parties; he never had any skill with what passed as light conversation. Particularly not with the Dutras, who were so boring that they repeated every word in their many-times-told tales ("there there once once was was a a time time"), since they thought that their ears soaked up one set of words and their listeners needed another. They were carrying nothing but pictures of their son's wedding. José Francisco picked up one of Henrique's good-luck apples and tossed it up and down, trying to appear nonchalant as he signaled his friend to come to his rescue.

Too late. "So so! Looking looking forward forward to to the the trip trip?" asked the rotund Senhor Dutra heartily. He would have clapped José Francisco on the back had he not stepped aside, gesturing more wildly for Henrique to save him.

"Right," said José Francisco. He paused, forgetting whether

the Dutras required the same verbal doubling in return if they were to hear anything. "Right," he added, to be polite.

"Tell tell us us," began Senhora Dutra.

Her torrent was blocked as Henrique, discovering that he had been seated next to the Dutras, threw the glove-udder at his friend's head. Under the shower of lima beans, José Francisco was able to escape.

Henrique tracked him down near the entrance to the fig orchard. "I'll strangle you," he said. "Mother of God—the *Dutras.*"

"Eh—wait. Henrique," said José Francisco, the huge sticky fig leaves in the trees like hands over him in the twilight. "Can you tell me something? I've been told that anyone who goes to sea must be careful not to taste the Soup of Sorrow. Do you have any idea what that is?"

Henrique thumped the side of his head with fingers swollen to the size of trout, as he always did when trying to tap a memory. "I've heard that a person understands what it is only after he's already drunk it, and then it's too late. That's one of the things that makes it sad." He shrugged. "Sorry, I'm a landlubber."

"I was just curious," said José Francisco, returning to his party before anyone could comment on his absence. Father Teo Eiras was, as usual, allowed to work at the grill. He was never expected to bring anything. Cooking was ostensibly his contribution, but everyone knew that it was really a distraction to spare them all, because conversation outside of food was so difficult for him that he broke into an awkward sweat. If he perspired over a fire, no one would notice, and busying his hands relieved much of the need for talking. José Francisco decided to swallow his usual (and silly, according to Conceição) dislike of the clergy. Maybe Father Eiras was a repository of wisdom about the Soup of Sorrow and could counsel him. As he approached, though, he noticed the priest pilfering off the grill and taking a bite out of something that he then slipped to Maria Josefa. José Francisco turned away in disgust. Better to drink a vat of the dangerous soup than to ask a grill-pig for advice!

Everyone was eating and drinking, and Conceição, despite her pregnancy, was moving about and laughing as she capped the filled glasses of the guests with heels of bread to ward off flies. She was better with people than he was, and strong as a cabbage rose—small but hard-muscled, with a bow at the nape of her neck and a birthmark of a wine-colored candle in the cove at the base of her throat. He managed to endure the dinner and the endless toasts with wine, which he drank until a fuzziness could transport him away from everyone but her.

Alone in their room, they made love while standing, with her legs wrapped around him. Suspended and clinging to him, she felt as she did when they had first met on a boat—tough as a barnacle fastened to an anchor; completely around him; feet off the land. He liked the sense that he was penetrating something he had uplifted. Lovely Conceição, whose eyes, brown, the size of sparrows' heads, flew inside everything; who swam naked; who slept with a pillow between her knees to keep the cartilage from grinding together.

"O, mine!" he cried from the suddenness of realizing how long he would be gone.

That night when she saw him standing by the window, she left their bed to go and put a hand gently on his arm. "It's perfectly fine to be a little afraid," she said.

"It's not that," he said, then lowered his voice. "Listen, dear—have you heard about the Soup of Sorrow? Do you know what's in it? No one can tell me, and I was thinking that if I figured it out, then—then wouldn't I have enough warning? To avoid it?"

She thought a moment, leaning on the windowsill next to him. The moon painted white caps on the trees as they looked out together. "My grandfather mentioned the Soup of Sorrow once," she said. "He said it was different for everyone."

"But what happens? How will I guess if I've had it?"

"I think he said that the taste would never leave you. You'll end up searching for it, needing to drink it forever. Teachers who taste it in their schoolrooms must teach forever. A poet who drinks it while writing must work on verses until he dies. Sailors who have it at sea must keep returning to the water. That's all I remember." She grinned. "If you do find some, don't drink too much."

"It doesn't sound bad, if I like to sail in the first place," he murmured, kissing her forehead to hide his confusion.

The next morning as he embarked for Nazaré, he forgot momentarily about the Soup of Sorrow. He could think only about how far he was going, and he had to be pried out of Conceição's arms. The waving white handkerchiefs of his friends were like violent slices of cloud, like a release of manic doves.

JOSÉ FRANCISCO CRUZ watched the women of Nazaré stretch sea-dampened nets dyed cobalt, olive, and orange over the shoreline's mosaic sidewalk. The women wore brightly flow-ered blouses with plaid skirts of unmatching shades and were like a troop of moving garlands as they worked. He sat in the long line of fishermen mending tears in the nets with lilac thread, or jade-green, or whatever anyone felt was the color of the day. At a distance, farther down the row facing the beach, the thread was invisible to José Francisco as arms guiding needles swayed in unison to give the ocean a concert with ghost violins. The violin playing was slow and even, and the song of the men was so elegant and silent that it seemed mournful.

He was already homesick and felt out of place because he was not wearing trousers and a shirt in jumbled plaids like the Nazarean men, and his notes as a musician of the nets were jittery and a step off-key because too much was new to him. He considered asking the fisherman next to him about the Soup of Sorrow, but the man never glanced up from his work as salt dried lime-white in the weave of the strings and the creases in his hands, and he had cataracts that were like sea haze drifting across his eyes.

I should ask him, thought José Francisco; it looks as if this guy has drunk barrels of it.

But he was afraid of how his islander's accent would sound. He took refuge in a nearby café. A waiter brandished a bowl of fish stew at him, and although he was hungry and the steam was laced thickly with the smell of peppers and onions, he hesitated. It might be the Soup of Sorrow.

"Forget it. Bring me a steak with a fried egg and a bottle of wine," he said a bit harshly, in case he had to show that he knew the waiter had been trying to trick him.

Dismay at his brusqueness with the waiter made José Francisco eat quickly. He missed Conceição: He could picture her leaning over to admire the abyss near the village of Biscoitos, where jellyfish parachuted, their quivering heads growing round at the water's surface. He saw her brushing her hair while bent over to entice him into climbing onto her from behind, or dabbing vanilla as a fragrance behind her ears, or chewing dried fava beans during the cravings of pregnancy. Longing clutched in a fist inside him.

He grabbed his knapsack and as an apology to the waiter left a tip that was more than the price of the lunch. Once outside, he had to restrain himself from waving at the docked boats painted crimson, sienna, cream, and sky-blue and decorated, as the Phoenicians had done to protect voyagers, with eyes on either side of the prows. The eyes, in spite of their flashy sockets, seemed to grow heavy as the boats bobbed in the water under the rhythm of the violin concert of the men. Pursuing the secrets of the Soup of Sorrow was futile—that much he suspected—but he could not resist running to the ship's cook, who was heading for the gangplank with a cauldron and utensils bundled like sticks on his back. José Francisco was sure that long after storms died, the cook's deeply wrinkled face would still course with filled riverbeds.

"Sorry to trouble you," said José Francisco, pointing to the forks and spoons tarnished and bent as if they had stirred acid, "but do these prepare the Soup of Sorrow?"

The cook laughed and set down the cauldron. "This again. Look, nobody can prepare you ahead of time, because what turns out to be the Soup of Sorrow to one man is nothing to another. Relax. You won't understand it—"

"Until I've tasted it! And then it's too late! I know!" cried José Francisco. He wanted to ask what exactly everyone feared about it, or why a sailor should worry about a soup that might enchant him into returning to the sea, but he was tired of riddles. To be safe, however, he resolved that once on board he would consume nothing but dried meat, maybe chickpeas, and avoid anything that might be a siren's song.

IN THE FREEZING waters around the Grand Banks, José Francisco fished in his own dory, like the other men alone in theirs, before returning to the ship in the evening. They pushed increasingly farther afield in pursuit of the harvest, plowing through the rows and acres of codfish. One morning he disappeared in the fog, but he was smart enough not to row aimlessly. He would let the ship read the currents and find him. There was no cause for panic. Settling into the boat's shell and, to keep from being seasick, staring where the horizon occasionally split the impenetrable curtain, he ate raw cod, and when he was thirsty, he would wring his woolen cap to drink the mist out of it. When he urinated, he tried to hit the fish. It was cold but not unpleasant, and the night arrived as wondrous as a cave that gapes in front of a boy, but as the second night approached he felt helplessly unmoored and spoke his name aloud, hoping to stamp it in large letters on the heavens. Instead his voice mixed with the groans of the dead sailors that are inseparable from the winds because the weight of their bellowing is too massive to ascend. His name was torn up in the flurry and swirled lost within the last words of the dead. Where was his rescue? He would never get home! Would the fish abandon him to starvation? Would he have to save the last one's dorsal bone to pare strips of himself to chew until, half-gone, a man of latticed muscle, loneliness would drive him to plunge a hand through the prison bars of his ribs and squeeze his heart to end his misery?

As he curled up inside the hull, creatures bumped underneath to overturn him and black waves curled over the edge like claws. He had to replace ideas of carnage with living red memories—reds that could flare out of his head as a summons to the ship: Redness of his birth. Red bloom of childhood—Mother had shrunk her days into little red pellets by whining steadily of minor ailments. *Ai, ai, ai. AI* was marked naturally on hyacinths. Good on flowers, tedious from mothers. Brought her roses. Forgot to check them for insects. Said, "Stop screaming, Mamãe. Ladybugs are good luck!" Caught measles. Was wrapped with red flannel to draw out poison. Built a fort with crimson brocade pillows. Mosquito bites. Mixed baking soda with burgundy wine for poultices. Useless. Drank the wine. Better. Got slapped red by Papai. Worth it. Tomatoes (relish in eating them destroyed when informed they were slang for *testicles*). First kiss (Luisa, age ten)—got slapped red. Worth it. Eyes inflamed circles from reading Dante and Cicero. Tried a trick of the ancient mariners one night: dipped hands in a red tide while on a boat between the islands of Pico and Faial; held fluorescent hands over a map in the dark to read it. Lobsters. Paprika. Cocks' combs. Conceição, red flower, red lips, wine-colored candle. Declarations of love: blushes. Red flushes.

His Tio Mario had his throat slashed in an argument over a drink. He died with a smile of blood on his neck. José Francisco took it as a warning that he could say, "Life is a narrow red grin." Or he could say, "Life is a prism and its spectrum throws down everything from red to clearness."

He stared upward, waiting to see what the air above shed on him. The white stars soaked up his red thoughts and changed into the color of the Azorean night wish:

> *Sonhos na cor-de-rosa.*
> Pink dreams. I wish you pink dreams.
> Rest in a light that is a gentle shade.
> *Steer with our pink lanterns toward morning.*

He slept soundly as an infant in a crib under the redness he had spread as a blanket in the night, under the shining pinkness it tucked around him in return, as the swells rocked him.

The sky was like pale opals when he awakened with the absolute calm that comes from dropping into the middle of terror and continuing to fall through it and out the opposite side. He assembled the best possible celebration within his reach by squeezing the moisture in his cap into a tin cup and flavoring it with some cod bones and a twig that floated along, a vegetable already salted. It was the perfect banquet. He slid a wet strip of his shirt back and forth between his lips to blow music from a cloth harmonica and leaned back in his shell as the surges of the waves kept time with his pulses.

He sat up with a start. A swimmer in cold water is in the greatest peril when in the midst of stroking along he seems to enter a warm, well-lit tunnel. His core temperature changes and he forgets where he is. He does not realize that he has invaded a bright but dangerous dream until it is too late, because while there he thinks, I'm not at sea, but in a safe harbor.

Actually in succumbing to the dream, he is lost to all but the dream.

He will want to stay with its serenity even if it kills him.

He will need to keep searching for it if he reenters the cold.

José Francisco sealed his face with his hands and sobbed. "For me it was a bone and a plant and a fog and the sea, but I have made myself the Soup of Sorrow."

He was enamored of water.

It was like the taste of Conceição.

Love condemned anyone who had drunk of it to return to it, somehow, again and again. The beautiful shackles: the embrace, then the sadness of the embrace gone.

He wiped his face and stood in the dory. The ship was drawing closer out of the distance to retrieve him. He would be rescued, although not from the dream into which he had fallen, and not from the melancholy fate lurking within all passions. He would be taken home, where he could go on learning the longer sorrows of love.

THEY WHISPERED WORDS over the crib to open their daughter's ears—*mão, são, pão; sim, mim, latim; nó, farol, girassol*—and any words with the swallowed letters and hummed endings that would mix with air to create a chiming cloud. This cloud was referred to in Portuguese lands as the white sound, the mist of reverberations that rose from the throats and guts and mouths of speakers to hover in a white buzzing overhead. High over the marketplace or plaza, the white sound hung like a comfortable canopy. José Francisco and Conceição thought that steering some white sound toward Clara might penetrate her deafness and tap its soft rain on the stiffened drums inside her. She had been born with both hands clamped over the sides of her head, and although her arms eventually lowered, she appeared to hear no noises and offered no sound.

Every morning when he was not at sea, at home on the island of Terceira in the Azores, José Francisco took her, dozing against his chest, to visit the corn. The green husks in a tight clasp over each ear reminded him of children with their hands raised to block out clamor: The corn was deaf and sealed away. "Here are your brothers and sisters, Clara," he said. He sang hymns and chanteys until his bones vibrated with music. "Can you feel my singing?" He had not guessed that sorrow would take the form of invading her, or that it would rob him of her cries.

He wondered if she sponged up his quavering when he spoke to her about the night of his red thoughts and the stars that had turned pink, because although she uttered nothing as the years passed, not a cough, not a sigh, she mastered color adventures: She became yellow when she ate mashed carrots, her mouth curving in soundless amusement, and she especially liked beets for making her lavender. Conceição was proud of her daughter's insistence that foods would be paints.

Like steam from a teakettle, Clara was light but sharp, directed, and uncatchable. Soon she was roaming into gardens throughout the village of Agualva to lie prone and inhale the coffee grounds, prawn shells like peelings of sunburned skin, lemon rinds, and eggshells that were stored in canisters in all the homes until a homemade-brandy odor signaled that the compost was ready for mulching. No one could teach her not to wander into places uninvited to stretch inside a square of sunlight. With her animal patience she could sit against churned earth for hours, like a tiger calmly awaiting its prey. Maria Josefa Magalhães, during sessions of scrubbing the black shadows on Agualva's pathways, convinced that they were traps that would snare the rabbits, often came across her holding silent court with the corncob dolls made by her father, their milk-teeth dried into ridged jewels. Maria Josefa could never remove very many shadow-traps and needed to protect something: She would cover her own eyes and trace pretend-tears down her cheeks to caution Clara that she must not stare directly at the sun. She believed the girl had ordered her mother's womb to shut down and leave her an only child—in mangling her ears, it had lost its right to try again. (Some people said that Clara's ear covering at birth had been to deflect the screams of the world, but Maria Josefa sided with those who felt Clara had come out refusing to listen to anybody.)

One morning when José Francisco was singing, Clara bolted around, touching the floor so that sounds could travel through her palms and soles, or up her spine as though it were a xylophone. She lowered her ear to the ground and smiled.

"Keep going," said Conceição. "You've reached her."

He sang until his lungs almost burst from flooding out notes and white sounds while leaning down to let Clara position her head against his ribs, without moving from the rise and fall of him. Every night after that he danced with her for a serenade from his bones, pressing her head to his heart so that she could feel his ballads and nonsense-tunes converting him into whirring tissue and purring skeleton, a body's lullaby.

Once while listening to the roar of the sea caught in a nautilus shell, it occurred to him that if the ocean could throw its voice into objects, forcefully enough for them to retain a maritime song even when they were on land, then he could do the same. He practiced projecting his melodies into the chorus lines of limpet and conch shells that he strewed through the house. They jangled, Come dance! Dance with me!

When Clara grabbed the ones he had set astir, he and Conceição were elated.

By adjusting the angles of the shells, switching them around on shelves, or heaping them into pyramids, their reception of his voice improved. How quickly Clara clutched one to feel it vibrating told them which were the first to spring alive with tremors. He also wanted to reach his wife and daughter from a ship, just as the sounds of the sea could still inhabit shells inside someone's house. Once he commanded them from close range, he sang from the chicken coop until Conceição leaned out the window to yell, "She's grabbed one up! It's working!" He pushed into farther territory, projecting from down the road, or the market, or while ocean swimming to test how well he would fly to them from the water.

Conceição smashed uncooperative shells with the hammer, mixed them into a paste with water, and molded new shapes, cubes, donkeys, and bowls, scattering them until she detected where they thrived as collectors of music. She stretched the curtains to the sill and nailed them into taut eardrums. The prize receiver and transmitter was a queen conch, its puckered lip facing outward on the mantel and its own anthem of the ocean blending with the harmonies of José Francisco.

When the shells were stubbornly quiet, Conceição filled a fountain pen with lemon juice and drew jottings that soaked into the paper. She then held the seemingly blank paper a close but safe distance over a burning candle, and rust-colored bars and circles appeared, converting the unspoken messages of the lemons into visible designs. Clara would run outside, return with an armful of lemons, and stamp her feet to urge her mother to make every one of them speak in shapes.

The mightiest success with the flight of music happened when José Francisco went pier fishing with Henrique Cerqueira, whose hands were so bloated from milking that José Francisco had to help him bait his hook. They drank beer and spent the afternoon untangling their lines as Henrique, gesturing with his enormous hands, told once again his favorite tale of the big cow riot. "It started when we untied them one day and fed them sunflowers, since we had run out of grain," he began.

"And having guts full of sunflowers made them stampede outside to turn their faces toward the sun!" thundered José Francisco.

"Whose story is this?"

"After you."

"We couldn't catch them. The flowers and the heat had made them too drunk, and—"

José Francisco rolled laughing on the pier. He knew how it ended.

"Zé, would you quit interrupting? The best story of my career, the finest—"

"Shut up and go on."

"They went crazy sucking one another's udders. We had to tie them up, but it took ten men at a time to pull them apart. We were soaked with milk by the time the riot was over."

The two men pretended to be lovesick cows and howled loud

opera, their heads thrown back under the brilliant yellow cape of the sun. Patches of algae glittered like eyes in the distant water.

When José Francisco was returning home, humming fragments of the afternoon's songs, Conceição rushed to meet him. "Hurry," she said, grabbing his hand to pull him along. "Keep singing and hurry."

Clara was posed in front of the mantel, with her eyes closed and face tilted skyward, egg yolk–smooth. Her arms were raised high and unshaking above her head as antennae, and she did not move. They could both see that silence was no barrier to their daughter being someone who not only loved a triumph but who liked to declare it in a grand pose.

"She's been like that for a while now," said Conceição. "How did you do it? You skipped over the shells and went right through her arms and into her." She stroked her daughter's waves of brown hair. Behind them was the queen conch, like a trumpet from the sea. Maybe reaching toward it had taught Clara to extend her hands upward to claim her father's music as her own.

Though they tried, setting Clara in the same position and having Henrique on the pier (to his delight) retell the tale of the big cow riot, followed by the same renditions of opera, her expression did not again contain the same signs of such a transport and possession by her father's music. It was a onetime gift that did not bleed over the edges of the moment in which it had occurred, but it was enough for José Francisco to banish thoughts of sorrow, forgetting how it bides its time and feeds upon joy before performing its works.

MARIA JOSEFA MAGALHÃES had arms like ropes from scrubbing everywhere that shadows stained her house. Black pools crept over the floors and the chair where her husband drank whiskey and snored, black drips surrounded the dishes her children left in the sink, and the sun threw its mud on the walls. She could not understand why she was not winning her battle with the shadows, since blackness appeared in the water pail when she wrung out the rags. Obviously she was trapping some of the shadows but not enough. Her chores were interrupted one morning by the discovery that young Clara had stolen into the house to eat sugar from a sack in the cupboard. Ordinarily Maria Josefa would have swept up the spilled grains quickly and, tongue clicking, sent her home, but she was exhausted with being fastidious. She cupped some sugar and held it out to say, "I'm glad you're my visitor! Take as much as you want."

Maria Josefa was not exactly sure what was prompting her to try to speak with sugar to the little girl. Maybe it was the impulse to be sweet, or simply to use whatever was at hand. So great was her sudden desire to get through to Clara—to get through to *someone*—that she was not in the least surprised that Clara immediately understood this sugar-language and added several grains to the mound in Maria Josefa's hand to say, "Thank you."

Maria Josefa divided the sugar into equal amounts in each palm, trusting that this said, "Don't worry. Everything is shining. We have invented a new language."

Clara pressed these sugar-hills flat, letting cascades run over the rims of their clasping. The sugar sealed itself in a sandy glimmer between them. ("I agree," or "I take hold," or "Life is too brief to marry shadows.")

After that, speaking with sugar seemed so easy—desiring to understand each other was all it took to learn it—that Maria Josefa wondered why no one had thought of it before. She and Clara got together for sugar-speaking every morning, and they conceived many other sugar-phrases that were soon adopted by the rest of the village of Agualva, including:

a mound of sugar with a thumbprint in the center	=	"You may rest here."
a pinch of sugar tossed in the air	=	"Welcome," or sometimes, "What a nice dress."
salt mixed with sugar on the tongue	=	"I'm so hungry" (+ gesture to stomach), or "I'm so thirsty" (+ gesture to throat), or "I'm so sad" (+ gesture to heart).
sugar stamped underfoot	=	"No," or "I don't know," or "You're as stubborn as a tar stain/the other Agualvense in this village."

a sprinkling on the speaker's head	=	"Come kiss me."
sugar dissolved in water	=	"He/she/it drowned," or "He/she/it died."

Some words were patted into rough shapes with sugar—*cat, cow, eggs, boat, ferns, lava, wine, lobsters, America, Virgin Mary.* The nice thing about sugar-pictures was that they retained the essence of the words they had been, even after being frugally scraped back into their containers, where they intersected other sugar-pictures so that when used in cooking, within flans and cakes or suspended in coffee, there drifted lobster-cats, wine-filled ferns, the Virgin piloting boats to the New World.

José Francisco spoke to Clara in rock sugar. (Large crystals studding a fig = "Let's pick up some figs before they turn the orchard into a purple carpet." A treat afterward: The sugar rocks dissolved into syrup to sweeten the fruit.) Sugar-speaking did not prevent him from also calling out white sounds, and her name; nor did it curtail his concerts. He taught her to hold his lips so that fingers bouncing in the right cadence could touch upon the lyrics.

When she had her first period, her expressions contorting in terror, since she could not scream, her mother made sugar men and women to explain love and birth. Clara drew her finger in a jagged edge around a circle of sugar. ("What?" or "What a joke," or "Monsters?")

Eugénio, Maria Josefa's thirteen-year-old son, liked to scatter a sugar trail up to Clara. ("Let's go exploring.")

It was not merely the humidity that slowed their walks, the heat making their feet squish in their shoes like flat, moist abalone, but because this was a time of peace. They loved to inspect the houses, to compare what people used to brace open the windows. Every sill was an air-altar, with cowbells, scrimshaw teeth, Buddhas from Macau, pumice sanded into oxen, and bulls' horns that acted as the grunting Atlases under the weight of wooden frames. Windows with tropical warping rested like stuck guillotines on bottles that had been put in trees to have sex with blossoms and now held full-grown oranges. Through these openings into houses, Eugénio heard loud arguments and also caged canaries trilling, advising Death that they were the house's smallest animals and should be taken first, leaving the family's children unharmed. He and Clara both saw peach-colored straw hats, crocheted antimacassars, *oratórios*, saints' statues painted with new dresses in thanks for favors, cutwork tablecloths, miniature windmills made from fig-tree wood shaved into strips, and faceless corn-leaf dolls. (Eugénio said of these, Round of sugar with a jagged edge = "Monsters.") They smelled lemon oil, garlic, cinnamon, corn bread, and spider-crabs, and they tasted white São Jorge cheese anointed with hot piri-piri sauce on bread, handed to them through the windows. Arcs of flung sugar followed them as they walked, like rice at a wedding. ("Pleasant sailing!" or "Sweet rains to you!" or "Visit me again.") What to feel? There were the rain-stiffened sheets hanging from clotheslines, no longer soft ghosts, but ghosts hard and starched, feeling as dried potato-water does on the skin. Eugénio chewed the rain out of the women's underwear dancing on the lines, while Clara's hair leapt with electricity to meet the empty trousers. Afterward, collapsing, they poured sugar inside their shirts. ("Rapture!" or "You are good to me," or "I was airborne, wasn't I?")

Part of him wanted to kiss Clara, but mostly he pined to be the sea traveler José Francisco Cruz, who was modest as well as brave and surely needed help in telling his daughter about his famous revelation at sea when the stars above him turned pink.

Eugénio was not sure how to convey this, but he arranged rock sugar like clear castles tossing down prismatic moats to say, simply, "Hues. *Colors hide within everything, including the night.*" He covered sugar eyelids with leaves to remind her that she must not steal the sun and wear it for eyes. To fill her ears with mist, he spoke words that quivered: *hortelã, lã, rã, lençol, coração, derramar, Cruz,* said *Croo-sshh.* The hum of the words mixed with the air and turned into the white sound, the cloud of invisible speech where nasalized endings go. Even when the heat hung its anchors on their limbs, sinking them against a tree and lulling Clara into a nap, Eugénio kept her ear pinned to his chest and whistled to palpitate her dreams, and he fought sleep until his own head, leaden, dropped like a ripe fruit onto the brown nest of her hair. They awoke with their arms fastened where puddles of sweat gave them the suction cups of an octopus.

Going home they passed houses where women watched without being seen behind sun-blackened bay windows and balconies in the vanguard like high stone-and-iron jaws. Eugénio understood that beauty hid on the other side of the dark glass and the gratings that were like the grilles inside confessionals. The women emerged to lean against the balconies for suitors who stood under them in the streets below, but the barricades still covered their skirts, letting only small cotton arabesques or lancets leak through the wrought patterns.

O, thought Eugénio, staring, there are women who from the waist down are nothing but flowers and crowns.

"Eugénio!" they called. "Clara!"

"Good evening," he said, but he wanted to yelp, The hell with the flowers; stand on the railings and lift your skirts!

THAT SEASON IN Agualva a new jealousy lurked in the air: It was said that Conceição Cruz would, in a matter of time, claim a part of the New World. Her uncle in California had bequeathed to her the entire large parcel of his land. It rested in the town of Lodi, not too far east of San Francisco. About five years had passed since the last American soldiers had withdrawn from Vietnam. Some Azoreans had caught glimpses and a scent of the war because of the huge United States Air Force base on Terceira. They had heard about the terror abroad and the unrest in the streets of America from their relatives in the States and in Canada, and those who owned televisions had seen it, but even stronger than these impressions was the willful sense that the New World was large enough to absorb its scars, and though it was perhaps no longer a place of absolute peace, it had at least returned to being as they had always dreamed it—a shelter of abundance. Conceição would get to eat ice cream, play pinball, and have a washing machine, and Clara could grow up in a paradise of clothing, shoes, elbowroom, and limitless hope.

To avoid ambushes of this chatter, Eugénio took Clara to the dim drinking house owned by the Cabrals, a tribe of thirty leathery cousins with pointed beards who could barely speak or move and cared nothing about the outside. They hardly noticed Eugénio and Clara contentedly speaking in sugar at a table so blessedly greasy that it moored the granules. The Cabrals' place was known as the goat-bar. Women drifted past outside, deathly slow in their black cowls and capes, with baskets of cut azaleas. An orange cooking oil was suspended in floating dots throughout the bar, as if droplets had rained from the ceiling, nodded off part of the way down, and stuck to tabs of air at different heights, giving the atmosphere of the place the feel of loose orange kapok. Goat-men sat at a marble-slab counter that displayed jugs of cherries whitened and bloated like cows' eyeballs in the kirsch. Lemons, shrunken and brown as huge walnuts, were stacked near a pile of wilted kale droning with flies. Horse mackerels that had been rolled in corn flour looked as if they had struggled and died on a beach. They were now waiting to be fried.

To Eugénio the goat-bar had the lumpy, sour comfort of a glass of buttermilk. Supreme over all was the goat-girl hostess, startling, radiant, with a gold tumble of hair, chestnut-eyed, clear-skinned, her flesh spongy as mushrooms instead of stringy like her cousins': out of goat-parents, sometimes the odd diamond.

Clara roughed out a sugar-arrow and pointed from Eugénio to the goat-girl. ("Love.")

Pinch of salt dashed to the floor. ("No!")

Fingertips pressed onto the old love-arrow. ("Don't try to fool *me*.")

Another salt pinch thrown.

Sugar-arrow + Clara pointing to herself. ("*I* love her, then.")

The hostess was like the magnetized soaps in the houses with running water: With a round of metal shoved inside, the cakes could dry clinging to the slender metal arms projecting over the basins. That was their goat-beauty—a steel core, but on the outside elevated and mild as spangling foam. And how she was drawn to Eugénio and Clara when they held out their arms to order! She brought them fried potatoes sliced in half-moons with mayonnaise and vinegar. To open their fizzing pineapple water, she jammed the marbles plugging the lips of their bottles downward, and they drank with them rattling, trapped inside the glass like drowning sailors.

"Do you like it here?" Eugénio asked the goat-beauty.

"Of course," she said brightly. "Where else is there?" Though new to sugar-speaking, she always took care to pat the word for *yes* on the table to be friendly to Clara: Whatever you would like, whatever you ask: *sim.*

The goat-bar's thickened air saved the hostess from the intrigue and sometimes the incest fated for some girls in other goat-areas. On occasion the goat-men lunged for her, but the oil dots formed a cushion around her and they gave up. She was too lovely to be taken, and the men, in sadness, discomfited, needing to work their hands, stirred with the powers of *maniflautistas*. Clasping and unclasping, massaging and chafing against one another, the woodwind fingers of the goat-men drunk on kirsch made shrill andante flute noises that seemed to say, How pretty is your hair/How like a butterflied prawn your lips.

The whiskey drinkers rubbed their thin fingers to sound like lips straining to blare the right wetness against the reed, and they pulled their baby fingers to add fife music and frantic scalings that released, I am taut as a flute/With breathing holes spouting like a dolphin's/Run before I savage you.

The hand concert continued mournfully until the musicians sighed and dropped into a spent slumber. Eugénio and Clara rested too, and when they raised their heads from the table, mixed-up sugar-language was glued to them. They read each other's features, tracing the new words, Eugénio glad and Clara with her noiseless laughter at the funny confusion of arrows and other questions, finely sprinkled with the *yes* of the Beauty.

During most of his visits to the goat-bar, he asked the Beauty for a hair.

"Why yes, love," she said. This was a typical request from the goat-men. He took hairs from Clara's head too. Later, with enough remnants of the Beauty, of Clara, to entwine into a true flowing lock, a part of them rebuilt in his room, he felt he had preserved something of these splendid drowsy days, these days of flute choruses from hands in frictional prayer.

Hᴉs ᴅᴀᴜɢʜᴛᴇʀ ʙᴇᴛʀᴀʏᴇᴅ so little of herself that it took three scenes, aligned together, for José Francisco to grasp why she was distressed. He had thought at first that the unrest about when they might move to the California land that Conceição had inherited was affecting Clara, but then he spotted Eugénio with a young girl in a café, asking that her initials be branded with the hot iron onto the milky skin of the custard. The next week he observed Eugénio with a different girl in a field, splitting the yellow-and-brown tortoiseshell scorings of a pineapple to expose meat engorged with juices. José Francisco noticed, finally, that Clara hugged the queen conch long after its rattling with his voice had ended, as if too preoccupied to remember to put it down, her head hanging despite his experimenting with the most idiotic chants he knew, drinking tunes and childish rhymes. She would not look up when he sprinkled sugar down his shirt and then shrugged, his palms upturned. ("Rapture?" "Aren't we airborne?") She had that look of shock that comes to those who are being instructed for the first time that stubborn desire is not always sufficient to get what one wants. When she was older, would this harden into a bitterness, an immobility? That was the danger of deep passions, thought José Francisco: When one is young, disappointment may still be manifest as an unwillingness to believe that the world refuses to cooperate, but when someone of passion grows older, disappointment hardens into a defiance, and then a terrible grief. He believed in staying even-tempered, and he feared for the lack of compromise in her forces.

To help her forget about Eugénio, he took her to greet some aromas and visions that might uncoil from her an exclamation, some noise of happiness. They headed for the Serpa Pastelaria, where the ovens exhaled an air clotted with a nut perfume, like the hot waves that bake the almond trees of the Algarve in southern Portugal. Beneath a waxed-paper hymen nailed to a slanted metal frame, a cache of cream horns, rice puddings, marzipan dragons with shrunken marzipan animals in their jaws, Abbots' Ears, Nuns' Bellies, Tongues-of-Mother-in-Law, and sweet-potato cakes sat like tide pool life under a pane of cloudy water.

Senhora Serpa tossed some sugar into the air to welcome them.

Clara pointed to a dragon.

"A dragon and a red-bean *queijada*," José Francisco said to Senhora Serpa, whose arms were like legs of mutton, floured and knobby with fat bumps.

"Too bad she still doesn't talk," she said, handing the pastries over the counter. "Such a lovely girl, and almost grown, too."

"Shh," said José Francisco, "she understands everything." Every now and then a glimmer in her eyes, a half smirk, or an unguarded trace of befuddlement made him suspect that his daughter might be able to hear and speak, but so far (as stubborn about some things as her mother) she had seen no reason to bother.

Clara plucked a marzipan mouse from between the gumdrop teeth of the dragon and handed it to her father. He poured a mound of sugar into his hand and added a few grains. ("Thanks, dear.") He nestled the mouse into the center of his tart and finished it in two bites.

She took his arm as they went to visit some of the lava-rock walls that crosshatched the island and were thickly sown with hydrangeas to turn the walls into a dazzling purple net extending over the fields and hills in a great arterial jumble. The fire that hid in the volcanic rocks heated the seeds until they erupted into lavender and amethyst blooms, and the net shone because each hydrangea's star-shaped flowers were clustered in a sphere that created a compound eye. The purple walls were one of his most beloved sights. "They'll watch over you when I'm gone," he said. She was tall enough now to lean her head against his throat, where his whiskers might inject his words farther into her ear.

Once in a dark room he had held a lantern near his face, and the light had projected a picture of the backs of his eyes, the contents of his vitreous humor, onto the walls: a violet tangle within the jelly, a compact internal version of the hydrangea-walls. Both were landscapes of purple arteries that blossomed far back and split into many branches. Veins penetrated the cruxes of other veins; bulkheads plunged into forks colored mauve and orchid—until José Francisco could not tell which were the intersecting male walls and which the splayed female ones. He stood with his eyes dreamed inside out and spilled onto the earth in configurations of mating, pleased that to behold his island of Terceira mantled with intercoursing flowers was to imagine the veined bedrock of his eyes spread out, making constant love under the sun. Walls, branches, the gelatinous parts of eyes—all contained sketches of union. Clara was studying the purple mesh, but he did not know whether she could learn from this net that Eugénio would be a passing grief, lost among the many other possible filaments.

MARIA JOSEFA CAME to the Cruz house almost daily to teach fish-scale art to Clara. The lessons were for solace, now that her son and Clara had ended their walks, but mostly Maria Josefa was grateful to her mute neighbor for taking her from a preoccupation with shadows to crystals. Skill with sugar grains made them adroit at using tweezers to pick up the scales, most of them translucent with iridescent shimmers and others tinted various shades and stationed across the table in paper cones. As they glued the scales into flowers, birds, and livestock, Maria Josefa no longer viewed living as a fight against muck: Days were small chapters, rounds of clear light shot with color that could be compiled into shapes that added up to a picture.

José Francisco watched his daughter assemble her artworks with a cool patience, piece by piece, and this was the image he preferred to keep of her: She was not volatile when she settled down to construct joy, as if it were a basket, ready to contain whatever she wished to carry. Her face was rapt with concentration but untroubled. Her expression and her work prompted him to form his theory for tearing down sadness. If beauty could be built by placing round upon round, then there was no reason why sorrow could not be dismantled one plank at a time, until the whole labyrinth of it was gone. Griefs could be pulled off, counted, and stacked like boards, one at a time off the maze, until there was no danger of wandering lost inside it. He would devise a system for calculating what each unhappiness was worth toward reducing the total allotted to one's lifetime. (Publish the results? Fame, money! Doctors and teachers for Clara. Bribe to Conceição to sell the land and stay here! It might be better to keep his theory to himself while testing it.)

The rip in the chicken coop, a brief annoyance, was worth

only one-half point of sadness to be subtracted from his life's total.

Eugénio's invitation to Clara to join him swimming earned her one hundred points—thirty for being reminded of his abandonment, twenty for the false hope that the old days with him as her guide had returned, and fifty when she realized that they had not.

Twenty sadness points for José Francisco's failure to comfort her. (He pledged these to her ledger instead of his.)

Eating lima beans, one-quarter of a point (for Conceição's ledger—a bighearted move, since she had inflicted them).

Thumb smacked with hammer, one point.

A one-week Atlantic fishing assignment triggered an argument with Conceição about when they would move to California. For distressing her, seven points plus for his side (per bout). Instead of subtracting sadness, it was only fair that he exact penalties for himself when he heaped aggravations onto someone else. His side: The land was not going anywhere. After a few more years at sea, he would be resigned to working in a dairy. Her side: *Resigned?* Was it a punishment to own land? With Clara almost thirteen, they had to move before she married and settled down in the islands.

Three points for the discomfort of admitting that he was admired for his bravery in going to sea, but that was in a sense the *known* unknown, while Conceição was courageous about the pure unknown.

Twenty—no, thirty points for suffering with Father Teo Eiras's unerring ability to arrive at mealtime. He showed up one morning as Conceição was serving chicken broth with mint leaves and unborn eggs, extracted that morning from Maria Josefa's butchered hen. José Francisco scowled. He was selfish when it came to soup with the tapiocalike pearls still rich from soaking inside the chicken, and he did not trust the clergy. He had not yet forgiven the Jesuits who many centuries before had conspired not to resist the Spanish conquerors sent by Philip II and had therefore been blamed for betraying Terceira. (Others in the order later played a role in the island's liberation, but José Francisco ignored this.) He considered modern priests to be grabbers of virgin land: the little kings of their quadrants. Did one need to come around now, stealing his soup?

"I am absolutely famished," said Father Eiras. He was large and yellowed, with an expansive face. Clara joined them at the table and studied the priest. She was unruffled, but he always seemed nervously quiet. Like those who appear neither happy nor in misery, he was as impassive as a drain that will drink the whorl over it but cannot go looking for water itself.

"Well, help yourself," José Francisco grumbled.

Conceição nudged him. Men and their quarrels! Butting their heads. There was enough soup to go around. She handed a bowlful to Father Eiras. "Take as much as you want," she said to him.

No, *fifty* points.

One hundred points, to be divided equally between Clara's and Conceição's accounts, for his fear of the water acting like a spurned lover if he told it good-bye.

José Francisco lay awake in bed with the nagging sensation that he had to face the truth: To what final figure were these credits being applied? He had been thinking that since a life had a certain total of days, there had to be a finite limit to the sorrows it could contain, but he had left this calculation gray and unnamed. People generally trusted that over a reasonable number of pains, they could not possibly be asked to go. That was ordinary hope, but it was hopelessly untrue. He awarded his distress over this not a single point. None.

Conceição often envisioned the land awaiting them, solid and dry, and she had a keen desire to see American freeways and skyscrapers, but she herself could not entirely evade elements of water. Her eyes had river-vision. It began during her childhood on the big island of São Miguel. She had had to use a wooden outhouse raised on blocks, without benefit of a stream or pit, with the pigs and chickens feeding beneath. One day, while crouched over the caked perimeter of the hole, with one hand catching splinters where the paint had worn off the side board, she heard her aunts outside cackling at her the old joke about which pigs produced the best spareribs in the Azores. To vanish from her body, she funneled herself, her eyes, and her shame into her river as it splashed onto a snout below. She entered the waiting mouth of the pig and rested her sights in its warm stomach, a much closer and darker hiding place than the outhouse. After that she learned how to follow her eyes and swim away, into whatever could help her disappear into the center or deepest recess or often the origin of a thing. On the one hand, she had a desire to strike out fearlessly; on the other hand, her river-vision would sometimes take over and spirit her away on a journey. These were her two great warring forces.

While returning home one afternoon from collecting a supply of fish scales with Clara, her eyes dived into the shirt of a farmer ramming his burro into a witless man. The silver milk cans over the animal's back clanged as she flowed backward through the fabric of the farmer's shirt to cotton plants in a faraway field. Her river ran past a stray silk thread and glimpsed worms spinning in a tree and continued over muscles bulging with the fish and percolating with the wine of his last meal. Her eyes sped along the rapids of wine and bumped over the noses of the fish, but they returned to a clear focus and snapped to attention in her head in time for her to burst out, "Leave him in peace!"

Clara was already a jump ahead. She marched to the burro, slapped its muzzle, and pulled its reins so that the farmer had to lean forward. She reached up and slapped him too.

"Goddamn it. Little bitch," he said, too surprised to do more than hold his face.

"Get out of here," said Conceição evenly. She would go mad if she stayed on this island!

Clara, again a step ahead, pushed the burro and its rider on their way and seated the childlike man at the roadside. She pressed scales onto his fingernails and held them up to show him how they blinked in the sunlight. He giggled. When he clapped and shed the scales, he laughed even harder. As Clara redecorated his fingernails, Conceição sank to one side. What could she offer her daughter, who never seemed to need her? At displays of threats or wrongs, Clara was on her feet to fight, her green eyes throwing green blankets over anyone in her way. She was small but made strong and fierce by high cheekbones. Her brown hair was wild. When it came to silent touches, she was leagues beyond them all. Her face could instantly knot into accusation or brazen intolerance for things out of place, and it was odd that she was also ruthlessly patient—or perhaps not so odd, Conceição reasoned; her daughter seemed to know instinctively that calculation, timing, and impassivity in proper measure were much of the battle in having one's way. In any case, the days of impressing her with lemons that squeezed out invisible shapes were finished. She had to give something that Clara would not even be aware of wanting.

California: If Clara could not embrace her mother, then let her embrace her mother's dream. That would be almost as good. In California the air was supposed to be thick enough to hold guitar music a few beats longer than normal. She would find a guitar that could open Clara's ears, and José Francisco would be too charmed to miss Terceira. To keep him reconciled, they could build a house with a moat, filled with goldfish big as horses and sea cows (a compromise), and he could stay girded with water. They would have curtains of floral prints and watch the night sky for astronauts.

Clara stood to lead the man home, and her mother rose to follow. They each grasped one of his hands. Conceição's eyes swam into the starry nails on the hand she held, burrowed through muscle, and emerged through the stars that her daughter clutched on the other side of him. There Conceição's eyes rested, two eggs incubating in Clara's palm.

AT HOME, CONCEIÇÃO found José Francisco bathing in the tub he had set on the kitchen floor, gargling a song into the water he was ladling over his head, and she grabbed the metal rim to dump him out.

"Hey!" he said.

"Right now," she said. "We're going to settle right this minute when we're going to California."

"Let me get dressed and we'll talk."

She lifted the towel beyond his reach. "Talk from there."

"A year from today. From this very day. I promise."

"No," she said, standing over him. "Two months from today." How could he spend weeks and months at a time on a boat? A man who hated the slowness of cooking rice and ate the kernels that still wiggled in the unabsorbed water like bees in their moist hive. Who then burned himself and screamed murder.

It took ten minutes to make her consent to sit on a chair so they would at least be on a closer eye level. Negotiations continued as the water chilled the metal of the tub. They agreed that he would leave for two weeks as scheduled on the tuna boat that would be docking soon. Then one more trip to the Grand

Banks, followed by a short excursion on a trawler heading for Madeira. A final trinity—one journey for him, one for her, and one for Clara, over five more months. That would be plenty of time to pack and finish processing their official papers. José Francisco felt serene. He and Conceição made fun of his skin, wrinkled as an old man's as he stepped from the water. He was perfectly calm and warm as he dressed. When he next embarked, he would tell the ocean that their affair was over, he had chosen his wife, and that he was not a bit sorrowful about it.

THE FIGS HAD been dropping faster and more thickly down the length of the Cruz orchard than anyone could eat or preserve them, and on the day before his farewell on the tuna boat, José Francisco invited everyone for some purple sleigh riding. The fig trees in the orchard were lined on both sides of a narrow, open corridor that rolled downward for about one hundred meters. The trees, good sports, seemed to fling their mushy bombs onto the middle of this runway. José Francisco stood at the crest of the fig carpet and roared, "Hurry up! I am the master of the purple slide!" (For Clara: rock sugar surrounding a fig.)

"Climb onto my shoulders," he told Lourenço, Maria Josefa's youngest boy, while sitting on a burlap sack at the top of the slope of seeded glue. They pushed off with José Francisco singing "Row Your Boat" in English, which he had learned on a ship out of New Bedford, until they spilled over, flipping and shimmying downhill like the sardines poured into barrels at the dock.

Eugénio shyly sprinkled a sugar trail up to Clara. ("Shall we explore the slide?")

Fingertips firm on the trail. (Emphatic "You won't beat me.")

He sat behind her on their burlap sack, his arms encircling her waist and his legs forming pillars that guarded them on two flanks. She put her head against his knee, and he crooned as he had done for her so many times. She had always been fond of how well his notes traveled through her skin. Suddenly, she caught herself succumbing to him, jerked her head up, clutched the sack to give it the curled front of a toboggan, and let herself fly forward. Halfway down, she braked so that Eugénio fell off, then she continued alone, skidding to the end.

Some of the children brought their own sacks to race, and others watched as José Francisco, with Lourenço piggyback, finished a stanza of the national anthem while coursing to the orchard's end without a hitch. He set down his passenger and, while picking their sled off the runway, tapped him on the back to make him take a bow. The children applauded.

José Francisco was triumphant. One did not need the water, it seemed; only the gladness of a new adventure.

At the farewell dinner they ate *cracas*, the sea animals that bore into rocks. Each *cracas* rock was a chunk that held a few of the creatures and looked like a mossy candelabra that could easily fit in the hand. Everyone poked horseshoe nails through the apertures in the brittle shutters that were protective seals, sucked the meat off the nails, and spit out any bits of shell. Into the emptied burrows, Henrique poured burgundy to wash out the scraps. "Health! Future!" he toasted, holding up a wine-brimming rock. He and all present drank from their unwieldy chalices, their uneven panpipes, red brine coursing down their necks, and after that loneliness somehow crawled into their food. Eugénio glanced at Senhora Dutra scraping the veins out of tiger prawns and slipped outside to touch the artery the length of his penis. When Maria Josefa took some *catalinas*, their valves edged with plum color and split open to offer tender nodes sparkling in salty juice, she shivered with aloneness. Clara put her head against her father's chest as he spoke, but her face did not show that she heard anything. Conceição's river-vision spurted into the wine and flowed back to the green, bluish, and brownish grapes as they were yanked from the vine by the winemakers. The grapes being crushed under their feet were like eyes being squished into rivulets of blood. The *cracas* rocks were red-running from their drained wine, like sockets with the eyes pulled out.

What could the river in her not bear to see?

She was so stock-still that José Francisco leaned over to tap her just below the knee with a crab mallet to test her reflexes. Although it made them giggle, the spell of the party was over.

That night he hoisted Conceição onto the roof of their five-foot shrine of the Virgin. It had become their custom when he was about to depart that she would perch with her legs parted in an arch over and around the Virgin's head because a moonbeam through the kitchen windows never failed to strike at such an angle, and with such a glow, that she was given a round moon on her shoulders in place of her head and, dissolved in a circle of light, softened in the luster, she would have to forgive him for leaving. It turned her into a beacon, and he could burn her into his sights for the time he would spend staring into the night sky from a ship's deck. He could put her luminous face above to watch him as a star.

"Good-bye, I will be back. I will bring you sunken treasure," he always promised.

And she never said good-bye but would close her legs around his shoulders, would guide his head to her belly.

They made love as they always did at farewells—standing up—but this time he wanted it to last forever. They tried to come without moving, just from being glued together. From thought—to practice coming when they were apart. José Francisco broke down—he had to move, had to stroke her insides before he died. Naked that night they walked sedately through the fog to the fig-slide, their backs curved and pretty as chicken meat, and away they glided, without crashing, managing to move in a slow rise and fall, holding hands, the length of the purple undulation.

IT WAS THE custom of José Francisco and Clara to say good-bye in sugar in such a way as to keep the other person guessing the true meaning for the duration of their absence from one another. On the dock, as Conceição, Henrique, and Maria Josefa joined the crowd on the pier, Clara gave her father a sugar rock wrapped in paper. It might mean:

("I have enclosed within me the stories they tell about the night you drank the Soup of Sorrow, when your thoughts turned the stars the pink of dreaming.")

("I will hold the castle for you while you are gone.")

("One day I will write in the language I have been given.")

He gave her a single grain, which she placed in a handkerchief. She thought of several possibilities:

("Find the colors in the smallest things; they are there.")

("What you must be more careful to guard is the most precious.")

("Like me it is merely one grain, but it is yours.")

On the pier he let his bones sing to her, and he kissed Conceição. What was within him as he took his leave was not good-bye but: Is it possible, then, that sorrow may be defeated if joy is this great? For I am not just a man who played a ghost violin; I have been a conductor of the sea, from the time I was given all of you.

To BOOST CONCEIÇÃO'S spirits as she waited for his return, Maria Josefa and Henrique visited many times to rest a shell against their ears and announce, "I hear his singing!" But the tones, if there had been any, dissipated before a second person could add assent, and they figured that they were listening not to music but only to the quivering of their own need to hear. Clara shook the queen conch, but there was nothing.

The morning the fleet was due home, Conceição awoke with her eyes in terrible pain. They entered a glass of water on her nightstand and flowed down to the beach and far off to a storm on the ocean, where they watched a stupendous whale gliding in a deep current, its body swelling huge as a mountain until it was an exploding earth; and when it burst, all the fish and wrecked galleons, the living creatures and the dead, were coated with the mass of the whale and its spermaceti and the gel from its spheric eyes, and living or dead, all the creatures glistened like stars in water, signaling her, saying, There is no need to greet the arriving ship. I fought as long as I could. Never fear, though: I will make it gleam down here to light your way to America.

Chore pedras: Cry stones, say Azoreans.

When grief is that heavy.

Let the stones rain on you; wear them as a crypt; shed one thousand for everyone you miss.

Let them hurl from you to the ground to erect headstones for those thrust into unmarked graves.

They say that the sea is salty because of the tears shed on Portuguese beaches for those whom no one would hold again.

SHE GRASPED THE ax imbedded in a stump and dragged it over the streets of cobbled black waves. In the sanctuary of the

Church of the Assumption she plunged the ax into the skull of Christopher, the guardian of water crossings. The metal cleaved his head, and she smashed him against the altar until he splintered in half. She chopped up a plaster Joseph and beheaded Brendan the Navigator, who sailed seven years to find the fabled paradise of the Isles of the Blessed, said to be the Azores. The ax sundered the harp from Cecilia and turned the saints into a rubble of painted lips and gold-leaf tunics. Severed noses littered the heap like limpets and cloven parts stabbed her feet, but she would not stop hacking them to pieces, not until they were specks that the air would obliterate. All the saints would blow away, destroyed:

Farewell to Gerard Majella, one of the patrons of mothers because he could read minds and be in two places at once.

Farewell to Catherine, patron of fire prevention because she lived ablaze as Christ's mystical bride, and to Teresa of Avila, patron of headaches because Satan tossed her around rooms and interior voices gave her raptures.

Farewell to Adjutor, beloved of sailors because after his sea journeys he became a recluse, and to Marculf, whose prayers dashed Saxon pirates onto rocks when they tried to invade his solitude on the island of Jersey, and to Venerius, who guards the lighthouses, and to Anthony of lovers and lost things, and to Jude of lost hope, and to James-the-Cut-to-Pieces, Matthew the winged man, the Holy Innocents, and the legions who had failed as intercessors. Why had they never stormed the throne to chant:

> Your craft has broken our hearts.
> Your craft has broken our hearts.
> Your craft has utterly broken our hearts.

Conceição ground them to dust underfoot, her face a monkey wavering in the shine of the blade, but when a gust of wind carried off some of the powder and sawdust, the ground-up saints proclaimed to her how they would rise again: They would sift as a white chalk into the earth and reappear inside plant shootings or the oozing milk of corn.

The chickens would peck the saint-bran and lay beatified eggs. When a woman starched her collars with the whites, the saint-dust would usurp fabric and closets. If a cook boiled eggs for a party, the saints would infiltrate the bodies of guests.

These guests might travel to a place where they would piss motes of saints under a chestnut tree, allowing them to grow through the roots and season the crushed-chestnut broth drunk on Saint Bartholomew's Day, when the Devil infests the countryside with lice and no one ventures into the vegetable gardens because God needs time to fight unobstructed.

The saints not sucked into the plants and trees would slink into water veins that would run to the sea and saturate the fish. The particles would find themselves slashed, marinated, and boiled in tuna for the midnight eve of Saint John's Day.

The Saint John revelers would then shit away the saints in the raised outhouses, and the pigs feeding beneath would absorb the holy microbes until slaughtered and served with garlic and cumin. The saints would seep from the stewed organs back into human entrails.

As for the saint-flecks stuck on grass blades, shepherds would eventually collect them as clods for mounded ovens. Saint-soot would rise from the fire and fly into the sea to penetrate some *meixões*, the eels that enjoy resurrections following three drownings after death:

The first drowning in water when they are cleaned.

The next in oil when they are cooked.

The last in wine when washed down the throat.

All Conceição had done was speed the saints toward a hydra of rebirths. Her ax had freed the statues to subjugate the trees, weave themselves into clothing, or assume real bodies by growing inside the islanders.

The pieces of José Francisco might rise from his ocean grave, filling the fish and water, driving toward shore to reach her— but she wanted him whole. Let the saints straggle around in fragments, but not him.

She threw a votive lamp at the Virgin, whose heart was pierced with seven sorrows and yet who remained unperturbed as she burned. Father Teo Eiras entered through the rear vestibule to investigate the noise as she struck the tabernacle with her ax. When she seized the red sanctuary light to hurl flames at the tabernacle's unassailable door, Father Eiras seized her arm from behind. He held it fast. "Fire belongs to God," he said.

HER LUNGS STRAINED. They stretched like trapped wings, and with every flutter the sharp powder she had inhaled lacerated her. She lay down under the revenge of the army of dust as it alternately cut her and punched up and down the length of her body to cover her with swellings. Maria Josefa applied hot compresses to Conceição's legs, arms, and abdomen and fed her unsalted food to ease the puffing out of her skin. Father Eiras checked on her progress and set up a makeshift altar.

When she sank into fever, Henrique borrowed an idea from the old story of the prince who brought his Scandinavian bride to southern Portugal, where she missed the coolness of snow. The sweltering winters left her suffocating and near dying. Her husband sowed the countryside with almond trees, and the spectacle of the blossoms falling in a thick white blanket across the Algarve saved his beloved.

Henrique could not find almond trees, but he and his wife shook dozens of hydrangeas from the roof of the Cruz house so that Conceição, propped up in bed in front of the window, could be soothed by a purple and pink snowfall. She smiled at the drifts sifting down. Clara sat beside her with a tray and sugar, and the sun beyond the pastel snow turned their words to a glaze:

Udder-shape, and a few grains added on top, roughed out by Conceição. ("Thank Henrique for me.")

Clara's fingertips on udder-shape. ("Of course.")

Square. ("Do you want toast for dinner?")

A + sign traced in the square, by Clara. ("Sure. Whatever you'd like.")

Conceição began to form a sugar-arrow, then stopped. No, saying "I love you" might send Clara scurrying off the bed. She

44

wanted to hold her daughter's hand but had never been able to figure out how to ask for it. Clara liked frankness as long as the emotions were buried rather than worn like frills.

Moth-shape, by Conceição. ("The night fliers will come for me soon.")

Clara shook the tray to wipe out the message. She threw a pinch of it on the floor and crunched it underfoot. ("No.")

Part of the trickery of being a mother was in eliciting a "No" that was close enough to be "I love you." Conceição relaxed on the pillow.

Clara dipped a comb into a glass of water, where the teeth were magnified into underwater black rungs. She shook the excess out before drawing it through her mother's hair and wrapping one lock at a time around her finger to be pinned to the scalp with Xs of bobby pins.

Conceição's eyes flowed toward Clara's fingers as they worked like a puppeteer's, dancing above. She was afraid to invade without permission, and her vision settled for attaching like strings to Clara's gestures. Would her daughter live in a welcoming land and descend curving staircases, to an audience's ovation? Would people use silver tongs to drop sugar cubes into glasses of champagne to honor her? Or would she wear large hats that obscured her face as she wrapped her scrub brushes in newspaper and tucked them under her arm as she went to clean houses? Would she come home to the knife she had left coated with marmalade in the sink? What a miserable business, that dying for love was easier than living for it. She wanted to hang on, to ensure what Clara would become, but the army of dust was too relentless. Besides, she can take care of herself; you would only get in her way, taunted the swellings on her face and chest. And overall was the faint calling of José Francisco: Come, my one-more-than-everything. Come to the place free of poisons where I search for you.

The hair curling was over. Clara stepped away. Little crossed swords were flattened against her mother's head for now, but the following day she would be luxuriant.

Father Eiras dropped by to pat Conceição's hand, saying, "There there there. Now now now." It was completely within her power to care for her child. Didn't Clara deserve a future? A girl who could not hear or speak needed space, time, a place to grow. Maybe in California—a change might trigger her voice. Could Conceição figure some means to help him provide? Which he would gladly do, if she requested it. Poor child. She would need a guardian. In fact, there was probably a means of taking care of Clara *and* making reparations, painless as a tithe, for some of her profanation in the sanctuary. The exercising of maternal goodwill and the cleansing of her sins, just like that! "Even the dying should perform good works," he said.

She pointed weakly to a desk drawer, and Clara watched him elevate, as if in consecration, the deed to the land. Conceição propped herself up long enough to agree that she was lucky that with one stroke, one selfless act, she could make her life a clean slate in the mind of the Church while also giving her daughter a new world.

"I wish you could sign it in her name," said Father Eiras, "but she's only thirteen. It won't be legal."

She raised her eyes to him.

"I'll see that she's cared for," he said. "It will be her home."

As she signed the papers over to the Church, he promised that she had greatly reduced her Purgatory time. He wanted to save her from the fires entirely, but only martyrs were exempt from the need for some laundering. Such were the laws! He wished he could do more, but some things, he told her with a smile, were beyond his grasp. He waited until she slept before stealing away. Clara was already curled up by herself in a corner, like a cat.

That night she climbed into bed with her mother. Maria

Josefa, who had been keeping a steady vigil, had gone home to sleep just for a few hours, and it was as if Conceição had been waiting to be alone with Clara sleeping beside her.

In Portuguese death, the soul flies away as a moth, white as a snowflake. It first perches on the lips, then hovers and ascends. Conceição, trying to inhale the beating wings, fought so hard to swallow them that she spent her final hour kissing the empty air. Clara awoke to feel her mother's hand groping, desperately searching for her child's hand so that her work could be done with the two of them bound, but as Clara turned to reach for her, the moth paused, touched its wings together, and then abandoned its station. Clara was frantic—she had not held her mother's hand in time! She had seen the mouth in spasms but had not kissed it properly! Her mother had never gone on ahead—not anywhere—without her! The swords were still arrayed in Conceição's hair, not yet ready to unveil the new waves of hair being coaxed beneath them. They were to have been undone, the beauty under them released—by Clara—tomorrow! She found her voice.

Mouth a jagged black world.

She released a sound enormous and sharp-edged.

Her cry burst so unnaturally past tissue that had been determined to stay inviolate that her ears were startled into turning a violent red, and she slapped her face, trying to put out the flames that had risen to its surface. Her cries came out in long streams and drove birds from the trees. She was shrieking as she ran outside, scooped hydrangea petals into an empty pillowcase, and returned to fling them over her mother so that her moth would not have to fly away alone, but it had already escaped. It was the bellowing protest Clara had refused to give at birth like everyone else.

The flapping and cawing of the birds woke Henrique a kilometer away. He fumbled to dress in the dark and run to the house. He knew, the way a father can hear his child in a distant crowd, that it was Clara unbottling her insides, Clara delivering her alarm.

The commotion brought Maria Josefa running from next door, in time to see Clara kissing the dead lips. It was true, then, that the girl was not ignorant of colorations of sound but had simply refused, until now, to speak the language of the known and brutal world. Now the world had forced her to join it, to speak as it insisted everyone speak, and she was in a fury. "She knew you loved her," said Maria Josefa, pulling the screaming girl away from her mother's body. "She did; she did."

MARIA JOSEFA ADMITTED that the signature on the deed was genuine; there was nothing to do but insist that Father Eiras promise to care for Clara. There were no relatives nearby, and she knew that Conceição had not trusted any of the ones, on either side of the family, who were scattered in Faial and São Miguel. Maria Josefa wanted to adopt Clara but was afraid of tying her to an island when her mother had planned to give her a whole new state. She helped her pack, petting the girl's back to coax her stream of noises into discernible words, but there was not enough time. Father Eiras had booked a swift passage for himself and Clara. Taking her along would by all appearances keep him in compliance with Conceição's wishes.

The morning they departed, Eugénio, knowing the tradition of José Francisco and Clara in leaving each other with a mystery on the docks, handed her rock sugar tied in a handkerchief stitched with cornflowers. He ignored the speech strangling in her throat; he preferred their speaking in sugar and wanted her leave-taking to be crystalline. The sugar said:

("I am sorry, Clara, that the world is stitched full of flowery distractions.")

("The cornflowers are blue, like the ocean that will be between you and me.")

She used a crystal dipped in water to trace an arrow on his cheek. Written on him was:

("Marked with affection—first by me, then by many.")

("Love will be where you cannot see it. It will mark *you*.")

("Remember how we spoke this private language.")

Maria Josefa and Henrique stood with him on the pier until the ship pulled away and the departing figures shrank against the sea. The arrow cracked on his face, and he thought, Your home of hydrangeas says good-bye. Farewell to you as you battle with the way the world talks and sounds and looks. Good-bye from your country of bright and sudden explosions, from your nine islands receding into dots; good-bye from the friends who will faithfully sing to you. These are such powerfully strange drinks that are handed to us.

TWO

People say that life is a river. But if life were a river,
we would not also have sleep. Life is a mosaic, with
sleep the black-grout stripes that slash our light with bars.

The nine islands of the Azores are a mosaic.
It is said they are Atlantis, rising broken from the sea.
Many Azoreans have marks and patches rising on their skin.

Bleu cheese is a mosaic food with its moldy veins.

Portuguese books are stringed
necklaces glimpsed at the bottom of a stream.

Latin is a mosaic language, with each word a tile that may be
freely moved in the line, and yet the sense remains the same.

You are a mosaic: ornamental parts made
one portrait held together by the white grout of your bones.

> *How to Read a Mosaic:*
> *To stroll along a Portuguese street*
> *Of black and white stones under one's feet*
> *Is to train with care for long and short sights:*
> *See the big picture, see each tile's delights.*
>
> *Look at the swirling pictures imbedded in the*
> *dragons'-teeth sidewalks before you. Stare down at every*
> *individual square, an isolated gem edged with a*
> *border. Then obey the rule for preventing seasickness:*
> *Lift your eyes to the horizon. The*
> *gems blend into a panorama of ships, griffins,*
> *hoops; and you will have read yourself inside them.*

I N S U G A R G R A I N S and rocks she poured out her story to Glória Santos, a neighbor in the town of Lodi who visited the guest house where Clara lived alone on the edge of a vast rolling stretch. Father Teo Eiras had opened his rectory in the main house on the hill. Sacramento was fairly close to the north, but Lodi was sunk solidly within California's inland, where it was dry and hot, and to Clara the more glamorous nearby cities of San Francisco and Sacramento did not hold out much promise of escape.

Sugar-arrow: ("I had love.")

Rock-sugar castles, throwing down colored moats: ("My father discovered one night that colors hide in all things.")

Jagged sugar-rounds. ("Monsters. Monsters crossed the water and crushed the castles to say no.")

Sugar dissolved in water. ("The monsters drowned the castles. Everyone in them died.")

Glória knew that all this had something to do with Clara's past, but she did not understand why the girl formed patterns of sugar on the table and then swept them into a glass of water that she was now saving on a shelf. She needed help in talking; that much was plain. On a piece of paper, Glória showed her the letters that people speak that look like fishhooks scattered on a white beach. All the sugar and sounds that Clara had ever swallowed, that anyone had ever hummed into her ears, turned into fishhooks in her stomach as she tried to imitate the letters and force them out. Her gut grew immense, and the letters burst from her mouth.

There was so much crowding and swelling inside her that the white sounds she had collected since her childhood, those hummed parts of words that should have ascended out of her and condensed into clouds, got caught on the hooks. Glória, who had no children but felt that as she approached the end of her childbearing years she had at last been sent one, wrapped her in a warm white blanket to melt the hooks and drink them out of her. It turned black and heavy and Glória dragged it outside for burning. Clara's white sounds were freed.

With the fishhooks changing more and more into real letters that could slip through Clara's throat without snagging, Glória danced her around and around, light as a hummingbird. The letters in Clara were stuck into Portuguese words, but if she was twirled enough, these would be scrambled and their letters knocked free to mix and group together to make English words, the way fat globules in milk break their skins and churn together into large clumps of butter. Stray lines and dashes would blend to create the unfamiliar k, w, and y necessary for English. There was no danger of the letters being made into another language, just as butter churned in California came out Californian, not Finnish.

Every day Glória visited to give Clara her lessons, leading her in a dance that would churn the girl's insides and rattle the

Portuguese words deep within her until they slapped together and the ending letters of one word and the initial letters of another spelled out words in her new language.

"*Estou cheia de saudades,*" mourned Clara to the air. "*Cá estou e pensando muito em vocês.*"

Glória danced her around, hoping to bang *estou* against *cheia* to form *estoucheia.*

Estoucheia poured from Clara's mouth. She looked confused.

"There! There's the English word *touch* hiding in the middle," said Glória. She danced Clara more, until the *es* and the *eia* fell away. Clara's hands were small, like the rest of her, but they had a tough grip.

"Touch," said Clara.

Glória then danced her harder so that every one of the letters inside her would become free-floating. More words opened and banged against one another and agitated and whisked themselves into English: *Pensando* got so shaken up that the letters could form *an, do, sad, open,* and *sand. Cá em de* was reshuffled during their wild dance steps into *made, came,* and *deem.* The letters in *cheia de* got mixed up and created *idea, he,* and *I.*

"I made an idea," said Clara.

"You have indeed! Wonderful!" shouted Glória.

Week after week, after a dizzying amount of whirling, all the pieces from her old language rumbled completely loose through Clara's body, and letters joined other letters to build increasingly complex sentences in English:

"I came to open a voice."

"The air here is thin and dry, Glória, and at night I do not sleep."

"Father Eiras stops by on Sundays to see that my well has water."

She could even translate the sentences she had uttered at their first lesson:

"I am *full of* saudades.

I am here and thinking so much of all of you."

To celebrate Clara's entry into the language of her adopted world, Glória lit the wood in the guest house's stove. She took the dissolved sugar that was Clara's captured past in a glass and boiled it in a pan, adding more sugar and water until it thickened into ropes. They pulled what had been sugar-language into doves. The legend of the Cruz family had not disappeared, but now it had wings. "Everything stays right here with you," said Glória, who was not yet sure what the "everything" in Clara's glass was, only that it was a drink of longing.

"Yes," said Clara, "but with a different shape, and more added."

"You can speak English now," said Glória, "but that does not mean our dances need to stop. You'll like it here. In the fall you'll start high school, but first, in the summer, we'll pick apricots. If we bring hot dogs for the Andersons' barbeque, they'll let us swim in their pool. Doctor Anderson runs the dental clinic. I'll take you to the park and we'll play Wiffle ball, softball, and badminton."

"Thanks. You've been very patient."

They put the sugar-figures on the shelf where Clara stored her clothes. Next to this history made into birds, she put pinecones so that the smell of California would go into her nose at night and instead of waking in shock she would think:

This is my home.

I flew on the backs of sugar doves into a land of new words.

No one knows my plan yet. I must learn how to wait until the time is right. Even with my childhood practice with years of silence, it's tough—this biding of time, this never forgetting, until what I carry within me can be put beyond words and into action.

CRABS AND ARTICHOKES were served as Father Eiras presided over the groundbreaking for the Transfiguration Church's winery. Men cracked the shells and pulled apart the legs to get to the pliant ocean taste. They tore the leaves off the artichokes and slashed through the choke and the sheaths that fluttered like butterflies out from the heart. Red-streaked chips like shards of glass flew over Clara as she sat at the end of the long table where the parishioners feasted.

There were whispers about her luck: The land had been dormant for years, and now, thanks to Father Eiras, she would make as much as ten percent of profits that would not otherwise exist.

She pretended to have trouble speaking when they asked her a question, merely shrugging when they inquired if she would like more. Actually she was ravenous. It was hard not to laugh at how easy it was to make Father Eiras blush. All she had to do was glance in his direction and he looked hurriedly away. She could not overindulge in this game, though. The key was to stay reserved, without turning a single accusatory face at him, to be calm and clever in winning him over, or he would only be frightened away. As the trays of crabs were being passed, she practiced the most maddening test of patience—to wait without any betraying twitch or premature lunge when whatever was desired was close by. She could barely restrain herself from leaping across the table, grabbing the tray, and cracking the shells one by one under her teeth! Amusing, to sit so quietly that no one knew how hungry she was. More? Hmm. Well . . . maybe. All right, if you *insist.*

She drifted to sleep that night proud of her composure until the sound of pincers' castanets jolted her like a summons. The darkness was crow-black, not an air or a filminess, but something full of hard, hiding figures. Crows were all over her chest, drilling. Needlelike beaks were partitioning her front with holes. Jets of blood spurted from her. "Sorry, sorry, sorry!" the birds shrilled, merrily digging up her inner wells.

"This is the worst you can do, crows?" she said impudently, although she was scared. "Harvesting the soft hairs on my chest and leaving me nothing but holes? Thank you! I've been wanting a body of gems, so I'll just plug your drill marks with jewelry! Every scar will shine! You can skip my navel—it's prepierced. A gem front! I'll make it the newest craze! Girls, girls! Whenever you get stabbed, decorate the puncture with a pearl stud, turquoise, or dangling silver. For every hole near the heart, plant a ruby. Your eyes hollowed out? Wear diamonds for a dazzling look! Tattoos with texture! Crows, thanks for the fabulous business idea. I'm going to love America, I'm going to win my fortune! I'll start a whole new industry: body-piercing jewels. Girls will be comparing torso earrings, neatest drills; we'll wear our bodices open. (Clothing will have to be redesigned—more profit.) Jeweled ladies in undone dresses, queens wearing their crowns in an exploded setting from breasts to mons. Mons demonstrate—"

Monsters.

Stirs. Clara stirs.

With one sweep of her arm, she knocked the birds of night off her chest and kicked like a swimmer needing air. Let me wake ache ache.

She sat up in her bed, lucid and unflinching. It was quiet in the guest house.

No drill marks on her chest. No more banquet.

No crows pinning her down in a midway stratum between sleeping and waking.

(No precious stones decorating her body either. A money-making idea dead before it started.)

She must have vigilance. Vigilance! She liked the inaudible

trumpeting of the word. Ears, open! Eyes, nose! Nerves! Breast turrets! Boulder of brain! Vaginal snout! Tongue, keep your belly low in its swamp. Be alert!

But she knew that bodies made of dreams are stronger than watchfulness; there would always come some winged attackers sweeping through the dark, especially for those who were alone. Despite this foreboding, she swept from her mind, as sharply as she had slammed the crows off her body, any thoughts that her plans would spring with leaks. It was impossible that she would fail. Father Eiras was weak, but *she* had conquered the messengers who flew out of stark trees.

Yet in the haunted morning she cried, "Mother! How could I have not reached for you in time?"

SHE WAVED AT Father Eiras whenever she saw him in the distance, striding over the slopes, inspecting the vines that had taken root. After a few days, he timidly waved back.

She planted rows of corn outside her guest house, hoeing the irrigation troughs with hard, clean strokes, pushing each calloused seed into the ground with a single drive of her pointing finger, so that she could be outside when he was. She smiled and brought him water from her well, and within a week he was sending a vineyard worker to bring water to her.

It was powerful if dismaying evidence that kindness could be the force of choice to trap and crush victims. This made her sleepless, first with horror, then with confidence, but she had failed to reckon that her plot would include so much loneliness. A strong sense of purpose could fall prey not so much to a sharp deathblow as to the slow drainage of anticipatory hours; that was the real test. Her long days at the high school seemed wholly beside the point. She would have to remain firm, resourceful, inventive. But what a dreary place to accomplish that! The guest house where she lived was a single large rectangular room, entirely pine, resting in a shallow valley. Sunset struck from the west's quiet vista, a low tide of foxtails with thickets farther beyond, and the door opened onto this, but the eastern side had no door or windows. A ridge there blocked the sunrise and was practically flush with the guest house's sealed backside, forming a barricade in the direction of the main house, which was three waves of land away, on enough of a hill that it could peer down at the pine box without the scrutiny being returned.

The only windows were in the narrow north and south ends. Parish women contributed mirrors for Clara to hang on the long, windowless east and west walls to substitute as widowpanes. Crammed into one end of the room were a water closet, a sink with a trickling faucet, a bed, a telephone, a miniature wood-burning stove—like something out of the past century!—a table, and one unfinished pine shelf for her clothes and the doves that she and Glória had made, which she handled when she missed the feel of sugar. She drew some of her water from the hawk-nosed pump outside. That too struck her as primitive, because the girls at school talked about using curling irons in the privacy of their own bathrooms. Under the sink hung a dirty cotton panel, stamped with daisies, to hide a few pots and dishes crowded around the metal intestine of the drain. She had no use for the bare half of the room, except when Glória's visits transformed it into a wooden dance floor. Very little announced her presence, but for her purposes she thought that was a good thing. The surroundings were more arid and brown than the greens and purples of home, but also more immense, which she liked. It was a plain canvas, stretched out, suggestive of more possibilities.

Clara spent many hours reconstructing her Tio Vitor, who had once owned this land. He would be about seventy now, if his life had not been shortened by sadness. They had never met, but she had seen him in a photograph the color of caramels from the 1930s that her mother had kept on her desk. He was tall, with the hair, smartly parted and crimped, of someone who belonged in a café. A fob stretched across his waistcoat and his suit was neatly tailored. Next to him in the photograph stood his father, short, with short-cropped hair, and rumpled, though he was wearing his Sunday coat. His creased forehead suggested continuous discomfort. Vitor's left arm was extended almost its full length across the gap between them to clasp the hand of his father, who held his arm slightly and stiffly out from his side, suffering his son's pink hand to collapse around his fist.

She invented a story to link the photograph and the buildings on the land:

Vitor had constructed the guest house and the main house to

capture what he had felt about that pose with his father. It was an angry repayment. His father was the squat plain fortress, sunk in a depression, its visage flatly reversed, bearing absolutely no witness to the fine tall manor—Vitor was stately and serene where his father was hunched and square. He had placed his father forever within view but ignoring him, as a reminder that winning a modest fortune with land speculations could not tear down the structures imbedded in his heart. His father would always refuse to face him and had never come to visit. (Some consolation: Let the half-buried guest house stare toward the west! Let the main house look down its chimney at it!) Vitor roamed his land, wondering why he had not braved the European continent and contested his wits against the cream of society instead of sleepwalking through this outpost where the dairymen and farmers knew he was just an island boy in fancy dress. He never married. His vacant property intensified his solitude.

Clara had one more character in mind for her story: her mother. Conceição had met Vitor only a few times in Terceira, when she had been very young, and she must have idolized him. He was the romantic escapist, a noble pathfinder. She was the family member who wrote him out of love; the others begged for money. Or maybe she was the one who seemed the most practical about the value of land, the most driven to wander as he had. Whatever her tone, he saw her as something of himself.

Saddened about her unknown Tio Vitor, Clara could not bear the empty half of her room. She cluttered it with huge gray rocks, some so big she had to roll them through the doorway. When Father Eiras slept, she sorted through his garbage and washed out tin cans, filled them with water, and nestled them among the rock piles. Bits of metal reddish with corrosion, tinfoil, buttons, nervelike wisps of fennel, and debris left by the workers in the new vineyards or at the construction site of the wine cellars worked very well as anemones inside the tide pools of the cans. Every morning, she greeted her seaside, and the musty smell of scarcely rustling waters made her feel less suffocated.

One morning she awoke to find Tio Vitor languishing on the rocks in a dapper suit with a green silk vest. He wore spats. No wonder her mother had found Vitor enchanting: With his mild hangover and liquid body, he was terribly inviting. "Come, Clara!" he said. "I know the most splendid breakfast drink, and one simply must take it out in the gorgeous sea air!"

She was glad that adding an ocean to the guest house had attracted him. Perhaps he had come here waiting for his father to arrive, so that they face each other at last and walk together to the main house. "Yes, I'd love to join you," she replied, running across the room. With a snap of his fingers, he summoned forth a table with a white cloth, china, tuberoses in a squat crystal vase, and covered silver trays.

"You speak English quite well," he said, seating her and presenting, with a flourish, a linen serviette.

"Thank you. Glória helped get all the letters out of me."

He poured pink ribbons of champagne into flutes, stirred in minced lily petals, and leaned forward. "Do you know why her husband João's arm is missing?" he asked in a husky whisper.

"I heard there was an accident at the dairy."

"O, something like that! It's delicious gossip—they screw so much that he's always falling asleep at work. One day a cow lay on him, but he was in such heaven that he couldn't feel anything until it had crushed his whole arm completely off at the shoulder." He laughed and dabbed his watering eyes with a corner of the tablecloth. "O my—some days I'd kill for a good love story like that, wouldn't you?"

"Why, they're so old! They're over forty!" said Clara, mock-scandalized.

They belched champagne-and-lily froth to drive away any stuffy people who might be thinking of crowding toward their prime seaside view.

"Ah, now let's see!" said Vitor, shaking the sugar bowl. "In case you get tongue-tied, Clarazinha." He lifted the lid on the silver tray. "Every morning they scrape the nautical animals off Triton's body and stew them into a porridge for us. It's an acquired taste, I suppose. Maybe you'd like me to pick out the whelks."

"No, I'll try anything," said Clara.

"There's a good tough niece!"

He became serious. He knew what she was plotting against Father Eiras. Her silence and calm covered desperation—he could sense it—and that meant she would go to any lengths with a cool relentlessness. "Is defeating Father Eiras worth ruining your life?" he blurted.

She was startled at how clearly he could see through her, but she trusted him. "It would be ruined only if I didn't try," she said. "Listen, if he were strong, he would not wear his guilt where I can see it. He'll be easy to trap."

Tio Vitor shook his head. "Let me handle it. I'm trying to persuade the spirits in the roots and the ground—"

"Don't try to talk me out of it. I was hoping we could be allies."

"Do you know Doctor Helio Soares? The dentist who comes here from Stockton once a week to work in the clinic? He's also a grafter of plants."

"I've heard about him and seen his work, but we've never met," said Clara.

"Maybe he'll know how to graft the grapevines to something that will turn them into crabgrass. Get him to help."

"Why should he? It's not his fight."

He looked miserable. "I already know I can't stop you."

"Vitor," she said. She grabbed his hand; the delicacy of the veins in it was tearing her to shreds.

His fingers clasped hers. He gazed at her directly and squeezed his other hand over the two of theirs wound into one. "It is glorious to rest with you by the side of your ocean," he breathed.

EVERY MORNING HER great-uncle lolled on the rocks and tapped a silver fork against the crystal vase to rouse her when she overslept. She so enjoyed their breakfasts that it took a while for her first to notice and then to admit that Vitor was indeed growing paler and more drunken by the day.

"What's happening to you?" she demanded.

"Nothing, Peaches."

"Tell me!"

"Don't be cross. Champagne?" He poured himself a glass. "Stop fretting. I'm busy putting myself into the grapes."

Funneling his spirit into the fruit and vines to claim them was threatening to sap him to the vanishing point before they were victorious. Clearly he was stepping up his operations in an attempt to conclude matters before she went after Father Eiras herself.

"I have to be a little older before I have a chance of succeeding. Wait until I can join you," she pleaded. "Or get your father to help. Aren't you together with him now?"

She regretted her mistake. Out of his waistcoat pocket he shook a silk handkerchief the size of a parachute and, sobbing, buried his face in it. "My father? I'm afraid not! He doesn't think too highly of me, you know."

"Have my mother talk to him. She's good at persuading—"

"That's just it!" He choked, the handkerchief catching his redoubled weeping. "I would love to enlist your mother and father, and mine, but every time I reach for them, they drift away."

She put her arm around his shaking shoulders. "I know how that can be. Is there anything I can do? I hate to see you so unhappy." She was angry at this revelation that melancholia did not automatically end at death.

"Look at me, carrying on like a child," he said, blowing his nose a last time and straightening up. "There. All better!"

"Are you sure?"

"Yes," he said, but the next morning he had faded to a voice gasping over the rocks, "Go introduce yourself to Caliopia Silva. She lives to the south of the Transfiguration land and can teach you how to occupy hidden parts of the landscape."

She trembled with excitement. It would be a means of priming the ground, in a sense, in preparation for her great battle, a way of helping him conquer the invisible aspects of the land.

"She can also teach you how to cry on command, and every morning she does the weirdest thing you'll ever see," Victor wheezed out, and then there was not even a purring.

The next morning, there was only silence, and Clara woke with her face and neck wet. She touched the moist patches beneath her eyes and the little streams running from their corners. Had he leaned over to kiss her a tearful good-bye? What was happening to her?

Maddened by the increasing noise of tractors and workers on the hillsides, Clara stormed out to rip some vines up by the roots, but as she clutched a handful, she feared that she might be strangling Vitor. Why did he insist on beginning the war without her? Was he hoping to win the applause of his father? He had already won her admiration, and she released the vines so as not to risk hurting him.

OUT OF A shaft of bottomless black, where a stone might fall lazily, never striking an ultimate plane, Caliopia Silva struggled to rise and awaken. She pressed the corners of her eyes with a finger and flicked grains of dried mucus onto the carpet. Should be enough bedside now to have formed a hillock. Whither all detritus?

She padded to the mirror. Caliopia, in the full flower of her morning glory. Checked for overnight hair sproutings. Mouth without teeth looked like a sorry sinkhole. Doctor Helio Soares from Stockton was due on Friday for his day at the clinic. She'd ask for new dentures. Despaired of belly of gas. Ah well, license to fart was one advantage of a lifetime alone. Why was belching forgivable but farting not? She had never made it to the flatulent stage with a man, never been with one long enough to breach the polite silences. (Maybe once; fled, red-faced, ended all that). Most telling of the several expressions used to assess velocity, tenor, aromatic properties of intestinal treachery: *abrir*, the verb "to open." Openness, access, ease with a man, to be receptive and giving, could be described with a word that also meant farting. All intimacy was relief, Caliopia decided: Ah, forthrightness. (How did others manage their first time? Did they say "pardon me"? Did they agree to be totally open thereafter with each other, and was this tacit or discussed?)

Never mind. Her job was to mourn the body.

Though an expert in the tonalities of the grief that accompany someone falling alone into blackness, she was no longer an official mourner in Sete Cidades, on the big island of São Miguel. No one in California hired her to keen at funerals, but they employed her vocal skills for other commerce. Running cattle auctions up in Sacramento, she would trill quickly, wildly. Today she had another gopher job: She would fall to the earth, screeching with sadness, and up the rodents would pop from their holes. The farmers would blast them with shotguns. She ignored the jokes. Being over sixty, she had to rely on what she knew to pay her bills—though she would have liked to know why grieving brought gophers surging from their lairs but had never successfully raised a buried human.

Caliopia brushed her white hair, thick but soft in its peaks, like beaten cream. Maybe if she had focused upon these inspiring flames over her head, over everyone's head, instead of upon bodies, she would have had the fearlessness to find a suitor. No, she was too trained in the apocalyptic and would have fallen apart at the least sign of a quarrel. How, even spared that, could he have comforted her when she cried?

Luís, his toenails like the tap shoes of a ghost on the linoleum, responded to his mistress. His warm nose, leaking from its apertures, rose for her petting. "Looo-eesshh," she cooed. He loved her. She loved him. Someone had kicked one of Luís's eyes out of its socket and abandoned him as a puppy. She had adopted him, naming him after Luíz Vaz de Camões, the epic poet who lost an eye during military service.

"Are we ready?" she asked, adjusting his eye patch.

Luís jumped and barked with a dog's constantly renewed ecstasy in what is routine. It was time for the daily changing of the hats in the chicken coop. Caliopia could not stand any form of unrest, including the natural disputes among animals. Every note of anguish, even from hens, added to the cacophony bruising the lining of her head. (She was not, however, pure of double standards. The violence she promoted against gophers was in clear violation of her temperament.)

She plucked tiny bonnets and felt derbies off the clothesline. The scent of fresh laundry was a singular happiness. "Nice?" she said to Luís as he sniffed them. It was his role to inspect and approve that day's helmetry. He bounded to the coop and settled in front of it, his signal that she could proceed. She switched the hats on her dozen hens and rooster, taking off the old ones and putting on clean ones, as she did every morning to confound the pecking order. With their heads hidden, they were born anew and unrecognizable, too confused to harass one another.

The banty ruffled her feathers while receiving a top hat.

"And here for you, Regina," Caliopia said to a white hen, replacing a gingham bonnet with a pilot's headgear. There was always a slight sadness as she completed this task, as if morning had been continuous and omnipresent and now became a litany of things past.

While throwing an arc of yellow corn, she noticed Clara stepping out mesmerized from beyond some bushes.

"Say hello," said Caliopia.

Clara started to greet her, then realized that Caliopia had been addressing her chickens, who cackled, the hats on their heads bobbing.

"Good morning," Clara said, a little stunned. "I hear that you know some secrets about mourning."

"Now why would you want to learn that from me? There's enough unhappiness around to teach you."

"Maybe if you show me something about it, I'll be better prepared," said Clara.

Caliopia set down the feed bucket. "All living eyes, including ours, dig tunnels out of the landscape. Draw two marks on a paper, almost the full width apart." She tried to demonstrate using grains on the ground but gave up when the chickens kept pecking at them. "Cover your left eye and stare with your right at the blot on the left-hand side. So far so good. Everything is visible. But then slide the paper back and forth from your arm's length to your nose, and you'll see that there is a point where the blot on the *right* disappears. That's our warning that the world is not a nice smooth picture. It's all in lace. There are black holes everywhere, but our eyes are always moving fast to blur them over so we won't go mad." She pointed to the hens. "Now, see how chickens walk? They jut their heads out and keep their eyes fixed. Then their bodies snap forward to catch up. They're stepping carefully so they won't fall into the missing parts of the lace. They gave me the idea that I could be less cautious and throw my spirit into the gaps, and it's scary enough to make me cry. From there it's easy to mourn for someone whose whole body has fallen in."

"Aren't you afraid of getting stuck in the holes?" Clara said.

"Sometimes I fall in too far and have to scream louder, until the echo bounces me out," she said, "but I've never fallen in as far as the Egg."

"The *what*?"

"Or Eggs, if you wish. One is the essence and the others are the specific aspects. Like saying *mankind*, and then *James, Peter*, and so on. Other than that, I'm not too sure what it or they are about."

"You seem to know quite a lot," said Clara, hiding an amused smile.

"No, I've fallen far enough into sadness to see it or them lying way below, but if you ever find yourself on its or their level, it is because you've gone past sorrow into anguish. I've never lost a loved one—even my parents are still alive—so I've never had more than sadness or vicarious grief. The Egg or Eggs are fragile little worlds and therefore they are lessons on how life works. You have to go so far into pain that you hit an end that must be seen as a beginning if you are going to survive. That's the Egg, I think. A land of trying to find birth out of death. It or they crack easily and bleed their hearts. So they're a nightmare of agony, but they also contain a little yellow sun that can help everything grow again. That's hard to believe when you see it or them spilled, though. The temptation is to crawl into your own shell." She clutched the hexagonal wire and looked out at Clara. "Would you like some tea?"

"No, thank you. I have to get to school."

"Good-bye, then," said Caliopia. "Thank you for visiting."

"Good-bye," said Clara. She thought that Caliopia's strengths amounted to heroism. Why the chickens wore hats remained to be explained, but she ignored it as a minor mystery in the face of Caliopia's lessons, which were to be defining points for the rest of Clara's life. She practiced seeing everything as lace, but rather than tumbling into the blind spots, she stayed attached to outer light by a thread as she dangled over the cutaways and blind spots around her, holding to strands fragile as the filigree caravels or crosses made by jewelers back home. She saw no Egg or Eggs and for the time being forgot about them.

She was a spider, with the courage to break into the rectory one night to look for a picture of Tio Vitor while Father Eiras slept. She entered the priest's bedroom and watched him sleeping, mouth open, inhaling the whole room with each breath. He did not feel her standing over him. Though she clawed through closets and drawers, she could find no trace of her great-uncle. Nothing! With a knife from the kitchen, she chipped the polished wooden floor; at least she could steal the veneer to use as agates in her tide pools.

THROUGHOUT THE GROWING vineyards, right under Father Eiras's nose, she used her newfound skills at falling into the lace in the landscape to tumble in and out of her parents' land as if it were a sieve, her green eyes rumbling below his feet like rollers just to amuse herself. The waiting to put her plan into action was difficult, but she was convinced that she had to be patient until she no longer seemed like a child. Already she suspected that this would not be a moment that would announce itself with a clarion call. She had picked her graduation from high school as the day of irrevocably crossing the line, because she recognized in herself that human insistence that at some points the broad sheet of time wears our cryings-aloud, that it stands physically marked with vectors of place and occurrence, with rites of passage, their knots forming a web to catch us.

We might as well write with sticks on panes of water!

We have no choice but to write with sticks on panes of water.

She missed Tio Vitor, and her days were consumed with a ruthless yearning. Merely touching the hair around her labia set off aching that she tried to cure with endless nights of anxious gyration and a waking but never conclusive hunt for satisfaction: She came while climbing trees, did unspeakable things with towels, and once spent a day with a small toy soldier hidden in her underwear so that she would not go a single moment without piercing touch. She figured that after coming a certain number of times she could be done forever with depravity, but when this did not appear to be happening, she had visions of herself as an unsated old woman, still sliding down banisters, still burning. She was afraid that all her lower holes might split together, and for consolation imagined that she could reach up and pull her head inside out between her legs if she wanted some company.

She made men and babies out of mud, not caring that she was much too old for dolls. She gave them straw hair and invited them to tea parties, where she served sugar water infused with mint leaves still white from crop dusting. When the men dried and cracked in the sun, she mixed up new ones. All over the inner valley around her guest house lay the dust of the broken, their shattered arms and coal eyes. She soon tired of building a dumb and useless army and decided that waiting was a puny virtue compared with going out searching—harnessing something of the world, not waiting to see what it might send one's way. As Tio Vitor was doing!

She stayed out late one evening with a flashlight, planning to join Vitor as he plotted with the hills. Instead her light flashed

on a girl she recognized from her class in school. They were
caught in each other's beams and smiled. Sometimes the hand
in the dark was not at all the one expected, out where the
crickets with resined-bow legs serenaded the night.

It was Eva Amália Ferreira, motioning to her with a whiskey
bottle. Eva wore red lipstick and the shortest skirts in school.

Clara took the whiskey and held every swallow in her mouth
until it burned.

"I am drinking away my troubles," said Eva grandly. They
settled on the ground and lit cigarettes. "Mahoney, that pig-
bore, that fucking jerk, says that unless I turn in my book report
by Friday, I may not pass history." She tossed her hair. "What
are *you* drinking away?"

"Nothing," Clara said. "I'm drinking to get things to stay."

They looked at each other and laughed.

"Whatever," said Eva. Her family was from the island of
Pico, famous for its daring whalers. Perhaps it was the black
lava-rock Picaroto houses, with white grout and fire-red doors
and shutters, and the black sand pathways like a moonscape,
that inspired a certain vain toughness: Eva had a careless beauty,
hard where Clara's was smooth.

They drank with their arms slung around one another, talking with their twin fondness for the night. When Clara lay back
on the spinning ground, her hair spread in a fan of brown curls,
with flickers of red. She held out her arms to be lifted, but when
Eva clutched Clara's shoulders to help, Clara grasped Eva's
shoulders. Eva descended in equal measure to Clara's ascension,
until they were harnessed by their chests, breasts kissing breasts,
each flattened onto its mirror as if an object falling to water were
meeting its reflection on the surface, a reflection that was actually its own separate entity below and was now rising spritely to
meet a magnetized kin.

Eva's tongue was the animal straining on its leash, unleashing.
It was Clara's, all hers.

Eva had an outsized clit that worked like a cross between a finger and a tongue as she rubbed it against, into, becoming Clara's.

Finding it. Unnerving it.

This was how Clara imagined love: Not the sugar-figures her mother had made, with parts interlocking (she does not masturbate inside herself, after all), but nerve to nerve, shape confirming shape; let it be mirror to mirror; here were the feelings that made women agree to retreat from the world.

She almost cried out: I have found myself, and everything here is mine! We can never hope to own any country in which we have not made love.

Look at what can be dreamed up out of darkness!

WHEN EVA PRETENDED not to know her at school the next day, Clara was at first too amazed to move. She stood in the corridor clutching her books as Eva passed, chatting with friends. Eva had given her a place and sensation at which to rest and sweeten the dark, and that this could rupture without cause, trailing behind it only hostile silence, made Clara's breath stick in her chest, where it broke into many needles that tried to exhale themselves straight through her skin. Odd, she thought, her head throbbing, that loss turned so quickly physical.

Because she could not bear passing Eva in the halls again, she fled home to collapse numbly on her cot, wondering briefly whether this would transport her to the land of the Egg, where she would have to relearn the basic rules of life, as Caliopia had promised. When love no longer recognizes us, we fall into the strangest comas and outbursts: After lunch hour, knowing Eva would be in algebra, Clara returned to school with a plank and beat Eva's locker, crushing it in places where it would gather rust.

In her bitterest moments as the year passed, Clara concluded that Eva had been sent to her to confirm that love was a distraction, and that she had to harden her heart before she could accomplish the one thing she had come to California to do. Very well, then—she would clamp down on her ardors, wearing her secrecies over them like a fireguard. She would feel her own internal burning, but to others what would emerge would be a studied calmness of perceptions.

Her self-possession worked so well that one day, while working on a school project to clear an area for a football field, a coworker, without provocation, hit Clara on the head with a shovel. That it was a dark flash out of nowhere stunned her as much as the blow. After the school doctor stitched up her head, he peered at her and saw that she was going back and forth between worlds. When she later asked her attacker—a small, mild teenager named Mary Jessup—why she had struck her, Mary looked blank.

"Because I've never seen you cry," she blurted, as bewildered as everyone else.

From that moment on, Clara never doubted the existence of original sin. Nothing grew anymore on the slight crescent near her hairline where the shovel had landed. Later that week, Father Eiras sent her a T-shirt with a silk-screened surfer, a basket of apples, a check for ten percent of the advance on the first prospective wine sale, and a note reading: "A little something for you! (Heard about your 'accident.') Do you like the new iron grillwork around the winery?"

If he was asking her advice, or at least posing such an offhand question ignorant of its presumption, it was her cue that her time was approaching.

Ir HAD BEEN four years since the planting of the seedlings, and Clara entered her final year of high school. She sensed that fortunes were the province of the air. She could feel them shifting night and day: Wavering coins of moonlight were tossed through her windows, falling on her in bed. The coins melted through her fingers and covered her eyes as if sealing the stares of the dead. During daylight, golden bars of corn tumbled over the lips of the high-wheeled boxcars that rumbled through the California farmlands, and she joined the children in collecting whatever bounty littered the tracks.

One afternoon she stood on the rail ties as people trickled like black tea from the station. No one saw her as she walked a mile up the tracks. The train was due to arrive soon to pick up the first shipment of Transfiguration Chablis, along with Father Eiras and several of the winery's managers. They were going on a trip to pose for pictures as they shook hands with the owner of the first market outlet. She hooked her thumbs into the belt loops of her jeans and kicked at some pebbles with her tennis shoes. Then she picked up some ears of corn and stood perfectly still. The train started as a faraway dot before stopping for a while to load up at the station. She watched, waiting in the distance. The dot expanded. When it grew into a column, passengers leaned from windows, screaming for her to jump off the tracks. The train became a wall.

When Father Eiras appeared at a window, shouting something indecipherable and waving his arms, she lay on the tracks with the bouquet of corn on her chest and the train flowed warmly over her, with sparks now and then like candles blowing out in a cave. The railcars were too high to scrape her. (She had spent hours that week sitting in a chair with a knot that hit the middle of her back, to make it very straight, as an old woman back home had done to attain perfect posture.) It was like stepping bodily into one of the pits in the lace of the landscape where her mind often painlessly slipped. She sensed that trains rattle on the outside, much as people sounded to her when she had been young, but here below, where exhaust sighed around the black tires, there was genuine silence. These noises fit into a picture: a smooth, muted sphere inside a black jagged cylinder. Father Eiras's face had been a circle pierced with a mouth in a booming O. Light first arrived as a square below the caboose's body, and then the square exploded into a whole sky as the train careened onward. Because she was not even shaking, she believed that she could do anything. It took her a few days to observe that her cheekbones appeared to be rising higher overnight, as if trying to shutter her eyes behind bone.

WHEN FATHER TEO Eiras returned from his first wine sale, he was bothered that his hands would not stop shaking. He had never liked trains. What to do? They made him positively ill. While sick as a boy with rheumatic fever on the tiny island of Flores, he had begun his lifelong love of puzzles, and that and some brandy seemed as good a cure as anything right now. Crosswords were a favorite, and also the game that converted a word into its opposite, letter by letter, as in:

> LOSE
> ROSE
> RISE
> WISE
> WINE
> WINS

He unwrapped a package of thin square origami papers and, with tremors in his hands, changed a green one into a diamond with hidden folds that could be further crafted into two smaller overlapping diamonds. The California glare of midafternoon, the kind that made him dizzy, thrust its headache-prompting sword through the window.

Mother used to put treats in the separate depressions of a muffin tin to cheer him up when he was confined to bed. The joy of everything in separate compartments! Known to those with an essentially indoor nature. (Sometimes he hid under the blankets, poking out his head when she came into his room. Being a shepherd, dairyman, or fisherman had never been one of his possibilities.)

He opened a flap in one of the diamonds to create an elongated triangle sprouting pointed feet. He had to stop sweating or what he was shaping would be ruined.

Tio Leonardo could not stop himself from molding animals from chunks of bread at the table during meals; he walked twice as fast as everyone else, fidgeting, impatient, petrifying Teo with this example of the effects of island fever on a man of larger ambitions.

With a pause and a glower: Now what? There was always a point in origami when he made an error, the manipulations of his hand grew lumbering, and the points did not sharply meet proper points.

Tio Leonardo won iron-bending contests in the town of Santa Cruz in Flores. He piloted his rowboat, with a cow standing on the slats, to the nearby island of Corvo whenever bonfires there indicated that the three hundred inhabitants needed food and other supplies. He was not afraid of the isolation and primitiveness of the Corvense, as some men were. He could do anything.

Father Eiras gave the body he was making more feet and completed tucks folded inward on the underside.

"The problem with all of you is that you walk small, think small, you little nobodies!" protested Tio Leonardo when arrested for borrowing a rock shaped like a rooster from Corvo. It was draped with a necklace of gold coins once seized from a pirate. With the money he raised from displaying it on all of the islands of the Azores: Flores, Santa Maria, Graciosa, Faial, Pico, Terceira, São Jorge, and São Miguel, he had enough to buy not only medicine for Teo and new clothes for his family but several sheep and cows for Corvo. He had not stolen anything; he had brought about increase. "They're going to be reunited with their property, their stupid rock, plus interest," he said. "I take a puny fee—that's just business, you fifteenth-century codfaces. Where is my thanks for bringing them a new herd?"

The body underneath held many concealed boxes, creases, facets. Father Eiras added others, running his nail along the edges, and turned it over. The outside was smooth.

The jail was crowded with people bringing paper flowers, guitars, and candies to Tio Leonardo, much as people lavished tinsel and fruitcakes upon priests at Christmastime.

He bent the tail downward and pulled the head upward.

Tio Leonardo had time in jail to hone his talent as a guitarist. After his release he roved everywhere, playing well and distributing paper roses to the grateful women. He played well and traveled to the mainland and throughout Spain. How Teo had loved the postcards from him, admiring how completely he had wrested for himself a part of the outdoors! As a priest Father Eiras was transferred to the larger island of Terceira, not much wider a drink of cloud than Flores, though he thought that the girls were prettier. He could scarcely breathe, could not swallow a satisfying amount into his bottomless lungs.

The hands of Father Eiras stopped their disturbing spasms. He had made a paper turtle, the sharp points on the underside hidden by the smooth tent of the paper shell. (A bit inexact in some of the angles, true, but did that not add to its rough beauty?) It would grow dusty in a few days, especially in the patches where he had sweated. Later it would be thrown away; like a puzzle worked out in bed, it was meant only to help the illness pass.

THE DAY AFTER graduation, Clara donned a spotless white uniform and headed for the rectory. It was widely noted that although she lived without paying rent, with a small percentage of the wine sales, and could afford decent clothing, she did not dress in a way likely to attract a man. She had a few old-fashioned long dresses and some plain black skirts and blue jeans and white blouses.

She lifted her gaze to Father Eiras when he answered the door. "I see there's a new annex going up, and it's very busy now," she said. "You need a housekeeper." Glória and João and Caliopia watched out for her, but they could not do everything. She had to have an occupation now that school was over. Didn't he remember how her mother had trusted him to take care of her?

She cleaned, cooked, and taught Father Eiras to dive, tossing a gold hoop into the shallows of the lake outside town and then touching his shoulders and running her bare foot against the inside of his knees to relax him for the plunge. In water she had permission to put her arms around him, to hoist him for air. He had rings of fat from his chest to his belly, like cords binding him internally. She clung to these to help him rise. She pressed her breasts against his back, her nose against his neck, and hitched upward.

"Our swimming lessons are over," he declared soon after the heat drove her from a one-piece to a two-piece suit.

"Giving up? Before we're done with our lessons? Shame on you," she scolded. Now that he was preparing to build a Transfiguration pool, how would it look when everyone found out that he sank like a stone? What was he afraid of? Surely, like every good priest, he thought of water as baptism, renewal, the beginning of a new life.

"You win, Clara." He sighed.

When she forgot to bring a towel or change of clothes, she shut herself in his bedroom to undress while dripping and put on one of his long white shirts. Searching through his bureau drawers for pictures of Tio Vitor proved as fruitless as it had during her night raid. Father Eiras waited, pacing, in the kitchen. "Feed me, if you're the housekeeper," he grumbled, but first, with his shirttails curving over the backs of her thighs, she stretched her bikini to dry on the veranda. Then, barefooted, she fixed his meal. Swimming gave him an appetite for charred meat, potatoes, hollandaise, strawberry pies. She poured him different wines for every lunch, insisting that as the driving force behind the Lodi Transfiguration project he must sample what he was giving to others.

She rubbed down the rectory until it bristled. One would not think a man all by himself could do much damage, but she found plenty to clean. There were spiders' nests to swipe out of corners, lightbulbs to dust in their sockets, brandy decanters to refill. When she shook comforters to air them, she sweated until translucent patches covered her blouse.

"O my God, I can't get rid of you," he said, "can I?"

She weakened a moment when she surprised him squinting in amazement, like a young boy new to a forest, at the dust in a light shaft entering through a rectory window. He was thickening around the middle; enlarged pores made him look like honeycomb tripe. He had a soft face. People back home had snickered about him, but here in Lodi he was growing silver-haired and beloved by his parishioners. Everyone was truly defenseless unto death—but, she reminded herself, not everyone dabbles so freely with others defenseless *in* death, and the so-called forgiving God had answered Adam's plea for mercy by forbidding automatic sanctifying grace to all of history.

Alone in the guest house she squatted and inserted two fingers into herself, spreading them with steady pressure, like blunt scissors, to make sure that she was the one to win the war over her canal. Three scant blood smears told her that she alone would be the first, that no one could hurt her, no one could claim a single drop of her.

The next afternoon, steeling her spine as Father Eiras worked over the winery's annual tally, she pulled off her shirt and sagged like poured clay onto his lap, slumping like a grieving child. He buried himself in her.

During their affair, he satisfied himself many times, but her feelings were obviously not his concern. This was fine; she preferred the arrogance of him stabbing in and out, imagining that anything that pleased him had to be doing the same for her. He adored entering her from behind, and she was satisfied that he never once reached around to fondle her. It left her nerves her own. He loved to unfetter a torrent whenever she bent over with her scrub brush in the kitchen, flattening her face against the minor sea of the wet floor, and this was perfect because it allowed her to swim away and prevented her from watching his pent-up years coming undone, although afterward the blood stayed in his chest and neck as evidence.

She worked harder to stay absolutely motionless. If her back and legs remained unmoving, it was no longer just her eyes that could feel invisible, but most of her. She asked him to turn her face downward and tie her limbs to the bedposts with his cinctures. Prone, frozen, she could fly away entirely. Before anchoring her, he dressed her in his alb, as he might clothe himself, so that pressing full-length onto it, tearing it aside, was nothing more than ripping toward his own thin specter, reclaiming the half of himself immobile and denied. Even if she could have managed to dig her heels like spurs into his backside, she would not have existed in this embrace.

How Father Eiras could toy with life without thinking of consequences would always astound her. If the entangled vines on the land of her family were allowed to grow, then would they not produce wine? If all he can see is his own fucking, then does it not take a baby to make him see her?

They were face-to-face.

She reminded him of his religion classes at school:

First they were encouraged to perform acts of mortification for penance, and she had stuck artichoke thorns into her fingers in the hope of reducing some of her Purgatory time.

Then they had been told they could chew raw onions and traipse the perimeters of their farms on their knees forever and it still would not wash clean original sin. Some burning time in the fires would be required anyway. Hadn't he said this to her mother?

Hadn't he drawn a heart on the chalkboard to explain it to the students?

At first glance the heart looks blank and pure, until we realize that it must take its shape against a black background if it is to exist.

Although it was impossible to win, he had encouraged them to keep on fighting against the stain of what man was.

All she had done, she calmly reminded him, was provide the black background against which he could shape his heart.

"You'll go stay with the nuns!" he said.

"But I've commended myself to you," she answered. She had disappeared quite enough now, and she had no intention of being bundled off to the home hidden in Napa, where rain drilled the bad girls clean as they scoured their rooms with pine water. She was utterly through with looking at floors. When her child split her legs, it would not plop into the obscuring, willowing sheets clutched by nuns eager to make the baby vanish into the hands of a nice deserving couple.

He became shrill. "You'll do as I say!" he cried.

"I already have," she said.

Clara told half of Lodi her good news, although one parishioner would have been sufficient for everyone, down to the workers in the damp wine cellar, to know within hours that acts of love and grace can be actual, if not always sanctifying.

She grew rotund. Caliopia and Glória brought her soothing teas. She craved blackberries but ate so many without being gratified that she got the high-noon jitters. Her milk swelled, and the echoes of her sickness vanquished the distance over the waves of land and drove Father Eiras out of the rectory, holding his head on both sides so that it would not split, the pose with which Clara had greeted the world. The berries she vomited bloomed like reddish coral in her toilet. This was her sea.

THE PAINS STARTED as if she had eaten something bad. We should have extra pouches, she thought, like cows with their hardware-stomachs for the nails and wire that they swallow. They could make metal calves. We'd make barbed-wire babies from the bad things we picked up. Or we need bigger wombs, not this one folded-over piece of sponge cake. Pains like muffling a stick of dynamite blowing up in slow slow motion. I've changed my mind; I don't want to do this.

The head arrived a battering fist.

Matilda Nicolini, the midwife, swung Clara's red, jam-smeared, yellow-green, violet, and blue son upside down. His curved hands, pink, with nails miniscule as a salamander's claws, swiped the air. His arms flapped out like wings, but he was soundless.

Clara would not tolerate this evidence that she had given birth to herself, nothing but herself, silent, all over again. "Give him to me!" she demanded, trailing ropes of blood while clamoring off Matilda's kitchen table. She pushed the midwife aside and breathed sound into her child of colors. As he cried high notes, she focused on the wound gaping on his chest. He had been born ruined. It had taken her this many minutes to see and believe it.

She screamed: loud, long, across the years.

FATHER TEO EIRAS was transferred to a parish up north in Eureka, where he could begin with a clean slate, but this was a truncated victory for Clara. Though she had rid herself of the perpetrator of the original sin against her land, the bishop dismissed her demands, though he agreed that the child was entitled to a certain compensation so as not to pay overly much for the sins of his mother and her confessor.

She had assumed that with a large-enough sacrifice of herself, body and spirit, it would be impossible to fail to win back her land. That she could lose it more absolutely had not occurred to her, but what now glared more harshly was that she had never pictured anything beyond having the child, nothing outside of this culmination of events. She had been so foolish! Certainly she had never considered what it might be to love her child, and holding him without letting go, she thought, This more than ever is what I have done.

There was a split down the middle of him, from chest to stomach, so that he could show her his heart. Was this his self-sacrificing idea to soothe her bitterness by displaying slow, steady pulsing, a warning that she must not forget that everyone carried this at his center? That she had forgotten her own heart? *Forgive me*, she asked him, trembling as she tried to push the open flesh closed. It refused to heal. *I didn't anticipate far enough, you're right; I forgot during my schemes that you would be born a separate self, breathing and yearning. Since you are giving me everything that you are, I will carry your injuries in return. You weren't born wrong. You were born all heart, just right.*

She stroked his smooth, damp forehead.

She consented to Glória's invitation to live with her and João for a while. Alone at night as she nursed the unnamed and damaged boy, she whispered, "Shall we pose for our family portrait?"

Your Vovó José Francisco is an ocean skeleton. I hope that he rests near a sunken ship, with a ruby floating loose to glow as his heart and pearls shining behind his eyes.

Your Vovó Conceição flies with wings. I realize now that the swellings that covered her on her deathbed came from hours of directing inward her tears for my father. When Maria Josefa and I massaged some of her internal water away, the salt left behind must have burned until she had to cry inside again for relief.

Your mother used to have a mouth as rippled as the bottom of an apple. Now it is flattening. I had large rounded eyes, a face with curved sides, like hands being shaken in emphasis. I can feel myself growing thinner and sharper. Sometimes I think I see Eggs that say, "We are the origin of things, and when you have lost everything, you must fall onto us."

I see your Tio Vitor occasionally, especially when I follow Caliopia's advice and enter the black spaces. He is very faded, with grapevines covering his skin like veins, but says he is fighting onward!

Now there is you. For you I plant a sugar arrow. I have pointed it downward because I am finished with all love except for yours. Pity me, in need of blooms! Hold on. Survive. Grow through the straight stem that is strong but bare, lift yourself past the leaves, and rest above, where the arrow needs only its flower.

THREE

Guide us to the light within animals. The light that reigns over heart-colors, over the blue shades of dying blood and the scarlet waves that tremble chamberforth.

Guide us to the light bursting from animals, from us—the gleam that shoots these reds and blues out through our eyes to join the yellow of the sun. These are the primary colors that paint the earth.

Flowers and rolling fields are an impasto ocean.

Morning is vivid crimson and purple because the air is still wet from the night's spilling of hearts, and it harbors all the lingering pulse beats. To navigate this painting and music of a dawning is to see and hear the secrets of the light; the tones grow faint without mercy; we must enter into the kingdom of our heartsplashing.

THE COLOR OF the heart of Clara Deolinda Cruz as she prepares to carry her dying son outside to absorb a neighboring garden is immaculate; it is immaculate, the hue of steel. Such a sacred heart is known by these signs: It is swollen to twice normal size. It rages enough to glow visibly on the chest. Fire crowns the furrow between the heart's two halves. Above a ring of white pearls is a sword, the memento of what was cherished and lost, stabbed in too deeply for the surrounding aureole to dislodge it. A heart is not immaculate because it is pure, but because it is injured.

Clara wakes early, before the world has begun. Each morning lately she leaves Glória's and João's house and takes refuge in the guest house to lighten a mug of black beer with rock sugar and an egg and gulp it without pausing for air. She thanks her breakfasts for being sure, steady, thick true masses. Today, with her son in her arms, she swallows pieces of eggshell, but gladly, gladly—perhaps their starry edges will lacerate her stomach to drive the iron in the beer farther inside to make her stronger. "Ahh," she says, with vanilla-brown spume crackling like sea foam on her upper lip. "Ahh," breathes the infant into his mother's chest as toy-sized rain drips from the mug and cools his burning forehead.

"Shh," says Clara, dipping a finger into the beer for the baby to suckle. Conspirators! We plot! Together we raise our glasses! The baby's gum ridges feel like the inside of a nose: solid but pliable and much too easy to pierce—more of God's terrible design work. Bad building materials. Problem of absentee land-lord, ruling by thought alone. Trees got a better thinking-through. Certainly waterfalls did, and whales.

Her green eyes drop round pools into her son's green eyes (it is mirror to mirror, as it was when she loved Eva Amália) as she muses, Why was a mess made of everyone of us? For instance the empty scrotum. Scarcely tougher than a pig's bladder. How does it survive infancy without tearing? Being caught on a nail. Or on a low branch when a baby crawls. Ripped like an airless balloon. Then what? I ache thinking about it, about how you were made. You are red clay I would like to remold.

Come to me, you anything within and beyond me that has a voice, she prays; I cannot be this brave alone.

The child raises his hands and belches sugary beer froth.

"Shhussh, shh," says Clara. "Ahh, here now."

Ahh. Shh. Ahh. Long morning sighs. Sounds of embracing. Sounds of waves going in, going out.

They enter the peace of the garden.

Just as Father Eiras is banished, so does Clara dismiss thoughts of everything and everyone outside her son. The world narrows for a determined mother; the world is grasped com-pletely by a determined mother. Outside of her and him, she feels the waves of Tio Vitor as she rushes about. She is grateful he is with her but is too distraught to do more than register him. Her thinking is in blocks; she wishes to break the world into manageable squares, like quadrants on a map that facilitate finding one's location, like tiles that form a mosaic on a sidewalk to the sea.

SHE WANTS TO find a fruit that embodies the baby's womb-song. She takes him to greet the *amoras*, the blackberries whose Portuguese name is so close to love. Every berry has many tiny breasts, each with a saber of hair at whose base an unseen seed clings buried. A breeze shakes the *amoras* like boats tossing in the middle of an ocean of brambles.

His wound must have been caused by how fiercely her own longings for her family had pounded in her chest, wanting to burst out where her anguish could be touched, or maybe she had stretched her arms too wide to claim her land, snapping herself open. The child's body could not contain such straining full-nesses, and he had been born with a ventral split, wide and suppurating, that widened his rib cage and laid bare his heart, the muscle wet and throbbing. She could see it; she could touch it if she wished. He had been sent to teach her of the reign of the heart. Doctors said only: There is nothing for us to do.

The immaculate berries quiet the baby.

His mother's voice calms him still more. The baby will soon fall into black infinity, and she is worried about him being afraid of the dark. Tio Vitor had disclosed to her the full lesson of her father about what hides in the night, amplifying what she remembered from Eugénio's speaking of it in rock sugar. Now she explains to her boy that caresses and color lie inside every seemingly lightless place. Lovers stretch nights longer, shutting out daylight, hoping to slip under the cover of one unbroken night, where they conceal the redness of their embracing. So too *amoras* pull a black juice over their newborn redness. So too a child, when he is ash, should remember that he also remains a gardenia.

She picks ripe berries and murmurs, Look how easily the darkest fruits drop into my hand. They are the sweetest. If you are ever imprisoned in an endless night, find the lovers hiding within it. Will you call out when you find the red? And your own colors mixed in? Because blackness is not an abyss, but a sea of all shades.

Her voice quavers.

The berries bleed on her palm.

She knows that hunting for color in so much mud is a folly, but she cannot let her son drop into nothing without a fight. As the baby's eyes try to focus on her, Clara goes to war against the dark. She will compose her child a whole life, right now, from the gifts of the lighted world.

She must swiftly find the child's birth living somewhere in the garden.

A famous grafter, a Doctor Helio Gabriel Soares, a widower dentist, lives a number of miles south, in Stockton. Clara has never met him but knows that he helps out on Fridays in Lodi's clinic, and during his lunch hour he creates unimaginable unions in the outdoors. He is reputed to be a hopeful sort, of the quiet diligence that usually belies a person coming to terms with his sorrows. She points out to the baby the doctor's attempt in this garden to graft tomatoes with dental floss to form tubes that can give transfusions of red fluid to ailing plants. He has experimented with crossing pages of stories with corn so that the kernels will became a baby's letter-blocks. Though these grafts are not successful, he has not given up on the possibility of their future healthy births.

No skin grafts can repair the baby's fissure, and his naked heart fades to coral, fades in its pulse beats. His innards, mucus-coated as fish, float in blood like the fruits in sangria. A gelatinous seal keeps most of his blood from pouring out. "You're a pitcher of what I once drank with Eugénio at a picnic back home," she says, touching the baby's nipples on either side of his open chest. She had stroked the raised dots of paint on the sangria pitcher at the picnic to absorb her not knowing how to touch Eugénio, who had been covered with mosquito bites, scratching himself, crawling with nipples.

This dying boy has no name, because naming is an act of separation his mother will not perform. Once the animals in Eden were named, they were no longer creation, but themselves alone. Her baby is going where all is named nothing, and he named nothing will then be named all, much as her father, José Francisco Cruz, washed overboard became the whole sea.

She knows that her father is off somewhere, eager to care for his grandson. "But you'll never hear the end of what he thinks of the clergy," she tells the baby. "He'll drive you crazy." (Let her father do the ranting about Father Eiras that she now lacks the strength to do.)

She kisses the wrinkles on the back of the baby's neck. "Drink air! Fill those out!" she teases. Her son's head is a sunflower heavy on its stem. He is unwrapped enough for the liplike edges of his chest, rubbery as liver and shiny as a snail's gummed side, to receive her kisses; she wants him to know it is a beautiful wound. She admires her son for dying in the cause of shaping a human in a new form. Brutal trick, that babies come out wailing but not talking or singing. "I will be robbed of his voice!" she announces; she rocks the baby against herself and declares, more gently, "I should be the one with the open chest, to press you back inside me so that we can start again."

Though she could not hear a chorus of family voices as a child—perhaps *because* she could not hear them—Clara now believes that this is how life must commence. To bestow upon her child a full infancy, she gathers up more voices by telling Glória that the baby needs clothes made like nets so that his heart can breathe.

"Do you know fishermen's knots?" Clara asks. "Use soft yarn."

"What a scaly head you have, kid! Are you a fish, a fish a fish a fish?" sings Glória, picking up the boy. "I'll make him net-clothing with an opening for his chest," she tells Clara. "Into the weave I'll use a hook to add a giraffe, an elephant, and a bear to guard him. Why don't we have wild animals in Lodi?"

"They would eat all our flowers," says João, who has a flesh arm and a ghost arm from that cow lying on him in the dairy. He holds the baby with both to prove the substantiality of what is missing.

"Look what I've done," says Clara. The blood of regret drips from her words. "I have no family, so I made him mine and ruined him."

"You have us," says João hurriedly. "Did you know that onions and lilies are in the same family? Strawberries and roses? Who can say what belongs together?"

Her nerves are beating out the refrain: Delight him as a toddler, protect him from evil.

> *Bicho vai,*
> *Bicho vem,*
> *Come o pai,*
> *Come a mãe,*
> *E come a menina também!*

> The buggy worm goes,
> The wormy bug comes,
> It eats the father,
> It eats the mother,
> And it eats the baby too!

Clara walks her fingers up the baby's leg while singing this rhyme, and on the final line she attacks his stomach until he squeals with laughter. She is teaching him to respond, warning that he must not let *o bicho* get to his throat. It is good training for the worse night things darting through outer space. She has already met some of them. If she stares too many seconds at those red and white pinpricks in a dark room, they roll into constellations that burst alive—into pirates and dogs speaking guttural English. When they approach as she lies in bed with the baby, she quickly signs crosses in an invisible picket fence around her territory. The beasts yowl but cannot claw him. From behind her cross-fence she scorns them by saying, My birthmark is a scarlet animal erupting from my side. You will not snatch him before his time. I am not afraid of you.

Youth blooms; it is tinged with wonder.

She slits a calla lily's stem into two legs and places them in a vase of beet juice. The next morning, she brings the boy near the flower's mottled face. The white part has colored itself from taking in the juice below. "Look," she says, "the lily is so pleased to meet you that you have made her blush." His fingers graze the dye drunk into the tissue.

She is still bleeding from the birth.

The lily's cut legs absorb redness; she drips red onto white cotton pads.

This *Lesson: With Flower* was how Clara distilled for her boy a fast, complete youth—the time of first studies in art and science. Whether it is bliss and seepage upward or pain and seepage downward, she found it unsettling that opposites resolve in the same key: We redden the pale world.

Youth is the time of first stories. She tells him how she felt right before he was born. "I thought, A beginning! A beginning! This is greatness, I think—don't you?—to be so thrilled with what is happening that what might happen next never occurs to one."

Aren't the teenage years the age of spices and discovery? Time for first tastes? Clara, a taster of tastes, is an able guide to this realm of exploration. She has long enjoyed eating whole teaspoonsful of nutmeg, with its essence of honeyed wood, and handfuls of raw basil. Now for the baby's sake she buys a jar of cinnamon so dense that it is compressed like a red-brown paint, leaking a shield of oil. She samples some and breathes fire the rest of the day. "Aii," she yells, stamping her feet, "Aii—let's go exploring, pal. I'll be the dragon and you'll rescue a maiden in a tower."

She takes him to encounter hydrangeas, because when the boy reached a certain age, she would have taken him to the Azores to show him where she was from. Her father often took her to visit hydrangeas; she thought it was so that she would lose herself in some quality that purple had. (Now that she could speak, she wanted to scream, What did they mean to you, Papai? What did you mean for them to mean to me?) Hydrangeas more than anything else remind her of home. They are her father. That is what memory does: It captures the remembered person in certain sculptures that one can carry in the mind, like a figurine in a pocket. *Papai, eyes forward, toward the horizon, near hydrangeas.* That was the title of him.

Her mother had called hydrangeas "balls of yarn." Clara, for her part, thought they were like the blue world globe she had kept in her room.

As she and her son approach a hydrangea, she points and explains, "Many people think: color—purple; perception—flower. But you are now a brilliant adult. You should trust the real only when it is grafted to the imaginary, and as an adult you must occasionally try to untie philosophical knots. Here is one, young man: 'What the flower is imagined is what is, not the real hydrangea but the dreamed globe. If you are to be a man, you must learn, quickly, that an adult spends his time trying to outwit death by picturing parts of himself living beyond himself. If you paint your dreamed globe onto a chosen flower, you may call it your flowering world. The world-flower ornamenting the path becomes your true globe. By affixing your world outside of yourself, you dream your dreams real, and therefore you perceive that you do dream living dreams, and so first conceive no longer your dreamed world but the pith wherein you are all a dream.'"

My word, she marvels. Where did that come from? Frightening. Maybe my father is speaking through me? Or maybe my head is trying to break open like your chest. Am I going to be like one of those live monkeys strapped below tables in the East who get their skulls sawed open and while they screech their raw brains are eaten with spoons? No, no, no! Don't cry! I only mentioned the monkeys because you're a grown-up.

The baby, kicking, is trying to grasp something. She offers her chin.

My chin is a mountain, isn't it? Here, can you chew it? Look near your nose, at that perfect dot! Unbelievable that time was wasted gluing that on instead of sewing you closed.

Gestating within her is the desire that he will have lovers and children. She tells him that he is not a boy but a seahorse from the race of ocean dragons with external skeletons and tails that are used for anchoring. The males swell with their pregnancies and ejaculate more than thirty live babies at a time. The young are always, always hungry. The advice of the parent who carried them is that they should intertwine tails as they roam. Wherever the offspring go, they will be bridled to one another.

Out of her head, ruptured from the hydrangea-puzzle, she watches a seahorse sail. It wraps its tail around the baby's wrist, like a lover taking his arm.

After burgeoning new selves and children, what follows is the phase of dreams that are a mist. To Clara, dreams are shrouds that are meant to prepare us for life as a spirit. Having rushed the boy through adulthood and age, she is desperate to camouflage him. Instead of being put inside the earth, perhaps he can live invisible but moving on the surface of it. She has seen light-bellied animals do this by slipping inside rays of daylight. She knows that eyes are especially difficult to hide, because his have shined toward her at night. He needs to sprout a mask over them. There are shorebirds called turnstones that have these, a dark band that tones down the eyes.

She will call the baby a turnstone bird! If his eye were still to glisten as a point beneath a black arch of socket and brow, as a turnstone's does, Death passing over would think, Hold longer; this is to be sustained. We thought it was a child to snatch, but we were wrong. This is a fermata.

Clara is breathing hard. Milk darkens her shirt. Where can they go that is safe? Where safe? He is her child of colors. He is still red, yellow, and blue.

She is desperate to find a sanctuary.

The baby shits green.

"Earth colors. That's the spirit," says Clara. She changes him and puts a sprig of rosemary into his fist. "A bouquet. It'll help you blend into the bushes." How do fingers manage to come out right? Already wearing their nails. A better plan: Trade being born with nails for speech from the first moment. Nails could be grown at age twelve. Age of putting on armor. Parties to celebrate the appearance of first nails? First wine then too.

Where shall we hide? The Midwest? Too landlocked? Some states are shaped like dry toast. But we could soak them in coffee, right, cowboy? Maybe San Francisco. Or we could curl up together in the circle of the fish-hook stuck on Massachusetts. Since you're my Egg, are you taking me to an end or to a beginning? What are your life lessons?

She hugs the baby in a grove where no one can see them.

She is dying inside as she gives the baby the Azorean goodnight wish:

Sonhos na cor-de-rosa.
Pink dreams.
Sleep well, sleep in pink sleep.
Rest with such white light that you bleach the red world
    pink.
Rest in the color that my father painted the stars.

Clara stops repairing the giraffe, elephant, and bear in the net-clothes after the baby's thrashing tears them open. She takes him home to darn the animals closed but then exclaims, "Wait a minute. Now I understand! You're trying to make them be the same as you."

She and Glória finish opening the net-giraffe, net-elephant, and net-bear and hem their fronts into buttonholes. Clara bites off the thread ends and flattens them with saliva. The baby's whole face, pleased, scrunches into slits for his eyes and mouth. He and his animals look like the Earth with her fissures and openings.

The Earth has billions of mouths to receive bodies. When one enters her, she shouts glad cries. She has her fill; the man dissolves. The ants scramble like black notes on the clefs of his pelvic span and the double staffs of his ribs to turn his body into music. She opens the chest and he wafts as pestilence but also as presents sent back to his home: his eyes winking on land, arms quivering in trees, wounds gaping in canyons.

According to Clara's mother, Conceição (trying to get her to eat a meat soup one day), vitality and hope are said to be in marrow. This means that bones have a lightness inside that allows them to flee into the air.

Clara understands why the skeleton of a bird's wing is homologous to the bones of a man's hand!

The fingers of the dead, because of the lightness in their marrow, fly up to caress the sky. Since they do not want to scare the living, they long ago developed the habit of hiding within wings. So that's where the hands of the departed finally end up!

"Find a turnstone bird. Or any bird," she advises him. "Each one that passes, I'll think, There my baby goes! Clutching the air within those wings."

The baby has grown old and dreamed; now the galaxies have truths but not explanations in store for him. Such as: Opposites in the heavens wheel together and explode into light. Out of this united massive energy, new pairings may be born, pulled apart again into separate wheels of new removed selves, with new opposites; light either breaks down like this or remains itself, but it cannot mate with other light to create light beyond light. This is the type of ultimate sorrow upon which the universe is based. How then can a living mother burst with a dying son into one wheel, from which they can both spin brightness upon brightness?

She does not know, but she vows that dead or living she will never stop singing to this boy who is about to leave her. "Listen for me," she tells him. "Maybe this is how to turn you into light: I will call for you always, whether I am here or up in the stars."

She is in rebellion. She wants a new kingdom of imagined lights, starred beings, and such a carnal bind with the dead that the universe explodes in God's face as one fiery wheel. Most men never kill anyone, but God is the murderer of all. The living and the dead must combine forces to become light in order to detonate Him.

She would like to stop dreaming up big truths. She wants comfort.

Her new kingdom will offer solace for *saudade:* The cure will be quite simple. No one and nothing will be taken from anyone; desires will be fulfilled; looming absences will be corrected; everyone, everything will partake of a present, timeless feast.

On the dessert trays at the opening of the new kingdom, she will serve *Papos-de-anjo,* Breasts of Angel, with rivers of sugar syrup, and *Papos-de-freira,* Breasts of Nun, all bursting with egg yolks. Spilled yellow suns! Suckling of heaven and earth. (The only obese people in the new kingdom will be those who eat no sugar or fats.)

To greet the guests, the orchestra will play notes from The Book of the Songs of Heaven and from The Book of the Songs of Earth. An antiphon between the living and the dead. (God's current disorganized plan: Two warring choirs that cannot agree on a time and place to practice together.)

In her son's honor, boomerangs will be the major sport in the new kingdom. "Now I understand—you're splitting yourself into a boomerang to come back to me! Will you soar to the sun, then twirl around and return? What a victory, to shape yourself as a person who can sail away, sail back! I'll be ready to catch you!" she shouts to her boy.

"I'll do a better job grabbing you than I did with my mother's hand. Sometimes I cannot look at your chest because it is like her open mouth, kissing the empty air. Sometimes I wake up picking at threads in my blanket because I still have not taken the bobby pins out of her hair. I have never seen her full and finished."

She watches his chest to prevent his white moth from launching through the gash.

Viriato das Chagas, the postman, comes to the grieving mother with gifts of the spirit. He was a man of letters on the island of São Miguel and frequented the library of the Universidade dos Açores in Ponta Delgada, but in California he could only find work delivering the mail. He believes that the baby needs an internal army to come to his aid, that some of the creatures hiding within the child must be summoned. Viriato invokes the Lisbon poet Fernando Pessoa, who engendered breathing figments out of himself with their own birthdates, physiques, and histories, called *heteronyms* because they were his inner correlatives subject not to his natural laws but to the rules of released light. They were not dim thoughts but their birthfather's masters, who used Pessoa to write their own poems, each in a unique script and style.

Viriato sees three characters linked within the child. Because the boy is so near to the seal upon his days, his heteronyms are spelling out *A . . . men* in order to say good-bye. He introduces Clara and the boy to the heteronyms spiraling around the exposed heart:

Álvaro Augusto Alvo, always announcing anguish.

Rui Coelho, who had three nightmares with drill marks, empty black holes in the sky, threatening to engulf him. He drew this picture of his troubles:

. . .

One day he piled these drill marks together to make a huge telescope. "I'll find and destroy the place where nightmares are born," he said bravely, but this turned out to be the cave of the same monster who decided which children should die young. Cracking as Rui's fist tightened in horror, the telescope fell back into:

. . . ,

an ellipsis that speaks of what is missing.

"What else? What others do you see?" asks Clara, staring at her son's heart. She wishes she could dab it dry with a towel.

"One more," says Viriato, relieved to move on from the grimness of Álvaro and Rui. "Someone who knows about the stars."

Felix Texeira de Carvalho, an astronomer who found out why prayers do not reach God. Felix already knew that everything audible in history, from an eyelash falling to Ovid's pen leaking, remains circulating in the airwaves. While hunting for the ways these sounds are trapped, he observed that stars were the tympanums of huge ears, but endless prayers had so toughened them that they now deflected all petitions and noises. Apparently God did not care that the heavens no longer transmitted the human symphony.

Felix believed that the stars hoarded the hope and songs of the world. He remembered that after swimming, a stopped-up ear may be loosened with oil; on a mirror reflecting the stars, he smeared oil and waited until dew broke the slick into beaded notes. He copied them down and dedicated his concert to A-men, the Egyptian god of life and procreation.

Men had to unhinge star-songs!
Men should not feel like lonely bare melodies.
Men had to sing, whether or not they could be heard.

Visitors come as if summoned to the house, because the baby is fussing as blood sheds more heavily from his chest. The mysterious efforts of Viriato had given Clara a moment's hope—she too believes that everyone contains an army of other souls—but the baby is not consoled. Glória, Caliopia, João, and Viriato take turns helping her walk him up and down a fallow garden patch. They weep black spots into the dirt, scattering them among his falling red drops.

"All our splattering—look!" Viriato proclaims. He tries to convince them that on the ground they and the boy have sprinkled *A* and . . . and *men*, his heteronyms forming the name of the god of life, but everything has soaked in too fleetingly, and the others see nothing. Over the next days, in between vigils of watching the child, they dig furrows in evenly spaced combings, and the drops lie eclipsed beneath the lines of the newly planted seedbeds. The ground offers no *A . . . men* that they can see, though Viriato continues to insist that they have spelled out the great word of assent onto the ground, that it may be invisible for now but there is no erasing it.

One night, after lighting a yellow candle at Glória's and João's kitchen table in order to rest with her son near a glowing in the dark, Clara notices that for a sparkling of a moment the white tablecloth appears yellow. Then her eyes correct the yellow into a whiteness to match what her mind knows is white cloth. She sinks into a chair.

Well. Well, well. Did you see that, cowboy? Colors change! They can color themselves. The eye—now here is a secret!—can switch around its pictures if the brain does not stay stuck on what is known. If the eye can paint what is actually white cloth into yellow—or what is colored yellow back into white—why stop? What should we eye-paint the lace next? How about forest-green? Sky-blue? Hydrangea-purple? Sangria-red?

The baby, unexpectedly, clearly, gives her his first smile of recognition, not merely at a warm moving shape but at this woman unwavering above him.

"Angel!" says Clara, rising to her feet.

The baby leaks a blood drop onto the tablecloth, and Clara

knows he is saying, Yes. Mother! You told me to relieve the darkness with my colors. My red is on the table, under the black cover of night. Can you lead me to other shades too?

She eye-paints her son pink, the color of dreaming. She does the same for the waterfall trickling from the boy's chest onto the floor, but now what? How can she help this weight of pinkness in her hands to rise instead of fall? There has to be a means of putting colors to flight to make them scale upward. There has to be a key to giving sounds to colors to make them sing.

Then the baby can be a song of pink dreams flying up to heaven.

She asks the species of turnstone birds for help. They know how to pry up pebbles and flip them over to find food. They can teach the baby how to overturn the slab of a grave so he can fly out of the earth, since his bones, internally buoyed, will yearn to go upward. After demolishing the stone, the turnstones will look down and see a pink mass not for chewing but for carrying away on their backs.

The sound of them sweeping through the air with him—would that be a wind instrument? Flying colors?

More of the child's blood spills. Clara sees that time is running out and that she has no solution, no absolute link, no formula that will save him. Glória and João come into the kitchen in their bathrobes. João's ghost arm buzzes like a five-pointed eel where it ends in the invisible hand. He holds the baby with his real limb and tries to entertain him with the phantom one, zapping him under the chin, walking invisible fingers up him while singing rhymes. Glória dabs alcohol on the remnants of the baby's umbilical cord.

All of them are finally helpless. When Clara takes her son to the window to greet the dawn, she mumbles, "Your blankness—have I filled it? Have I?"

*　*　*

THE TIME HAS COME for Clara's agony in the garden.

Long labor, long stanching: She is weakened from giving birth and from the search for flying, singing colors. Covering her face with her hands, she longs for the landscape to dissolve into one black hole, where she can fall with him forever, refusing to let him go alone.

She spent months of scheming, then months of pregnancy, only to see that her life—or was it everyone's life?—was in danger of being boiled down to a recitation of its highlights. What disappeared were the mild hummings of tunes, the brushing of teeth, the eating of a peach, the pauses to feel the baby kicking, the frying of ham, the nights when, oppressed by a heaviness of spirit, she went to bed much too early, full of resolutions to begin afresh the next day and full of panic that she was acquiescing in her own defeat.

She senses that these small moments work like padding to soften the bluntness of one's bare facts (hers: unresurrected family, misfired attempt to win land, inability to save her child), and that is how one is tricked into going onward, buffered despite everything. God packed the world with laborious rituals, eating, bathing, and card games, to slow it down so that people would not rebel or break at once in the face of their stark truths.

Feeling it is possible to die of pain, with no amount of padding guaranteed to prevent it, she clings to this: She will still be able to say that she has had a full life with her little boy, and by bleeding red within the night, he showed her that her father's secrets about colors hiding within darkness are true, and that such shades lie under the rule of one's own eye.

She carries her baby back to the garden.

Clara's Psalm on Contractions

He thrashes and blinks with green vast eyes
Tightly shut, then wide and relaxed.

He signals the truth of repose:
All moments of note are time ticked out in muscular
  rhythm—
A contraction and clutch; a flash, a spasm—and then
  high-flying peace.

The heart is the muscle that tightens, then stretches.
Love is the pang that constricts before relief.
Birth is a squeezing and seizure, and finally surcease.
Thought is a closing-in, with sinews, and then the mind's
  throb expands.
Death is a cramping and then spirits untensed in the valley
  of repose.

My child is my pulse beat with green vast eyes
Opened at me, then veiled in a contract.
He signals the truth of repose:
All moments of note are those ticked out in a bond—for a
  contraction is also
An agreement and tie; a flurry, a sadness—and then bitter
  release.

While he blinks his green eyes, she traces the veins in his
temples, although what she really wants to touch is the gorge,
swollen, oozing, and the heart, Swiss-dotted with white fat,
contracting in clear sight like a wet bird under thin strings,
thumping its wings at her. The nerves strapping it converge in
a tender outer knot. A slight pressure with her finger seems
enough to push the heart back where it belongs, a massage
enough to relax the bird in its ruby bath. His ribs are only as
firm as gristle. When she holds him close, the bird flutters,
aroused by the steady rhythm of her breathing. They rock
together, soft-dancing, until she swells with peace to watch him
pulsate so surely in her arms. "You were no trouble being born,"

she says. "No trouble at all." Delicately she presses his sides on the chance that his chest will close, but the bird pushes its head angrily against the boy's rib cage. He is dripping faster, but she thinks it is a sign that the bird that fuels his chest is growing stronger.

And then he gave her his heart—he cried, face tight and eyes shut, and from his wound the bird flew entire to explode on her. It trailed cords that snapped and sprayed her face and breasts. When he went cold and limp, she clamped the bird dribbling against her chest. It was still attached to him by a few red reins, and she wailed out the blood he had birthed into her eyes.

She swam in the lake outside town, with ferocious strokes. The algae-slick rocks were like the backs of frogs, and the water made her feel swallowed within their evil green muscles. She tried to dive more deeply, holding her breath until her lungs heaved empty, toward that passageway lighter than clouds where her sexual nerves would flare from her toying with oxygen— how furtive the secrets that swimmers know for creating sparks of life within water! How varied! And grand! she thought, plunging, airless, as she tried to force her insides to bloom with a fullness and a kicking. Instead she landed within the white belly of another gigantic frog. She pulled choking and blinking toward the surface, out of the suffocating green, where the rudeness of day had to count as a sanctuary.

One morning, Glória gathered a bouquet that would relive the boy's life spans:

For birth, an amaranth, the imaginary flower that is also the real species named love-lies-bleeding; for youth, a jumble of bearded irises, squash marrow, bulbs of garlic teeth, morning glories with their throats, and beans with their pulses—because youth discovers its physicality in all things; for adulthood, fuchsias with their stamen and pistils housed within the same dancing girl's skirts, the sexes joined; for aging, a time of pursuing promises—a rose. She would wrap it in paper for Clara to open on Christmas. If she did not peek, the rose would stay unwilted.

When Clara arrived home from her swimming, Glória gave her the bouquet, putting it on her chest in the exact place she had been clutching the baby's heart when Glória had found her screaming.

Missing were the flowers of the afterlife and light; neither of them had any idea what to pick for these.

Clara's belly stayed distended and hard, sprouting dark hairs as if planting flowers on the mound that was his memorial. Some nights she awoke with terrifying *saudades* for him, because she could swear he was still inside her, the way João continued to feel his ghost arm.

Because loss always involves something that proclaims a disengagement from the world, Clara lost the ability to read and write. Letters were fishhooks again, but indecipherable. Nor could she recognize numbers. She could not count money or read a radio dial or a clock. She listened to the voices that had come to her during her child's life—to her mind awakened within her by her son's heteronyms, and the choruses of the earth—but none of them could comfort her.

The psalm has ended, psalm with its sounded and silent letters, psalm that stems from an old word for "twitching due to the plucking of lyres"; now the song is hushed. Now muscles are past. But must the living go on, twitching, sorrows, and all?

So be it.

To be like the other families, she busied herself by building a chicken coop onto the side of the guest house, the hammer ringing like yelps, and by buying some canaries. People also raised parakeets, talking mynas, or parrots. The birds gouged their cuttlefish and filled the air with trilling and cracked seed to match the high nerves of the houses, and outside the chickens squawked in bass agreement.

As if in rhythm with her frenzied exertions, the pipe under her sink began dripping, soaking the cloth stamped with daisies and flooding the floor, spreading as far as her sea rocks. At her request, Father James O'Brien, Father Eiras's replacement at the winery, called the plumber. The canaries chirped over the lake. Mr. Williams fiddled with the leak until it lay quiet. She was furious that Father O'Brien refused to pay for the repairs. She gave Mr. Williams some money, but since she could not count the bills or recognize the numbers on them, she had to trust that he was taking a fair amount. The next morning she needed him again. He had to return three times. The drips turned the hollow under the sink into moss, and at last the pipe blew up.

After shutting off the main, Clara carried her soaked towels to the rectory. She nailed them over some windows so that Father O'Brien would look straight into mildew, then returned home to stretch out on her cot and wish that he would disappear. She did not move or eat for two days; all was arrested. Only the birds soothed her, and their chirping helped her fall more deeply into her swoon. When thoughts other than the ones she needed to feast upon entered her mind, she pushed them aside with the aid of the singing canaries. She concentrated and pictured the priest vanishing. She knew how to feel around until she found a black hole and could fall inside it, going farther into her depression, quickening her inhalations toward that unlatching when her spirit could shoot from her body. Then all was cold and ebony, with a prickle of nausea.

After she fixed a picture of Father O'Brien's departure invincibly in her mind, she hoisted herself out of her secret depths. It was a matter of teaching herself to distinguish between fate, which could veer out of control, and strength of will. *Will*—that she had mighty stores of; that remained hers.

When she heard a week later that Father O'Brien had already tired of the wine business and requested a transfer, she led her birds in an aria.

If her willpower could tell a man what to do, could it tell God? She lay down again to create a swoon that could bring her to everyone she desired, to all that she missed.

Glória had the instincts of a mother. While dusting her house, it came to her that Clara needed help right away. She ran into the guest house, to find her stretched out on her cot, eyes shut, her bare feet cold as alabaster. Glória heated a kettle and soaked towels in boiling water to apply to Clara's ankles. "O, Lord, child, what are you doing?" Glória said, shaking her.

White stripes extended up Clara's calves and from her fingertips toward her elbow, and fleecelike marks appeared on her neck, where they grew in little white spears toward her cheeks. She lay as firm and untwitching as she had been beneath the onrushing train.

She was pulling up a winding-sheet inside herself.

"Don't do it, Clarazinha," said Glória, holding the towels on the dead white parts, leaving some tinges of redness but not enough to stave off the strong upward roll of the internal sheet.

"Don't!" She unbuttoned the front of Clara's dress and placed her hand over the heart to stem the drive of the chalky ribbons, and at her blockage in their stream they stopped, ebbed backward to regroup, charged toward Clara's heart again, and were rebuffed, to form whirlpools of zinc-white at the border of the firm hand. "Clara, dear," pleaded Glória, "I know how much you hurt, but you can't go. Don't leave us."

It was Clara's heart, held and protected beneath Glória's grasp, that ordered the winding-sheet to stop. As long as it could feel someone's hand, it was not ready to shut down. To surrender beneath paralyzing events was forgivable, but that did not have to mean dying; it could mean living stunned. She opened her eyes. "All right, Glória," she said, "I'm here."

Parts of the winding-sheet remained visible on her skin, from her feet to her scalp, in splotches and streaks where it could not be fully retracted, but the filled outline of her neighbor's hand over her heart stayed sanguine. That was sufficient for now to keep her alive, but she was no longer able to remain a spider, swinging freely over the dark blind spots in the landscape, fastening herself by a thread to the light. The thread of the generation behind her and the thread of the generation before her had been severed, leaving her without lifelines.

She was falling unattached, unanchored. There would come a day of rising for her, but it would come from someone without, from elsewhere. It would require the courage of a rescuer who could reach with both arms into a nightmare to pull her out.

Because she saw the point of absolutely nothing but a prolonged siege of absence, Clara lay down on her cot one day when she was alone and shot the lengthy hollow black tunnels of her optic nerves outward to probe the immediate scene for holes in the lace of the landscape, like the feelers of a lobster searching for food. When she found one, she rode the shafts into the blind spot. Once inside, she realized that her task was to discover the Egg. She dripped with the yellow and white of the newly cracked sun as she received this assignment, and a basketful of eggs appeared. "First," she told herself, "to enter the Egg, I must understand the feel of one." Like the pure milk from a cow in a filthy stall, the Egg that she selected was firm, cool, bone-colored, with a calcium wart, and had survived sharp beaks and dirty nests. Voices like the ones that had guided her through the life of her son emanated in a garble from the Egg. It lay as a gift on her hand—what an uneasy honor, to be trusted not to drop or crush it! To thank her gentle approach—was this the consolation of the Egg?—it became a lover in her hand, round, tapering to its tip and full at its base, of a streamlining that could glide without resistance through water.

"I know you!" she shouted.

She agreed with the guiding voices that everyone was part of the Egg. "Yes! Yes!" she said. "The Egg has a thin skin like ours, and liquid inside. A sun nourishes our centers. Caliopia told me about this level of sorrow. I'm not scared because I don't care anymore about anything."

"Then you are ready for a story from the history of the Egg," said the voices. "Long ago, in the convents of Portugal, the nuns starched their wimples and habits with egg whites. Because wastefulness is a sin, they needed to dream up uses for the leftovers. That is how they came to invent the yolk-heavy desserts that are made to this day."

"The Egg has a history," Clara repeated, her eyes bright and wisps of hair in rays around her face.

"Yes, and what else?" the voices asked.

The Egg grew warm in her hand. "If the Egg reminded you about the Sisters," she said, "then does the Egg have a memory?"

"It has *many* memories! Very good! What else?"

"I'm not sure."

"For the Egg to be full of all kinds of memories," said the voices patiently, "can it stay the same old Egg? How does it create different sweets?"

Clara was at a loss.

"For our Egg to take its many forms, it must be released from its shell! It wants motion, poor Egg, because it can't stay content while caged or unchanging. The Egg is the summary of life. You are ready for it when death has forced you to investigate other beginnings. Break one into a bucket of water and read your future," urged the voices.

She broke the Egg into a bucket, where it spread into two wings.

"Look! Your future is that you are a bird!"

Alongside the wings was a triangular smear that she read as an egg-tooth. It was her son as a young bird, open-mouthed, hungry, waiting, tapping his way out. She began to cry.

"Look at it this way," said the voices. "He is still attached to you. You are carrying him well into the future. It is your father's boat and your mother's hand, stuck on you for life. It is Eva, whom you had for a little while. Why not celebrate how they are with you?"

"Celebrate?"

"Every moment. *You won't believe us now.* You won't listen to the moral of the story of the motion of the Egg—but try. *Remember our warning that the poor Egg needs motion.* But for now: Take the Egg into yourself."

She saw the Egg enrich itself when mixed with brandy and she smelled its raisinlike sourness, clinking her glass against the table in order to hear the toast. After tasting the Egg on her tongue, she felt it shivering down her back, letting it become the five senses—was this consolation? Why did it not feel full enough? What was missing?

"A problem remains," the voices said. "We want you to celebrate, but there is another truth shown to you by the people behind the egg-tooth shape. They are telling you this: It is not enough for the Egg to be outside of its shell to make itself happy, because it longs for something else. For something unlike itself. For an other."

"Why?" Clara finished her glass of Egg.

"That is one of the most important questions anyone can ask, but no one can answer it. The best we can do is to take the Egg to meet an other and see what happens."

She brought an Egg near the flame of a candle. A candle works as an other because it is alive—it burns, fire moving down the hard length of it, as steadily as breathing. The Egg was entirely lightened in the candle's glowing, and the candled Egg revealed the dark speck that would branch out as shaky red lines on the yolk, the sketch anticipating the chicken.

"With the candle and the Egg together, we can see what was invisible," the voices continued, "and once the fragile Egg learns transformation, knows it can make itself completely new, it searches for ways to be permanent. Here is one way: The Egg and the candle form the egg-and-tongue design that often appears high and continuous in a rotunda."

That would be consolation—being repeated endlessly in an artful circle, thought Clara.

"When the eggs-and-tongues press against each other," said the voices, "the Eggs become round heads and bodies, and the candles are sturdy wings. They join to form birds that cannot stay pinned inside some mausoleum. They want to soar to the sun. Rise now! Friends await you outside." The yard was bathed in light the color of the brandied Egg, but the winery on the hill had darts of shadow. *This* was consolation: to fly on a journey with companions.

"You know what's next?" The voices were quaking with reverence. "The Egg always goes full circle. Did you guess this when you first said that you knew the Egg was your own? That was only in your mind, of course. Now the Egg must end as it started—imaginary."

Would she meet square raspberry-checkered Eggs? Eggs with harlequin designs? Eggs laid by tulips, or ones that sprouted arms to lead the forest in song? She marched to a clearing where a troop of mud men were saddling a sugar dove for flight.

"Good day, Your Excellency! General Custódio Diamantino Abreu, ready to serve you." Their leader saluted. He cracked slightly as his mud arm hit his temple. "You are to lead by air the charge toward the sun on the other side of the forest. We will carve out a path on foot."

Across their chests the men were arranging golden sashes bearing their names. Sergeant Ricardo Teixeira da Mota, moved by these good-byes, wept himself into a mud ball, which Corporal Afonso Alfacinha slapped onto his own stomach. He waddled over to Clara and said, "Hurry, Your Excellency. The sun is already slowly killing your dove, and to delay too long might result in a failure of the mission." She mounted her steed and felt her dove softening beneath her.

"Ready? Hee-yup!" yelled General Abreu, beating its tail with his whip of foxtails.

"Hang on! Ride hard and fast," shouted Lieutenant Pedro Flores, pinching Clara's rear.

With the mud men exhorting her, she sailed up, carried by wings flapping in delirious rhythm over the forest. She warmed at the thought of the lieutenant, which did not help her sputtering, heaving dove, battered by the sun and dripping syrup in a thick stream until there was nothing left of it but a glaze coating her thighs and the rest dissolved underneath and inside her as she tumbled from the air, clutching the candles she had hoped would guide her through any shady parts of the forest, plunging into a thicket. Bang! When she came to, General Abreu was patting her hand and Lieutenant Pedro Flores was fanning her with an oak leaf. Redwoods vaulted in a cathedral overhead.

"Clara, darling," Pedro said.

"Where are we? What now? I must be going," she said.

"Rest a while with me."

"Do you love me? Isn't it time for me to leave?"

"Can't you see how crazy it is out there? Look!"

He was right. The troops were in disarray, playing camouflage games against the mud, getting drunk on tree sap, humping vanilla plants and then fainting beneath the umbrellas of mushrooms. It was better to recline in this shadowy grove, with an admirer at her side. "Let's enjoy this peace together," he urged her, "before it's over."

And immediately it was. "Gentlemen!" cried General Abreu. "We are forgetting why we are here—to forge a path to the other side!"

"Onward!" Pedro cheered, leaving Clara in order to go rouse the others.

"Hear! Hear!" They stopped rioting and murmured their assent. The soldiers harnessed a squadron of hummingbirds—known in Portuguese as "kiss-flowers." The nerves of these birds are so attuned to the rapid motions of their work that, even without blossoms in sight, their wings will vibrate to a blur as their beaks frantically stitch at imaginary flowers. The flurry of their kisses quickly created a garden out of thin air, redolent with vines, bluebells, dahlias, and irises. Elephants emerged to help them stand this garden on end, propping it as a ladder that broke a shining hole in the forest's ceiling.

The mud soldiers and Clara waited in line for their turns in mounting the garden ladder. The first to ascend loosened showers of seed that caulked the lines of her palms when she held open her hands.

"How about some kiss-flowers yourself?" joked her lieutenant, offering his lips.

"You bet," she replied, following him behind the ladder to hide on the underside of the upright garden, where the roots, quaking under the boots of the unseen climbers, brushed against their embrace. His erection towered like a rounded hook above both their heads. "Climb on, dearest," he groaned, "before we both die." She wriggled, impaled on his hard mud, sliding him deeper inside until she could cling to the grass hairs on his chest. An elephant drove his trunk up her ass and another crammed a seed caught in its begonia-pink nostril into the back of her throat. "O love!" Pedro's elation rebounded in the forest as he released a geyser of hot mud and the elephants unleashed watery blasts that spun her away from them. She fell with a thud.

When she ran back to where she had been, she found that everyone had forged to a far height, and some soldiers, since the ladder's base was now slick with the muddy sweat of the troops and impossible to grip, were using a flowery lasso to hoist Pedro.

"Drop a vine for me!" she said.

His clay-thick tears bombed her. "I'm sorry! Sorry! I was sent to teach you the grief of happiness. Now—too late!—I realize that I love you! I do!" When he strained his arms toward her, they jerked him upward, dragging him out of reach. The mud men were traitors! All ambushers!

"Help me!" Her plea rang through the forest.

Though nearing the top of the garden, half-concealed in the flowers, Clara saw her mother, Conceição, turn, alerted to the merest tremor of her daughter's voice. She was carrying a child with an exposed heart but managed to stretch out a free hand, fighting to slide down to Clara, but the soldiers blocked her way. She noticed her father, José Francisco, reach through the hole to shake the whirligig seeds out of a maple bough. "Use them to fly!" he thundered, but the mud men intercepted the seeds and stuck them onto their own heads as propellers to fly up and herd both Conceição and José Francisco more quickly away. Struggling, shouting, "Clara! Watch over yourself!" they were flown upward, through the hole in the redwood cathedral that pointed heavenward, shooting its mud stream at the sun on the other side.

A wild boar charged from the underbrush, knocking over the garden ladder and kicking up tufts from the fallen and ruined bed. She wrenched out a scruff of the boar's hair before it galloped off, trampling more plants. The dome above her was mud-colored and plugged, and it was impossible to tell where the flowered incline had once rested against an escape into the sky. If consolation were continuous art and the journey together, then this was the end of consolation, fled like the curved-tusked boar.

To her surprise, she saw Tio Vitor, sickly and covered with vines, approaching through the forest. "How could I leave you wandering in such danger?" he said, putting one arm around her and pointing toward some galls that were like the oddly spherical eggs of the tawny owl, bulging from an oak. "Let's hide in these for a while, until we get our strength back," he said. "We'll each go into our separate ones. Rest—and then I'm coming to get you out!" They mutely entered their own Egg-galls to be safe in case the boar returned. Clara lined the inside of her Egg with the fur torn from the romp in the garden. A scruff would grow again on the boar's back, as if she had never clutched it! The cruelty of its ecstatic dance was that the animal would dash happily on, showing no trace of her ride, leaving her with only a souvenir.

She felt protected inside her Egg and saw no reason to leave it. In fact, when Tio Vitor came for her, she might just curl up more tightly and refuse to budge.

IT IS NOT only vision that can tumble into the cutaways in the landscape's lace, Clara mused in her gall, but time itself, which does not barrel on horizontally, event after event, as many believe. Time is, instead, a forest of threads suspended from between the pinched thumbs and forefingers of the angels of the Domination choir, the movers of the planets and the stars. She could see them through a crack in her gall. They intend that she and all the living should grab the threads as towropes and be lifted along the vertical poles that lead to heavenly lights, but few people bother to stretch toward them. Clara preferred to rest.

She watched the angels (mostly the unsupervised teenagers who grouse about wanting to join the star-moving teams) become easily bored and drop the threads. Safe inside her gall, she observed that time plummets, not arrow-straight but with curves and loops, as threads do. It enters geometry: The distance between the points at the opening of a curve is much shorter than the thread's span in its straightened full length. Hence time is swallowed in the bulges of threads that fall into the blind spots of the landscape.

In this way time is mutable; lives condense; whole days buckle and fold away. Seven years were to disappear in Lodi, and neither she nor anyone else would be able to say where they had gone. This was an appropriate reaction to the climate in the country, with its movie-star President, a time in which moral vacancies went parading as consumerism. Better to hide at seeing America carelessly fermenting despair.

One morning, Luís would fail to greet Caliopia, and she would find him dead, with white whiskers. It would appear that she instantly replaced him with another Labrador, but it would be actually after two years of mourning.

João would report that his ghost hand was slowing.

Eva Amália would marry and move to Seattle, and Clara would hear less about her with each passing year.

Viriato das Chagas, who had conjured up the heteronyms that spelled A . . . men inside Clara's son, would grow increasingly bored with delivering the mail and would open a trout farm.

Fifteen priests would come and go from the Transfiguration winery, which would continue its steady business and tourist trade.

Glória and Caliopia would take the short terms of the priests as a sign that Clara was alive enough to go in and out of swoons. They would debate whether to send for Doctor Helio Gabriel Soares to examine her; his knowledge about cavities teamed with Caliopia's skills with mourning might together bring Clara completely out of her blind black spots, but then they would see her around town, despite her inability to read or write invitations or to dial the numbers on a telephone, laughing at birthday parties, pitching a softball game, tapping her foot happily as she waited in the supermarket's line, and they would think that she had emerged.

Of course during these seven years she would manage such excursions out of her gall only to throw them off her track, and then she would gladly fall back into her private darkness. Her sorrows had leeched certain chemicals out of her, the ones necessary in keeping love thick in the plasma. She assumed that these were gone, never to be replaced. The pain of knowing this right as it was happening was acute, but even this immensity of sadness would soon leave, precisely because it was acute and therefore required the same heightened components that also went into the creating of love. When the sharpness of griefs can never more be tolerated, then the inverse apex of romance, the capacity for the elevated and the good, is also ground flat.

She would stay caught within the earth's lacework, trembling in her gall, her tempests compressed, visiting friends only to prevent them from being alarmed. One day she returned to her very core by patting out a sugar arrow, for fear that even this language would be entirely lost to her. It reminded her of the goat-bar's radiant hostess roughing out *sim*, the word for yes, as a comfort, and of the heat after the flute-songs from the hands of the men that made Eugénio and her take naps, their heads resting on the *sim* mixed up with other sugar-words on the table. Time and California's breezes spread her arrow into a fine scattered layer now, as happened in the Azorean days when with melting body she would bend down to wear on her face the confusion of the *yes* of the Beauty.

BOOK II

FOUR

The Calamity of the Ashes transpired centuries ago, when a volcano on São Miguel spewed mightily and the winds turned solid with ash and swept toward Terceira. At first the spots speckled the ground, dappled the houses, and imbued the trees with pointillistic shadows, but soon the dark arms of the breezes clasped the island more closely. For three days no one saw the sea, sky, or land, nor could anyone distinguish day from night, though it was summer. The vineyards became blocks of cinders, and it was impossible to find the fruit.

Anyone foolhardy enough to stray outdoors became moving carbon. Even a week after the main assault, everything was still wearing soot. "Mamãe," a boy was said to have asked, pointing to a flurry spinning down the road, "is that the storm, or are people under the ash dancing?"

DOCTOR HELIO GABRIEL Soares applied wax over the wound where he had grafted two apple seedlings together in his yard. They were both waning. Usually he preferred joining a weak plant to a strong one, but sometimes two that could not survive on their own each rallied to the cause of the other. That was gratifying; they became his special prizes. He smoothed the wax on the apple plants, watching it cool opaquely over the incisions and inserted stock, before securing the cuts with cotton string. He hoped to develop, among other things, tomatoes that would grow in pods, to keep them safe from being crushed or split. Peaches in a rubber tree would be nice, so that the fruit would bounce and not bruise when it fell. His most fervent desire as a grafter was to fuse separate species so truly that the parts would not only entwine but meld into a fresh order.

In his garden's shed, he opened the book where he was recording sunrise and sunset times, in case the numbers concealed a coded warning about the return of the Dark Ages. Yesterday's entries were #2751 and #2752. Doctor Soares had been devoted to science, logic, numbers, and magnanimity since age twelve, growing up on the island of Faial, when he learned:

In 1792, during the Brazilian gold rush, Joaquim José da Silva Xavier, a dentist called Tiradentes, or Tooth-Puller, was executed for leading a revolt against the rule of Portugal.

Gold was smuggled from Brazil inside religious statues.

Slaves were being brought in to work the sugar plantations.

Helio, overwrought with romantic notions of peril as a child, had been convinced that his ancestors were soldiers who had impaled pieces of Tiradentes on a spiked fence. He resolved to honor the martyr by becoming a dentist. Maybe curing rot and putting gold into people instead of taking it away from them could expiate some of the past. Furthering his wishes was the wooden pandy bat, once used on schoolboys, that had hung in his grandfather's study. Seven holes were drilled in the pandy bat's head to create a suction that would increase the pain of a blow to a boy's palm. The care taken to design a way to aggravate misery appalled Helio far more than the basic fact of corporal punishment.

Walking through his garden, surveying the peas, artichokes, and corn, he recalled the extraordinary record that had plagued his boyhood. Despite 5:1 odds against it, he found the hidden fava bean in his slice of the Bolo Rei 11 times (2 in dispute) in 14 years and had to buy the next Kings' Day cake an unfair number of feast days. He had vowed that the Magi and sovereignty would not squelch him forever. His first metaphorical wonder at teeth struck at a pastry shop's display of sea shapes of hard sugar encasing egg filling. He thought, Enamel protecting spongy pulp. Teeth are everywhere. He heard the theory that the bloody wounds of women were filled with man-biting teeth, but instead of being horrified, he was delighted to consider love as yet another part of dental training. At age 20 on 3 July at 3:06 P.M., he correctly guessed the number of dried favas (432) in a jar at the Imperial Dairy, winning 3000$00 *escudos* and 12 marzipan cows for his sweet tooth and dealing a blow to the rankling defeats suffered until then in the grip of favas and kings.

He forgot about majestic repression until his first year as a dentist. He had not stopped to think that dentists often make people roar with hurt, and cursing himself, reviling his inability to undo what he was, he often fell to the agony of prodigious nightmares.

Now he was the master of a garden free of favas. What a minor victory! But that was what men were allowed, wasn't it? The submission of their trappings, but slow servitude to their careers. He pulled up some onions by their shoots as if hoisting rabbits out of the ground. They were lovely, bulbous and bright white. Let his tiny empire bring him solace, then, if that was the minimum that men were granted; let small pleasures substitute for joy!

He was slender and nervous, with a threadbare mustache and straight black hair, beginning to thin on top and worn slicked back. His gold-rimmed spectacles often slid down his nose—which became dangerous when he tended his bees (the finicky ones did not like him to make any abrupt motions), merely a nuisance as he worked on his grafting projects. He had lived in Stockton, California, for twenty-five years, ever since his wife, Felicia, died in childbirth back on Faial. Their daughter had been stillborn. He had come to America at age twenty-seven, during the year of mourning for Kennedy, to visit relatives and had ended up applying for immigration. It made him laugh now to think he had imagined "starting over," as though what one's life had been fell back flat like a weak stage prop. He had written to his mother and taken periodic trips to the islands until she died. She had steadfastly refused to go to California with him. He regretted his stubbornness about going backward and hers about going forward. With her death, his family behind him completely vanished, as had the family preceding from him when Felicia and their daughter died. He was a little island and their waters lapped against him, front and back.

Inside the house, he sighed at the dishes in the sink. Leaving them there overnight had been an effort at being rougher and more spontaneous; his friends often teased him mercilessly about his bondage to order and neatness. He put on his yellow rubber gloves and filled the sink with warm water, adding three squirts of liquid soap. The congealed chicken fat broke down into a loose glue on the plate, but the skin of the pumpkin squash had hardened to it and he had to scrape the skin off with a spoon. So much for the wild life. He checked the jar of strawberry jam in the refrigerator and felt a twinge of happiness at thinking that he had accurately parceled out dabs for his toast so that the jar would last exactly one week (he liked generous helpings; he despised those who were misers with themselves or others). Tomorrow he would feel the catharsis of washing the jar and using it to sprout an avocado pit. After drinking a glass of port, he brushed his teeth and submitted to his private game of believing that if he took any *more* or *fewer* than ten steps from his bathroom to his bed (ten and he was safe), a spacecraft would come to carry him away while he slept.

Though he felt the stirrings of a slight erection, he decided it was better to ignore it. Coming alone was making him break of late into an incalculable sob, and this made the whole enterprise more troublesome than the relief was worth. Even when he told himself, Relax; you're not even sad! there it was anyway, unwelcome and unannounced, bursting up from his chest. It might be a service to mankind to tally the number of days one could go without making love before a given number of seconds of postonanistic tears would occur. (The study could include advice on how to figure alleviations granted through sex without love, or how memories of love might exacerbate the computation.)

Such an undertaking would be perfectly suited to a man in exile, which was how he thought of himself. Others thought of him as exotic, with his grafting and beekeeping and meticulous projects (or at least that was the impression the neighbors conveyed to his face; he was the saffron of the local soup), but Helio was fully aware that he was fifty-two years old and had filled his existence with fancy ways of hiding how fearful of life he had become. Sometimes his strivings made him feel as close to wonder as a man could be, but at other times they struck him as flashy hobbies designed to save him any of the normal evidence or embarrassment of being solitary. They were life-givers but also life-absorbers that did their job in helping him forget who he was.

He gave in to himself, and when he came, he managed to choke back any crying; then suddenly it erupted, because eyes are never denied their part of a climax, and small fountains ran past his temples to dampen his pillow.

HELIO UNDERSTOOD THAT he would never move on, never clarify who he was until he looked with courage at what he had been. He believed with his entire soul that unless we account for and love those in our past, we cannot expect our own lives to mean anything to those who will follow us. He crushed some dried lemon verbena leaves to make tea, took several aspirin, and unlocked the cabinet where he stored his father's notebook. Of course he already knew fairly well what it contained—his family's legends were partly a matter of public record, and his father's jottings were infamous in their own right—but he had never done much more than glance rapidly over the strange tales and sad scrawlings. He was afraid of catching whatever it was that had driven his father crazy.

Fear had to be behind him now. He had never known his father, Hugo, but if he wanted to attach himself to the human shoals behind him, he would have to delve into whatever history offered. No matter how repulsive or glittering, he would not avert his eyes. Sipping his tea, pulling on a sweater against the overcast morning, he opened the notebook with its leather cover, dry and crackling as oak leaves. He began with the first entry, the story of the acknowledged initial sin in the Soares family, copied by his father, when his script was still relatively steady, from a manuscript displayed at the Museu das Artes in Horta, Faial. "This is my great-great-great-grandfather, Captain Ricardo Pinheiro Soares," Hugo had written at the top of the page.

There followed the account of the captain's behavior as his boat was sinking during a pleasure cruise between the islands of Faial and São Jorge: He had not known how to comfort the twenty women and two crewboys who looked to him for help. For one thing, he had grown fat and listless on the heavy meals that his wife always packed for him, and until now his trips had been so brief and routine that he had not bothered to stock the most basic safety devices. The one lifeboat, a wedge-sized craft swaying aloft on a mast, made it clear that very few would be saved.

" 'Back and forth, gouging this one channel, while the men before me sailed many uncharted seas!' fumed Captain Soares. He had not asked to be entrusted with the lives of others!"

As Helio read these lines, a chill made seeds of sweat rise from his scalp and perch on the tops of his hair, like watery eyes straining upward on stems. He dreaded what he knew came next.

"A crewboy shouted, 'I must swim for help!' and leapt into the water's black swirling holes before the captain could warn him to beware of the sharks. Too late! The boy screamed as the beasts began to devour him, and no one answered his cries. Instead, a furious struggle ensued over the lifeboat that the captain loosed from its pole . . ."

Helio stopped, and the eyes of sweat in his hair burst, as if weeping in anguish. He could see the scene with piercing clarity—the quarreling, the pushing of rivals into the sea. He skipped those long paragraphs but made himself look back at the page:

". . . and when a woman heaved her own mother to the sharks, the captain's humors evaporated even more and he abandoned any pretense at trying to create order. Three women, one crewboy, and he survived, clinging to separate berths. . . ."

Helio could scarcely bear to digest the part about the red waves lapping over the faces and drenching bloody the clothing of the survivors, nor could he keep his gaze upon the part of the legend where his family's curse surely had its inception: The captain's disgust for human nature was so great that he threw overboard all witnesses to the wreckage of his voyage. It was pitifully easy, since the others were too guilty and petrified to join forces against him. Helio winced at the thought of the captain stomping and crushing the hands that reached for the boat's rim. The crewboy managed to emerge from a black sea-hole long enough to shout, "I shall come for you!" before he died.

Captain Soares forgot this malediction, however, during the sympathetic public inquiry. How he had suffered! How gallant had been his attempts, tearfully related, to save those who had been his charges on the pleasure trip!

Helio made himself a fresh cup of tea before reaching the blighted end of the tale:

"Though the captain went on to acquire a fortune from smuggling contraband into Europe, the round black sea-holes must have stayed inside him, riddling his dreamless dreams, multiplying, causing him to awaken in his dotage and shout, 'Devil take you all!' One day he could hold it in no more, and he vomited out the dark whirling holes of the sea and the round cursing mouth of the crewboy that had been stored in him for so long, and these black dots spelled out on the floor, in winding sentences, the true story of his crimes. His son copied down the speckled words that his father's spewing had spread out for everyone to see—the captain's history is a trail of blots that have marched from his life into ours—and that is how we have come to possess this tale of long ago."

Helio paused, too shaken to continue with the rest of the notebook. How staggering was this first and foremost blot imprinted onto his family! For many years he had put this original infamy out of his mind, without realizing that it had continued to weigh on his spirits. He closed the book and went outside to rake the yard. Gathering up fallen leaves would be a brisk interval before he had to go to the office. This morning, the Quinn children were coming in for fluoride treatments. They liked the grape and spearmint gels he used, and their eagerness about this, and in the comic books he would give them to read, would wrap for him a tidy parcel out of the hours.

Months passed before he could bring himself to fall into the recorded abyss of his father, Hugo Jerónimo Ignácio Soares, whose decline was triggered by his proximity to death while working in the mortuary owned by his cousins Gustavo and Chico in Angústias, on the island of Faial.

"My first day on the job," his father's barely decipherable script insisted, "my cousins made me throw a corpse over my shoulder. It exhaled in my ear, and they screamed with delight when I dropped the body. This was my welcome. I did not know that bodies have a last sweet nothing that can be burped out of them.

"I learned how to make a dead body smile by taking a stitch between the upper lip and exiting the needle through the nostril. I had to do this with Alexandra, Gustavo's goddaughter who drowned. He was sobbing too hard and couldn't get it right. I coated her with beige paste and Chico showed me how to use a piece of straw to give her lifelike pores. We drained her blood through a tube, but Gustavo would not let us throw it out. He sat in the corner patting the bucket, the way someone sends a child to sleep. That night I asked my dear wife, Adelinha, to scrub me with the wire vegetable brush because I knew I was becoming a potato."

Helio could scarcely discern the next words amidst the ink blots:

"I stuck two straight pins into the upper gums of a corpse to make it easier to brush its teeth with detergent. The lips drooped like a red curtain over a stage. Yellow footlights for teeth! 'Chico!' I called. 'Over here! Make a wish and throw in a coin!' Ha ha!"

Helio took another aspirin; the next entry was too painfully familiar. His father had come into work and found his cousins propping three dead milkmen, wearing caps twisted backward, around a card table. Gustavo made one body wave a bottle of bourbon at Helio and say, "Join us!" He did, and his team won 2500$00 *escudos.*

"At the Requiem for my milkman," Hugo wrote, "I wore a black suit and my shoulders were hunched as I escorted his widow to view the body. I was a comma, saying, 'pause with me, and then go on.' I was a cedilla, saying, 'pronounce softly the attachment above.' But it is truer to say that, like my ancestor Captain Ricardo, I carry my black marks within.

"Adelinha has insisted that I quit my job! Good! I have been reading the story of Captain Soares and *have stumbled upon a truth:* All my past actions, everything I have done in my life, are now stored in my brain, where they are hazy but shiny as a dream. That is how we contain memories.

"But don't stories that we've heard or read go to stay inside our heads in exactly the same way as memories? Pale washes stored like dreams? Then to hear something, or to think it, or actually to do it, amounts finally to the same thing! Something *heard or thought up* ends up existing dreamlike inside, the same as what a person has in fact *done!*

"Therefore in the present they *are* the same!

"Having heard the story of the captain, I contain what he did. Anyone who reads it must share the same guilt of having done it. (It existed as a dream in his mind, after he did it. It exists like a dream in ours.)

"Last night I dreamt that I mounted a goat. When I woke up, my dream had shriveled into a parade of many assholes of goats:

· · · · · · · · ·

"Therefore I have slept with goats!"

HELIO CLOSED THE notebook and headed for the apiary, where he trapped a bee and plunged its stinger into his wrist.

When applied during troubled times, the serum of bees worked like a vaccine. He was not yet ready to fathom the experiments his father had conducted during the final descent to his horrible end. When Helio returned to the house, even with the antidote of the bees in his veins, he could do no more than flip quickly through the pages, past the brown patches of dried blood littered near the last words. He came upon an envelope stuck into the binding. It was marked "H. Soares" and contained a baby's first lock of hair. He recognized his grandmother's handwriting, but was the hair his or his father's? This was the first time he had seen it. He placed its coil on his palm. It was dark and fine, curved in on itself, like fifty sketches of the inner ear in alignment. Remarkable! A part of him, unknown, foreign, delicate. Light. Or was he at last holding his father? He pressed the curl so that its tips touched, making it a closed circle.

Helio knew about his father's theory that everything contained a dreadful speck, just as men owned dark secrets, and salvation was only a matter of getting to this darkness and destroying it. Despite himself, he returned to his father's words:

"Think of cockroaches! They have eggs that hold the next cockroach, which conceals smaller eggs containing more insects, and so on to infinity. If I isolate the ultimate egg of every cockroach, if I find the final fatal point in everything and dig it out, I will master darkness and subdue it!

"To find the final black spots hiding in a fish, I slivered it with a razor, subdividing the scales, fins, and skin.

"ONE FISH can be made to cover A HOUSE with dots! Depression:

Do we have the TIME to chop everything?

"I chopped a kernel of corn. Thin yellow pieces covered the table. I reduced them further into white grains and attacked one particle until it vanished like dust.

"Awful discovery: Whenever I close in on my prey, it slips into the air! Yellow corn————white————GONE! Taking its dark spot with it, safe from my punishment!

"I cut up a rug string, a seed, a sow bug, with the same result. Trapped inside wood fiber were chains of dolls, laughing as I released them, dancing from my pursuit on their skinny legs. I sliced a period out of a book, cut it into sixteenths, into crumbs that stuck to my blade, and then the period disappeared. With no revelations! Adelinha complained that every surface in the house has a scattering of slashed things.

"Despair! I come close to finding the black spots that can be divided no further and they JUMP AWAY!

" 'Stop,' said Adelinha, 'this is not something anyone can solve.' "

Helio went outside and repeated one of his father's experiments, telling himself that this would be less painful than reading it. Water was indeed black in the pond, but clear when cupped in his hands, just as Hugo Soares had declared. Helio did not know whether to laugh or cry at the thought of his father grimacing at how darkness had once again eluded his capture. Helio flung the water down: Yes, his father was right. It left black splotches on the ground to ridicule him before sinking out of reach. Helio did not bother to trap water in thimbles—as a way of chopping liquids to force their specks out of hiding—as his father had done, because then Helio too would have to curse the air that sucked the thimbles dry.

Instead he felt a flare of anger. He had done a fair share of defending his father already! He remembered long ago fighting the village boys who pelted him with black allspice and disks of cow shit and sang, "What would your father do with this? What would he do with this?" He had uprooted bushes to flush out packs of taunting boys who raced home like scourged dogs. He gave them black eyes. His mother, Adelinha, had prescribed piano lessons to soothe him, but the notes and staccato marks reminded him of the ciphers he had glimpsed in his father's writings, and he pressed down the pedal to connect the scattered dots. He was ashamed of having a father who had suggested wild things about darkness and deliberately cut open his testicles and bled to death, and then he was ashamed of being ashamed.

Until now he had avoided thinking of the obvious: The trail of the Soares family led right up to him. Its dots had paraded across the decades to arrive at his feet. They were waiting like a row of seeds to see what he could raise out of them.

He planted a line of defense by grafting keyhole limpets to water-swollen squash in order to guard his house with aquatic volcanoes, but he worked so hard that he began to see spots before his eyes. By nightfall he was suffering with muscae volitantes. Everything in his sight appeared speckled. It was like being visited by his father's dotted madness and the cavities of his patients, pasted at the same time onto the air. "I can give in to this," he told himself, applying cold cloths to his forehead, "or I can pay tribute to my father by fighting back. I can't hide forever."

He seized every dot oscillating before him and pinned it onto paper with a point of ink. At first he was content with their capture, but soon he needed to fit them into some type of shape. He did dot-drawings of his hand: studies in minuteness, with freckles and hairs accurately rendered and dense dot-clusters for the shadows. After every session, when affixing the date on the page's lower corner, he glowed from work well done. Better yet, the work caught like flypaper all the mites that flew at him and, when he flipped over a completed hand with a resounding slap, he crushed them from view. His eyes were cured.

After many weeks of daily pictures, he had to clear his hands off the desk to make room for a new cycle. He turned the stack over and almost fainted with delight. "My first one is so crude!" he said. "I've been so close to the work that I thought all the hands were exactly alike!" But they had been too painstaking, too faithful to their given day to be static. He riffled the pile with his thumb, and each dotted hand was instantly alive and in motion. The earliest fingers tapered and curved slightly in one continuous reel as they aged across the span. He had captured his recent past, to be replayed at will! Helio resolved to dot a picture of his hand each day as it gnarled, dried, and groped toward his death. If he could not detect in his disintegrating flesh the secrets of becoming old, someone else might see his work and grasp the mystery.

His name was close to *soar*, "to sound," but this did not have to be a bell striking a toll from a mortuary tower; it could be a pealing from his heart like a cry of "Have mercy, have mercy!"——one ring celebrating every day of a man. Hope could combat darkness and guilt; hope could make a man discover new designs.

Because he wanted this hope etched onto his family's record—this would be *his* addition—he unlocked the notebook from the cabinet once again and in an elegant script contributed the legend of his whale-eyes, a gift that he had set aside for many years. Bypassing the stained pages, he wrote on blank leaves:

The Richness of My Eyes
by Dr. Helio Gabriel Soares

When I was seven years old on Faial, the men loved to shout, *"Baleia! Baleia! Baleia!"* from the shore to announce a whale sighting. Like everyone else, I tore some corn off any stalks along the way as I ran, because vats of whale oil were being heated on the pier, and we could boil the corn and eat it as we watched the whales.

Whales! I adored whales! The cries of the men seemed to envelop our house. Coming right for me! My mother and the aunt who lived with us would say, "Run along!" Off I would go.

There came a time of many false alarms. I would race down the hill and arrive at the pier, but there would be no whales off the coast. I did not always hide my disappointment and usually wanted to return home at once, but everyone pestered me to stay and eat more corn, and they badgered me with pointless conversations.

One afternoon, though, I slipped through the crowd

and headed home before anyone knew I was missing. When I reached the window of my house, I could not believe my eyes. My mother and a neighbor lady were lifting my old aunt from a tub, and her body and legs were knotted and twisted. I was shocked, first at her arthritis and then at myself because I had never noticed it before. She wore large, loose dresses and walked slowly, but this was too much! I should have known.

Then I was angry. Everybody, including my mother, was in on the hoax of pretending to see whales just to get me out of the house at my aunt's bathtime. I went away and returned home later. I would rather have died than to let on that they had fooled me, but I did not want to embarrass my aunt either.

That night I determined that I would wake up with a pair of whale-eyes. I had to know where whales were, as easily as most men could spot the horizon. I'd show everyone that I was nobody's fool. I would not rely on others to bring me whales. I would dream them up myself. A lot of Azoreans were given whale-eyes in the old days; this does not happen so much anymore. Nothing can compare with being on a boat with a sailor who stands there calmly, nodding when he means, Starboard. Veer east. Whales, when no one else can see anything.

The next morning I sat up with a burning in my skull. *"Baleia! Mamãe, Titia, Baleia!"* I called out.

I got my aunt out of bed and wrapped her gnarled legs in rags to keep her warm. She leaned on me as we hobbled to the beach. "What are you doing, you funny boy?" she asked.

"What's gotten into you?" asked my mother, clutching her shawl.

"Look!" A dozen whales appeared in the distance like

overnight islands, shooting their steam on high. "Papai's black spots!"

Mamãe agreed that they were glorious. My aunt was smiling.

Soon everyone in Faial heard about my whale-eyes. Sometimes a faraway ripple in the water or a heat in my brain signaled the presence of a whale. I would point in the right direction, and within minutes the whale's spout could be seen. At other times, a dome of halo marked the spot where treasure hid, and these were the most precious sightings of all. I could detect a flicker pretty much by wanting to see one, but the halos had to be granted.

Though I was offered many jobs aboard whaling ships, I declined. People laughed when I turned instead to bees, but I preferred to risk having creatures harm me than to harm creatures who pleased me so profoundly.

Halos should have appeared to save Felicia and our daughter, but this did not occur. After their deaths, I shut down the use of my eyes. Twenty-five years have passed without my calling on them. It is only today that I recall how much joy this gift gave me, when I exclaimed on countless mornings, *"Baleia!"* and my fellow Faialense hurried to see the pageant I had summoned to dance for us under purple skies.

H ELIO, I'M DYING for tea!"

Hissing wafted around the kettle he had placed on the fire. He wanted to relax after adding the story of his whale-eyes to the family ledger.

"Tea! A lovely cup of tea!"

"First, collect dried leaves. Wrap them in a straining cloth—"

"Helio, please, don't confuse me! Can't you bring me a cup?"

"Vovó, can't you ever be reasonable? Am I supposed to pour it on your grave?" he said, but the heft of the kettle staggered him, and the air was cream-thick. He lay stupefied on the floor.

His grandmother, Melissa Fabulina, strolled in, sat on his chest, and began busily writing her poetry. "What does a thirsty old lady have to do for some tea around here?" she said without glancing from her work. "Why are you spending so much time dotting your hand?" As always, she wore a ring of cameos on her high-necked Chantilly blouse, front and back, so that elegant heads could scrutinize in every direction.

"Vovó, what is it now?" He sighed, unable to squirm free.

"You forgot about *my* story."

He recognized the eye and head that swiveled to regard him. One day while retrieving a poem fallen by a cactus, a spine had pierced his grandmother's left eye and turned her into an axolotl: She had whitened from the pain, but the stab's reverse passage let her peer more profoundly into her brain, and a gold annulet encircled the black wound. Pieces of heart fanned out of her head like an axolotl's external red gills, where they quivered as wings that carried her, thriving in the fires one could observe through the porthole of her salamander-eye, into poems about the unexpected in our midst, poems famous enough to be housed at the Universidade dos Açores.

Although he was lying on his floor in California, a memory

of being a teenager back in the Azores possessed him. One day he had been hurrying to meet friends and had left his grandmother to butter her own bread, whittle her own pencils, and prepare her own tea. "Vovó, everybody's waiting for me! You can manage things just this once," he had said. He returned home to find sugar spilled, spoons dropped, and water sloshed on the floor. She had been lost in the maze of all the necessary piddling tasks for brewing tea and, overwhelmed, had retreated to her room to lie down and die.

"Was it on purpose? For not getting your way?" he squalled as he lay pinned beneath her. His immobile arms could not reach up to shake her fluttering red gills. "Or did you need me because you were ill? If you were ill, why didn't you say so?"

Instead of replying, his grandmother stretched full length on him and melted, gluing him to the floor. The scent of the dead woman now inside him attracted an army of bugs. Marching ropes of ants strapped him down. Cockroaches fed on his eyebrows, and their antennae siphoned moisture from his nostrils. Moths dined on his clothes, mosquitoes contentedly stuck him with their nose spikes, and flies dragged maggots into his navel. "Please, stop tickling. Let me stand," he begged, but the insects ignored him. Spiders swung on webbed trapezes between his chin and chest. Beetles laid eggs in fancy geometric patterns on him, and the termites, tapping to each other to signal a termination, tunneled through his festering spots to build galleries inside his legs. Outside their digging holes they heaped chewed muscle.

The moths finished eating his underwear and said, "He's all ours!"

His Vovó Melissa had a poem about memories being the only indisputable encasing against decay. Quickly he said, "No! I used to carve lemons into stars for my grandmother's tea! She was so tough that one day she pushed aside soldiers to bring bread into a quarantined village! My wife Felicia once wore a parade costume with hydrangeas as the puffed sleeves!"

"What nice fodder!" sneered the cockroaches. "To prove that everything is dead, we're going to rape you."

Maggots teemed over his eyes and clogged his nose, sounding like gently sizzling fat, jelly-white termites gagged him, ants trooped columns into his anus, and his sores bloomed into rivers. He swallowed the termites to be free to shout, "I remember beautiful things! Listen! One afternoon I lit the rocket at the festival of Saint Anthony, and it misfired and set the gazebo on fire. I was embarrassed, everyone was alarmed, but Felicia told us to stick our handprints in the wax flowers streaming from the gazebo onto the ground. I placed my palm over the warm impression that she left, and my hand over hers made outer ridges that stood up like petals. People layered their prints to make flowers, and bees swarmed—not stinging, but in amazement at our garden of hands holding hands. That was truly my wife! The insects knew that she was a master!"

She had been a genius at leaving impressions upon the earth. "Felicia!" he cried, "I am clinging to your last imprint, the one of you lying with insects in the earth; I am feeling you buried, disintegrating into your disintegration, making a flower from pressing against you."

His Vovó Melissa Fabulina rose out of him, and at the sight of her, the bugs scattered in a frenzy. She scrubbed the egg pockets out of Helio's skin. "Listen, chowderhead," she said softly. "Felicia has been gone for a very long time. If you don't do more than dot-pictures of your hand, I'm afraid you'll go as mad as your father. You're too squeamish to do what he did, but you'll come up with something else that will break my heart."

"I don't want to talk about him."

"You didn't finish reading his last words! You're all talk!"

"I know how it ends."

"But not the way it's told. Not exactly, anyway. Come on, I'll finish it with you."

Together they opened the notebook to the last entry of Hugo Soares. Helio read over his Vovó Melissa's shoulder:

"My wife, Adelinha, and I watched the fire-dancing at the Festas Sanjoaninas. The men vaulted with bamboo poles over flames that leapt unpredictably, throwing sparks like a pod splitting seeds. While Adelinha and I were eating limpets and drinking red wine by the pier, I suddenly thought of how every point in the fires had crackled with several tangents, sometimes visible, sometimes invisible. I almost upset the table as I jumped up! I ran home to light a candle. It was true! Fire has many double-points. Here is my diagram:

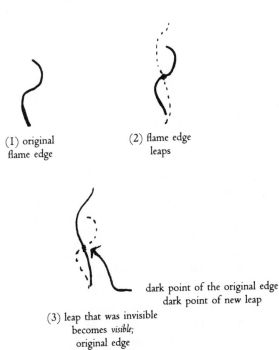

(1) original
flame edge

(2) flame edge
leaps

dark point of the original edge
dark point of new leap

(3) leap that was invisible
becomes *visible;*
original edge
becomes *invisible*

(4) double dark point
for the visible flashes

(5) double invisible point
for the ghosts of the flames
THAT WHISK DARKNESS
AWAY FROM
MY CAPTURING IT!

> = DOUBLE POINTS
> CONTAINING INVISIBILITIES

PLAN: Capture the dark Double Point! Open it! From this, find how it makes its invisible parts and thus ESCAPES INTO THE SKY! I BELIEVE I AM VERY CLOSE TO THE SECRETS OF DARKNESS.

" 'It's all too astonishing,' I said when Adelinha told me she was pregnant. I carried her around the house. I was amazed! I covered my panic pretty well, I think. I have to work quickly now; our child must find a world with its dark points removed."

"I can't," said Helio, turning away from the writing in the notebook.

"Just because we've come to you?" said his Vovó Melissa. She grabbed him by the shoulders and refused to release him. Together they read the final words of Hugo Jerónimo Ignácio Soares:

"Adelinha is in the bedroom sleeping. I am awake, dizzy with questions. Will the baby have her hair? Her nose? Or my hooked one? Maybe he will have one point that is hers and one that is mine, this child that is now no more than the size of a salt grain, a skin pore, a cat's pupil.

"My! O my my my!

"He is, like everyone else, a double point! A seething egg made from the meeting of two fiery lines! As I am myself! As everyone is!

"The answer is inside me! I must hunt for the double point that was my start. Then I will find where darkness becomes invisible.

"I have shaved off a fingerprint with a razor. It looks like a fish's scale. I'm finding nothing. I must cut off other pieces of myself. I must search my testicles for traces of goats. Those will definitely have to be removed. I can cure myself of my own dark points, even if it means opening myself into nothing. If I can stand before my child and say, 'Never fear! I have saved you from being from a dark house!' then I will swim in those cold waters. I will ride on fire down the river that departs, as all darkness does, into the air: the painful air! the watery air!"

Helio sank to the floor, too horrified for tears. Dried blood cracked off the final page.

"There, there," said Vovó Melissa evenly, which was more of a comfort than she had planned—she was a terrible consoler, and Helio laughed.

"You're very lucky, actually," she continued. "I've made sure that you are not entirely like the others in your family—"

"Please don't start in about my whale-eyes."

"I had to drive a hard bargain in heaven to get you a pair of those. Every whaling ship wanted to hire you."

"And I liked spotting whales as a boy. But I didn't want any part in hunting them down."

"Then put your eyes to some kind of good use. Forcing them to find cavities is such a waste. They'll see anything that's grand

and submerged. Use them to spot love."

"Okay, Vovó, but I won't quit dotting my hand either," he said stubbornly. "Are you going to tell me if you died from illness or because you're a mule who'd die just to spite someone for not following your orders and making you some tea?"

"Why not leave a poet with her mysteries, dear? Now I must be going." She kissed him and helped him to his feet; then her axolotl wings carried her away. She was right, as always: Hope was a state of receptiveness toward being alive, but redemption demanded action. Why had this taken so long to penetrate his thick skull? He did not want stories now, but a touch of humanity—to live the new, now that the old was written. Each scar on him had its own halo like an amphibian's eye, like a china rim around hot tea, like suns wreathing pitch, at last wrapping his body in a graceful cloak of mourning.

He was restless. He dressed for the apiary, because the humming of the bees often calmed him and a problem with one of the hives needed his attention.

He zipped his veil shut and went outside. Foraging animals, probably opossums, had sucked dry dozens of bees and littered the entrance of the plagued hive with empty white husks that retained their bee-shape. Disk-pans where eyes had been, the now-hollow slope to the sting—forms all preserved but all dead. He crumbled the pale voided hulls as if they were brittle candle drippings. Of the twelve hives in his beeyard, only this colony had no thick umbilical cord of bees to the perfume of the clover fields.

He would have to kill the queen. As long as she lived, her workers and drones would stay saturated with her unmatchable scent and could thrive nowhere else, preferring to falter with her in their diseased tomb. Bees were brutally loyal in remembering or defending their queen, and even if they ventured off, they would remain drenched with a bouquet that other bees would smell. He cracked the seal of the hive, and a few wobbly bees stirred among the ripped cells and moths on the ravaged comb. After crushing the large, thin queen with a wrench, he knocked the survivors free. "I'm very sorry," he told them.

The survivors of the cleaned-out hive tried to join the other colonies. Guard bees savaged a few of them, but most seemed to slip into their new homes without any problems, although it would still take a while for their queen's scent to fade completely.

It was time for his whale-eyes to find miracles again. To celebrate his plan of renewal, he cut himself a slab of dripping comb and ate it off a plate with a knife and fork, as if it were a steak. The rich sugar fermented in him like mead. It made him pace. What to do? Suddenly it was too much to think of sitting still! He worked the figure of the queen bee into the life lines of that morning's dotted hand—the first time he had thought of burying some remains of the day within one of his drawings.

He unearthed his father's notebook and paged through it fearlessly. "If there's a curse here, let's root it out," he said, surveying the dots and dashes that filled many of the pages preceding his whale entry. What could his eyes find in them? What could he make of them? He grafted stems, seedling peaks, irrigation canals, and diamond-shaped leaves onto some of the dark blots to change them into neumes:

"Look," he told his swimming head, "there are marks of time, breath, and music concealed in these dark things. My father did not leave panic for me, but the beginnings of music! These are scattered notes, though. Can I uncover a song here?" The grafter carefully spliced the notes he had made into a drawing of a whale singing in neumes. To enormity! To the gift of his eyes, reactivated! To this whale, melodiously free! To the lovely and huge! The sugar within Helio was speaking to him in a riot: Do not be afraid of darkness; rearrange it!

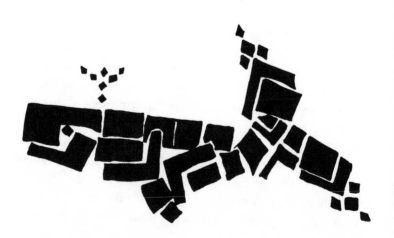

The problem with his desire to spring alive was that he was not sure how to go about it. He dressed in a linen suit, purple ascot, and panama hat, and got into his car. Flinging himself outward, without plans—wasn't that how to invite adventures? He headed in the general direction of San Francisco, but, as usual, became egregiously lost. This too seemed fine, although it was a pity that centuries of ancestral navigational skills had reached a state of collapse with him. Perhaps this meant he was the last in a line of aristocrats, the reverse ebb, the carrier of the banner of decadence. At least he was dressed for the part! His mood was sunny.

He found himself parking at the Oakland–Alameda County Coliseum in time to catch the early innings between the Oakland A's and the Boston Red Sox.

"We're almost sold out, man. You'll have to sit in the bleachers," said the boy inside the ticket booth.

"Splendid," said Helio. "That's where the *real* fans sit, right?"

The boy looked at him blankly.

Helio could tell that the boy was quite stoned. "Here," he whispered, handing over his bottle of eyedrops. He was never far from it, but—time to divest himself of all finicky crutches and props!

"What the fuck?" said the boy.

"Enjoy," said Helio. He turned to see people from the BART train station streaming out of the fenced walkway. He had snatched up one of the last tickets and had already exchanged pleasantries with an addled child; he strode eagerly into the Coliseum. The inner concourse echoed with the strolling crowd.

"Nachos and a beer," he said at the snack bar. The plastic cup read *World Champions* on one side and *Don't Drink and Drive* on the other. Well, he'd have just one.

His seat was behind four drunk teenaged boys who were building a pyramid out of their empty beer cups in the vacant seat next to them. Their language was foul enough for Helio to be forced to concentrate on the game. He found something wonderfully operatic about its slowness, which seemed to be its own point, and the sudden bursts of action. Clemens was on the mound for the Sox and Rickey Henderson managed to steal second and third on him. The boys in front of Helio stood up in one jeering wall whenever the A's Canseco struck out and every time he trotted out to take his place in right field. Helio refrained from joining the Greek chorus.

By the seventh inning, the pyramid of beer cups was threatening to block his view. His mind wandered to how insular he and his fellow Azoreans remained, how weighted with fantasies and chary of well-organized ambitions, even when they moved into the larger world. He had left his house today hoping to change that, and yet here he was, an island on the bleachers, timidly clutching an empty cup.

He set it on top of the pyramid, whereupon the whole thing toppled.

"Damn it. O, hell!" he said.

The boys rose up as one, with a hooting noise, which Helio could not immediately interpret as either hostility or merely their acknowledgment of a change in the landscaping.

"Thanks loads, old man," one of them said.

Old?

"How about a free round?" he said, pulling his wallet out of the inside pocket of his jacket.

As they nudged each other, he congratulated himself on his quick thinking. They were certainly easy to win over. As the least drunk boy went off to buy more beer, the others eyed Helio.

"What's that around your neck, your wife's underwear?"

The others laughed heartily.

"Actually, it is an ascot."

"Ooo, *excuse* us!"

"One of my ancestors took it off the scalp of a pirate right after beheading him."

The youngest boy leaned forward to admire it.

"Aw, you're full of shit," said another of the boys.

"Maybe you've just never seen a Maltese cross," said Helio. He leaned forward so that they could see it patterned in the silk. "I thought most people knew that pirates always wore this sign."

"Yeah? Maybe you've just escaped from a ward."

"Believe me or don't," said Helio.

When the youngest boy reached out and touched his ascot, Helio took it off and handed it to him.

"Do you like it?" asked Helio.

"I don't believe that crap about any pirate."

"Certainly not," said Helio, "but the ascot will make a fine souvenir just the same." When you've reached a high point, exit whistling: In casual encounters, that was a sound rule. He stood. "And now I must be going. You gentlemen enjoy the rest of the game."

"Hey—" said the boy, but Helio was gone before he could hand the ascot back.

Helio glanced over once more as he approached the concourse's tunnel and saw that the boy had fashioned it into an odd bandanna to keep off the sun. Together they had made a modern pirate, done up in silk!

He stopped in the parking lot. He had forgotten to check the score! He didn't even know who was going to win; how could he prove to his friends that he had been here?

Why did he so often feel the need to report to people, as if presenting the facts to someone else verified that he had lived through them? No, he was going to go home now, with the final result unknown. "Did you hear their remark about your underwear, Felicia?" he chuckled to himself. Felicia would have lifted up her dress and said to them, "No, boys, it's not around his neck, it's right here!" By staying forever twenty-five, she impressed and shocked him now. She would be almost fifty, but he could picture only a slightly grayer version of the dream he found familiar.

He started up the car and said, "But I must be going now, my love."

It had been an eventful day.

His whale-eyes provided no halos as he drove toward home, but in the distance he could sense flickers heralding the presence of glories.

Unfortunately he got hideously lost on his return voyage; he overshot home and landed slightly north, in Lodi. Since he was due at the clinic here in the morning for his weekly Friday visit, he decided to stay put, using as night wear the gardening clothes he stored in the closet. He tossed fitfully in the dentist's chair, and in the morning he looked at his wrinkled chinos and white shirt with distaste. This Friday promised to be mostly walk-in business and would be rather light. He would stick around a short while, quickly inspect his various local grafting projects, and head back to Stockton.

But his adventure was not over. As he examined a wisdom tooth he had grafted to a camellia to make wise beauty, he felt the discomfort in his eyes and the burning in his brain that meant a glimmering awaited. Some distant ripples came for him, spreading wider like sound waves and then contracting around him until he was wrapped into a chrysalis and reeled to the underside of a bush down the road, where he clung, watching a woman bent over her outdoor washing tank, her hips swaying as she soaped her laundry with fierce kneadings.

She was wearing a short calico skirt. The bare backs of her legs were like the dark peahens that glinted seablue and seagreen, just for a flash, when they caught the sun. A woman in a spotted skirt! Surely she was meant to be a cure for the Soares griefs. Yet he did not feel love at first sight as he had hoped he would, though she seemed entirely pleasant. He reminded himself that this was because he had not been in love with anyone besides Felicia for so long that he had forgotten what it would feel like. He watched her crack a walnut. While eating it, she let the butterfly papers that halved the meat flutter to the ground. Could he use this as an invitation? He hesitated. It might alarm her if he sprang out of the bushes to introduce himself. He loosened the ripplings that were wrapped around him, letting their expanding hoops carry him back to the clinic.

He could not go home as he had planned, however, because Sean Riley showed up with a loose filling. Helio, trying to sound offhanded as he plied his metal tools, described the woman to Sean and learned that his eyes had revealed a Filomena Mendes. Since no more patients appeared, Helio used a surgical scalpel to spiral the skins off eighty tomatoes. He left the pulp in clean buckets and carried the curling skins, damp in pails, to the yard near her washing tank. It took two trips. There he rewound the skins to form tomato roses and spelled FILOMENA with them on the ground. (He could see a plan unfolding: Tonight he would not be lonely at dinnertime; as he ate tomato soup in Stockton, he would, though solitary, feel buoyant as the arms of a windmill on this day of the declaration of the name in tomato-skin roses.)

He caught a few hours' nap in the dentist's chair and was awakened by Glória Santos, who had a gum problem. He asked her a few questions as he probed her mouth and was rewarded with the information that Filomena was at that very moment rowing on the lake on the outskirts of town.

"Port?" he asked Glória. He kept a bottle of it for patients who were experiencing discomfort. Next to it in the drawer were squares of foil, which he chewed on if children fussed as he treated them, because he could not stand for them to be alone in knowing distress in the teeth.

"You're a dear," she said. He never charged her anything for his services.

When she left, he drained two glasses of port, and every muscle spoke to him: Courage! Go!

He stood, tremulous.

Like all bold explorers, he took the precaution of bringing a gift with which to entice a fair chieftain of a new tribe—a strip of gauze, the only thing he managed to grab as he reeled out the door. While racing to the lake and paying to rent a boat, he rejected several clever things to say about the gauze. There she was, in the middle of the water. His shoulders ached as he set the boat into the shallow end, pushed off, jumped in, and began to row. When his boat bumped against hers, he handed over his present silently but with what he decided was courtly aplomb.

"What a nice bow," she said, tying it around her neck.

How resourceful she was! Undaunted!

She broke off a straw from her hat. "For you."

Psyche, I know you will spin it into gold by morning!

He introduced himself and undertook a recitation about his life, omitting mention of his whale-eyes (she might think he was some fly-eyed spy). He had never been rowing before, and the boat's nose would not stop sniffing in circles. He concluded, while attempting to steady his boat, by confessing that he had written her name in tomato roses that morning.

"That was you?" Her face sagged.

"Yes. Weren't you pleased?"

"Certainly. Yes. It's just that I was hoping—I mean, I thought someone else did it," she said.

Helio swung around to lie curled up on the bottom of his boat.

"Really, it was very sweet," she said, leaning over to pat his back as her boat knocked against his.

"Mmppp," said Helio, cursing the port.

"I'd like to be friends," said Filomena.

He winced and said nothing.

"May I explain?"

Why not? He had certainly filled her ears with a story. As he lay in the boat, becoming nauseated by the rise and fall of the swishing lake, she told him about Robert Paganelli, a married man she had been seeing on and off for eight years. She was unhappy about it, but more unhappy without him. She mentioned that she wrote pamphlets and compiled research studies for historical societies and was currently cataloging the locations of the California poppy in Lodi for a valley gardening center. Helio thought of the supply of red pulp waiting to be taken home. Tomato stews! Seedy desserts! Bread that bled. He did not blame his eyes for this miscue; after all, they were out of practice, and Filomena appeared rather nice, though she did go on a bit, as women whose lives were given over to waiting tended to do.

He returned to the clinic, shamefaced, ready to pack up his buckets of tomato pulp and flee, but Caliopia Silva came running to him.

"What luck that I caught you!" she said. "We should have come to you years ago. Maybe if we had, she wouldn't be so ill now!"

"Calm down and tell me what's wrong," he said, leaning against his car. He was starving. He was desperately in need of a shower, and his body ached from uneven sleep. It seemed like ages since he had left home. Obviously the problem with adventures was that one was not always permitted to be comfortable during them.

"Do you know Clara Cruz?"

He shook his head no.

"She's stopped eating! Her head went very far away and now her body's trying to follow—"

"What?"

"Her brain left the world and now her body wants to go with it," said Caliopia patiently.

"I'm not sure what you mean," he said, barely keeping the irritation from his voice, "and I'm not that type of physician anyway. I'm not a psychiatrist."

"Don't be so dense," said Caliopia. "Are you going to help or not?"

What was wrong with him, to be reluctant when someone needed his help? Hadn't he had enough of comfort, of routine? Skipping one day of dotting a picture of his hand would not kill him. He had promised himself to push ever toward the unknown, not merely at his convenience but whenever it came for him, and that is what he had to do now.

"Take me to her," he said.

As they drove toward the Transfiguration land, she told him the history of Clara Deolinda Cruz and about the black holes in the lace of the world (and about how Clara was falling too far into them), but Helio was half-listening: A dove-white halo, huge and domelike, had appeared just beyond the winery. The ripple that had drawn him to Filomena had not been a misfiring after all, but a point of reference, so that he would be able to distinguish a halo when he received one.

He was stunned. He was not merely being granted a halo in the distance; he was being sent straight into the center of one.

CLARA WISHED THAT everyone would stop rapping on her gall, demanding that she come out. Ever since she had found worms in her shit, she was more content to stay in blind spots, where worms could not be so clearly seen, but people refused to leave her in peace. Every week the midwife put on gloves, extracted a mingle-mangle, and let the little bouquet of pinheads dance on her sheathed fingertip for Clara to see. The shit-smeared worms did not trouble her as much as the dainty fibers on their pointed heads, which meant they were not an accident but creatures of thoughtful, feathery design. But wasn't the job of worms to spare the living and chew the dead? "Aren't I alive? Am I dying from the inside out?" she asked, worried.

She was dwindling to nothing. Glória and Caliopia (crying, "It's all my fault! I should never have taught you about griev-ing!") brought her almond-and-cinnamon cakes with sugar lilacs to cheer her up, but Clara was appalled that someone had shaped stems and petals that would become tenfold worms. Why had the baker wasted his time? Tongues were slugs. People brought her fish disguised in onion sauce as if it were not an early form of shit. Grilled sardines, tarts with pastry leaves, stew with herbs—snakes of excrement on her plate. Shit was clogging the earth, and her contribution to the world would be to give up eating.

On her third noneating day she had double vision, and apparitions shadowed all that she saw. Meeting ghosts was also supposed to wait until after death, but they arrived to roll her left eye inward, curving everything into folds, half-shapes, and cloudiness. Everything ascended a shimmer out of register. Even when she held her hand stock-still, it appeared to flutter as if trying to rub something out. Because it was a sin to violate her clitoris, she would kneel open-legged over a mirror and touch her ghost one, and the shadow-palpitating of her unmoving fingers made her real clitoris swell bright red and come from the connecting joy of its ghost. Coming did not flush out the caves where the worms coiled, but it spat onto the mirror the type of drips that ghosts were said to leave at the sites they haunted. The ghosts seeping out persuaded her to repeat this because she had a lot of slime to eject.

The midwife, hoping that Clara would not become pregnant again, gave her biology lessons using a dwarf doll that opened to show his interior. "Here is the organ that the ancients called the seat of desire. It secretes bile," she told her, pointing to his liver. Clara hated the dwarf. He was a liar. His insides were too clean and solid, and he had no penis. The harp string of his spinal cord did not connect to any lower regions. She had no patience when the midwife used the common expression *pombinha*, "little dove," to describe the vulva. She wanted medicine for worms, not love prettied up and served to her raw.

At the hospital she pulled the intravenous tubes out of her arm—more invading worms. Doctors proclaimed that although her body had stopped functioning, she was fairly healthy and could go home. On her seventh foodless day, Father Dimitro left the winery long enough to put a white corporal on her bed and pray, "Do not defy your intestines, your ovaries! O Lord, release this girl's soul, trapped in its lifeless body! Will you accept this bread and wine, Clara?"

"No," she said, lying down to wish him away. Her swoon would make him the sixteenth priest to disappear since Father Eiras.

She awoke to find Caliopia and a thin, disheveled man standing before her. He looked tired and rumpled, as if he had marched through a storm in a dark tunnel or been driving for nights to be at her bedside. Gold spectacles were sliding down his nose.

"Clara, dear, can you tell the doctor why you won't eat?" said Caliopia.

"Are you that grafter guy?" asked Clara.

"Yes," said Helio, thunderstruck. She was the most beautiful orchid he had ever seen. She had bottomless water, green, for eyes. She seemed buried under leaves, packed down in the floor of a thicket, but there was about her also a smell of fresh water. She was out of a rain forest, where water is a constant music and the bright animals rumble with it.

"Yes," he repeated, because that seemed the truest word to keep uttering in her presence.

"I've been having a nightmare," she said.

"Tell it to us, Clara," said Caliopia. "That's why the doctor's here."

"It is, yes," said Helio. He sat on the edge of the bed and took her hand. "Tell us where you've been."

"All right," said Clara. "You see I joined up with some men and women who went searching for jewels. We saw a sparkle far inside a cave and crawled toward it, but we slid into a pit where centuries of shit had created its own tides and undertows. We kicked to try and ride a wave, grab the shit hanging from the ceiling, and swing out into the sky, but we didn't have the strength. We had to taste the quicksand we were in, and we did not like it because it was bat guano.

"All the days were the same, and we gagged on so much guano that we began to understand its taste. It was like salted hay. To keep off the bats that flew onto us and to help each other to stay alive, we shouted great false encouragement: We dined on custard! The cream of black cows, a trout paste! The lies made us stronger, and we survived by forgetting our fate."

"Heavens," said Caliopia.

"Of course natural laws never stopped," Clara continued. "Our cells and organs, fed on this stuff, became made of bat guano. Soon we had guano skin and hair and a green guano film over our eyes. The bats, frightened and confused to see their shit flailing around in the shape of men and women, beat their wings and spurted into the sky so thickly that the air between their bodies solidified into part of their current. We grabbed hold and rode this living black stream out of the cave.

"The more tightly we clutched, the higher the bats charged to shake off this shit clinging to their fur. They stormed upward in a fist toward God, crying, 'Why did You make such awful shit? Are we dinosaurs or birds? Why must we huddle in caves? Why are we thought blind? Answer or we will keep hollering!'

"We were scared of being shit punching at God and wanted to bail out and escape punishment. We remembered that our diet had given us ten-foot tapeworms. We reached up ourselves and pulled out our worms as if we were jerking rip cords.

"As we tumbled free of the bats, the ground spun its colors: yellow and brown fields and squares of green blurred into peridots, quartz, and jasper. Here was what we had been looking for! Our fall whirled the clouds into ghosts. They saw that we had stupidly trusted the worms to make us open up into parachutes, and they tried to save us, but we fell straight through them. Our cave adventures, our diet, our helping each other, and our discovery of jewels—it added up to nothing. The land hardened beneath us. When we smashed on the ground, the ghosts tried to rake each pudding back into its own broken head, but each of us had spilled into smears of ourselves. 'How sad,' said a ghost. 'They have leaked the human shit they planned to defy. They have joined all those who fall as specks over the land.' "

"Lord!" said Caliopia. She soothed a raw white patch on Clara's calf, where part of her internal winding-sheet was still visible. Caliopia had not realized that one could fall past the lessons of the Egg into a deeper level of despair: people as shit.

Helio could not speak. Her hatred for life, narrated so

calmly, had shaken him. She had plunged to the bottom of the same chasm where he was more slowly drifting down. What was his own history, what were his legends, if not a minefield of black holes? He bent down and with both arms lifted her off the bed. Her body felt like a bundle of plant stems as he pulled her out of her forest. Her arms were bruised, and in the fruit of her he could feel the weight of the hidden stone. He touched her hands and chest, where bones floated like those bendable needles that poke unmoored in fish's meat. There was a small bald spot near her hairline, and some whitish streaks on her neck.

Caliopia stood, rubbing Clara's bare feet. "Will she be better soon?"

"I hope so, yes," said Helio. He carried her outside. Let them go to see the jewels on the land now, not in the moment of falling to their deaths. He knew all at once that the cure for their condition was that someone must come along and hold the other. The other must be held and offered up to the light. It was really quite simple. He took her into the sun, with Caliopia shielding Clara's eyes, which had grown accustomed to the dark and blinked in rheumy pain.

They stood there awaiting the first signs of repair.

"I think I'm very hungry," Clara whispered to Helio. "Are you?" He was clasping her head against his chest.

"Terribly," he whispered back. And again he added, "Yes, terribly."

FIVE

A Creation Story

In the beginning God made the first two bodies lonely on the earth. One died here and the other there, but already fate was at work to create life beyond life. A bird ate a spider that had chewed the flesh of the first man, who had done a pathetic job of burying himself and was sticking out of a bog. This bird therefore had in its stomach part of the man, which permeated its wingspan as it flew to the other end of the globe. A feather dropped over a riverbed. Desperate for a companion, the man's microbes in the feather slid down the quill and traveled on grasshoppers until they found the second man. (*The aim of the bird's feather had not been very true, but we should be glad that the first man's microbes did not land smack down on the second man. If not for the journey, this would be a story of pure luck and not one of desire and will.*)

The remains of the first man and the second man instantly made love (*from the start men could love men, and women love women, and the dead could be with the dead or living.*) They had many children, both male and female. All were marvelous swimmers, and many lived and died in the water. This spread creation farther, since tides could bring bits of people over vast areas to reproduce on foreign shores.

Whole beings sprang from the intermingling flecks, and the generations quickly expanded. Hordes of people were soon trooping across the land, which packed those who were the longest-dead more deeply toward the earth's core. They were stomped completely inside one another. But since this is the ideal of making love, to be contained with immense heat within someone else, they turned into fire. This is why the earth's center is so intensely hot and why it and the other impacted areas closer to the surface ejaculate in volcanoes and fissures to release their sighs. This, some argue, was how the islands of the Azores were born.

The planet spins to mix these deepest lovers more thoroughly.
We must admit this is nice but does not alleviate the distress and crowding on the surface.

Iᴛ ᴡᴀꜱ ꜱᴀɪᴅ that Lodians collectively returned from their seven years' lull in time for the great trout treasure hunt, thanks to the lifting of one of them by Doctor Soares: Holding Clara up to catch something of the heavens shamed the angels into dropping everyone some lifelines. He took her to eat sundaes at the ice cream parlor until both of them were in wonderful agony and had to hold their stomachs as if about to give birth. Then, after kissing the top of her head, he drove off, taking his buckets of tomato pulp with him. She could still feel his presence in the guest house. Her gall had been cracked open, and retreat now seemed as undesirable as oversleeping on the first day of a vacation. How her heart had flared upon first seeing the doctor, because she thought for a moment that he was Tio Vitor, sweaty but clear of vines, grown older but with his handsome and fragile looks intact, coming to say that victory was theirs. Helio's torchlike eyes gave him the isolated intensity of a light-house. Occasionally she had glanced away from it, but what was there to fear? She too was a keeper of a lighthouse, looking for survivors on the wide sea!

The guest house was so confining! A matchbox! No place for a twenty-five-year-old woman!

The trout party came along as a release for everyone. Viriato das Chagas had opened his trout farm in hopes of financing an early retirement from the post office, but instead he was going further into debt. His liberation (and everyone else's from the seven vacant years) arrived on a normal Friday in California, with the sun's rays acting as their usual palette knives, scraping swaths of color off the landscape and leaving behind white glare, when his wife, Carmen, lost her diamond ring in the trout pond. She did not know that it had slipped off her finger until she saw it blink in the arc of brine shrimp that she was tossing to the fish. She watched a trout swallow the ring and disappear into the gray-green fish amassed like boiling cabbage. She came into the house crying, but Viriato could scarcely contain his elation. They could cut up every lousy trout in pursuit of the diamond, coerce the insurance company into paying for their losses, and end this shipwreck of a business. All Lodians were invited to partake.

At Caliopia's house, the hens felt the excitement and had trouble standing still for their bonnet changes. Luís II barked and jumped. "Yes, it's going to be a party," she told him. "A real party!"

Glória and João decided that if they won the one-hundred-dollar prize for finding the diamond, they would buy more canaries.

The Sete Cús families repaired their trucks for the ride to the trout farm. (Their ancestors on the island of Graciosa had been so hefty that the nickname "Seven Buttocks" had stuck for generations, although the Sete Cús brothers in Lodi were quite thin.)

Filomena Mendes finished her second beer of the morning. She hoped this would ensure that she would not be tempted to drink in front of anyone at the party. Robert might appear—but with or without his wife? She went fuzzy-limbed back to bed. Before leaving, she would hide the bottles in the trash, beneath the wreckage of her name in tomato peels, in case Robert came home with her.

At the Botelho home, eight-year-old Fernando asked his father, Guilherme, "Can we take Mamãe down for today?"

"I suppose so," said Guilherme. Stored behind the family pictures on the mantel was his wife, Margarida, who was shriveled into a string with her head, stomach, and knees as round glass beads. He blew the dust off her and handed her to Fernando.

The boy had to wait until his father left the room and the sun struck a hammer blow through a window, throwing one of its little rectangular heating trays filled with dancing magnolia petals of light onto the floor. (The moon could also deliver magnolias, although the temperature was less intense.) He was impatient. Once he had appalled himself by thinking that he could sell his mother and buy a bicycle. At last a sun-tray appeared, and he planted the necklace in it. His mother's beads cracked like buds in rich soil and, rising like Venus again in the center of the light-magnolias, she rained kisses on Fernando. Her face still had a few bruises from the last time Guilherme had hit her.

"Today is a chance to be happy, Mamãe!" he shouted. "We're going to a feast!"

As guests arrived, Viriato was dragging a net through the pond and dashing trout onto the ground. He ordered his daughter Cristina, a nineteen-year-old who read silly magazines and worked on her tan, to cover the fish with rags and rap them with wrenches to curtail their suffering.

"Another big scheme of yours shot to hell," she said. "If you think I'm going to clean a single one of these fish, you can just forget it."

Viriato had to be constantly on guard that his disappointment in her would not turn into dislike. At her age, he had devoured every book within reach, voracious for what she dismissed as a bore. "You'll help out today, without your mother or me begging," he said.

" 'You'll help out today, without your mother or me begging,' " she mimicked. God Almighty, she couldn't even come up with her own retorts.

"If you plan to be horrid, Cristina, I am going to bounce

higher than the planets," said Carmen as she carried plates and utensils to the redwood picnic tables. She was what is known as a "good wife and mother," meaning that her husband and daughter remained fond of her but were no longer much interested in anything she did or felt.

"Good," muttered Cristina.

Viriato slung more trout at her feet as visitors filled the yard. The bodies of the fish arched into silver bridges and collapsed. Tails fanned the grass desperately. Jaws locked open, and in some the desire to return to the water forced pink air bladders to distend through their mouths. Viriato whistled as he helped the men gut the fish into buckets. They searched the slops carefully and released the pond's water with cheesecloth over the drain but concluded that the diamond must have worked its way into the flesh of a fish. Luís II sniffed the entrails, but Guilherme and the Sete Cús brothers shooed him away.

"Luís, I am going to sit on your head," said a Sete Cús brother.

"He's just helping you check," huffed Caliopia. "Come here, Luís."

"Careful," said Guilherme when she was out of earshot. "If the gopher-lady sings, we're dead men."

Caliopia joined Glória, Filomena, and Ethel Riley, the florist's wife, in scaling the fish. They wielded their knives back and forth across the gray skin like barbers sharpening razors on a leather strop. Clara, suddenly inspired, caught the shower of scales in a brown paper sack. She missed doing fish-scale art.

Father Maximillian, the new pastor, stood in front of her as she patted scales out to dry in the sun. He said, "What do we have here?"

"Quit blocking my light," she said.

Filomena was soaking the cleaned fish in olive oil, vinegar, eggs, and chervil and taking them to Sean Riley, João, and the

Sete Cús, who were working the fires. Yellow tears dripped and hissed on the coals as the fish were thrown onto the grill. Filomena scored slices of bread with a knife and tucked them around the fish.

"Look," said Fernando, taking his mother to see the bread's cracks widening from the heat. "The bread is so glad, it's laughing."

Filomena trickled oil from a teaspoon into the opening mouths of the bread. "It's thirsty too," she told Fernando. She would busy herself with many tasks so that it would not seem that she was waiting for Robert.

João's ghost hand could not grip the tongs very well to turn the fish, but it could sprinkle salt. Onlookers saw a tight white star rise within the smoke and burst into a falling comet over its target.

"Wine! The chefs need wine!" called out Viriato.

Carmen poured glasses for the men.

"The scalers! The scalers need wine!" admonished Ethel Riley.

They received filled glasses.

Filomena paused, accepted a glass. Just one. If Robert came, he would see her enjoying herself. If he did not come, the wine would be some comfort. But she drank it quickly and soon needed another.

"To the chefs!" João said, toasting them.

"The hell with the chefs. To us!" said Glória, joining Clara in chopping tomatoes with olives and onions for a salad.

Caliopia stole a trout off the grill and boned it for Luís II.

The men were drinking and talking and did not notice the smoke billowing downward.

"Hey, rattlebrains!" said Cristina.

The men slammed down their glasses to snatch trout off the fire.

"It's an offering by Cain," suggested Father Maximillian.

"Here," said Clara, shoving a basin of tomato salad at him, "go put this on the table."

"This was on purpose," announced Viriato, holding up a blackened fish. "Haven't you heard of Trout Diabo à la Sete Cús?"

"Kiss our asses. It's à la you," said one of the brothers.

"There's room now to throw Mr. Amaro on the grill," said Guilherme. Mr. Júlio Amaro owned the Lodi Sunlit Dairy, where many of them worked.

"He's so fat he'd really sizzle," agreed a Sete Cús.

"Gentlemen," said Father Maximillian.

"Time to eat," said Filomena. She sensed that Robert was not coming and wanted to hurry this party and go home to her beer.

Clara brought out artichokes that had been boiling in the house.

"Come with me," said Fernando to his mother. They saw Guilherme studying Filomena's rump as she walked past, and Fernando could sense his mother beginning to shrink inside her clothes. He hoped she could enjoy the party before she turned back into a necklace. "Watch me, Mamãe, I'm going to eat like a hog," he told her.

Father Maximillian said grace.

Artichoke leaves flew and the cooked-egg skin of the fish crackled under their teeth. Wineglasses clinked, sounding like a fencing match with crystal foils. Luís II begged for scraps, and a parade of other Lodians arrived, having followed the hand-lettered signs that Carmen had posted on the road. The entire pond would have to be eaten.

Clara waved when she saw Helio appear in the crowd. When she reached him, he bowed slightly. He *was* a lot like Tio Vitor. She knew that delicate manners often indicated someone who had managed to retain a fondness for life after some siege, making the fondness gentler, almost halting, and perhaps more hidden for being hard-won; delicacy was rarely the weakness people took it to be.

"Doctor," she said.

"It's Helio, please," he said. "I just wanted to make sure that you've been eating all right."

She could see herself through his gold-rimmed glasses, etched on his pupils like reverse scrimshaw. When he smiled, she changed into gleams on black pearls. "No more worms either. You came all the way from Stockton to ask?" she said.

"It's my usual day at the clinic," he said quickly, "but everyone is over here, it seems. I heard there is a diamond to find."

"There is," she said, seating him next to her at the table. He sliced a fish off its bones with a thoroughness that made her giggle.

"Are you a surgeon?" she asked.

"Yes," he said, gesturing with his utensils at the air. "Right now I can do anything. Everything!"

"Maybe you'll be the one to find the diamond."

He selected another fish for her. "Or maybe you will."

Volunteers fried the mountain of trout. Filomena went into the house to prepare more salad often enough to appease herself with sips of wine in secret but not enough to arouse suspicion. Visitors ate standing by the depleted pond or sitting in folding chairs.

"More trout!" the Sete Cús kept yelling.

There were comments about them living up to their name.

"I've had ten, and I'll have another," said Sean Riley.

"Everyone should eat like monks," said Viriato, gesturing to a full platter.

Father Maximillian sat quietly, pretending not to hear. Clara felt a pang for him; he seemed rather nice. Too bad he would have to be wished away like the others.

When every trout was gone, a cloud of frangible silvery bones covered the tables.

"Wait a minute!" declared Helio. "Who found the diamond?"

Drinkers lowered their glasses. The replete eaters looked helplessly at one another. Some pawed through the cumulus skeleton on the table and gave up.

"We forgot that we were on a treasure hunt!" said Caliopia.

"My poor ring!" cried Carmen.

"I guess that means no prize money," said Viriato.

"Since the diamond could be inside any of us, why don't you divide the prize money equally?" said Helio.

"Good idea," Clara muttered at him, impressed with his command of worldly matters.

"Goddamn it," said Viriato under his breath.

"Mamãe, we're all diamonds," said Fernando.

After the hunt on the feast day of the trout, none of them had any excuse not to say: I shall never again forget that I must find treasure; I am a diamond; I shall sparkle from this day forth.

Clara pieced together diamonds out of fish scales. Turned sideways, they were the doctor's eyes! (She would later give one to Father Maximillian, somewhat regretting that after one of her swoons he requested an indefinite leave of absence to visit his ailing father.)

On the diamond night, João held his ghost arm like a lantern toward Glória. He clasped her tightly with his muscular limb and his limb of ether. To love her with the real and the incorporeal (certainly those featherweights in heaven, the men who were only naked light, could not do this to her as he could), he entered her from behind, reaching his phantom hand around to caress the front of her. As she rocked against his flesh and his ghost touch, she fairly whispered, "The dance of our lives!"

Filomena sweetened her dreams with sips of amaretto.

Helio, off in Stockton, gave thanks to the gems of his whale-eyes for spotting the road signs that brought him to his place at the feast.

Certainly young Fernando shone that night. When his father rampaged around the house, Fernando led his mother into a closet and said, "Finish shrinking into a necklace so Papai can't get you." When the darkness helped her revert into glass beads on a string, he stuffed her into his shirt.

"Where is she?" his father yelled, slapping everything off the mantel.

"I have no idea," said Fernando. He stood tranquilly in a lightless corner where the fullness in his shirt could not be detected.

His father stormed outside and called, "Margarida!"

Fernando was fearless. He was like the gallant priests of old who carried the Eucharist inside their cassocks, in a sack hung over their chests, to the faithful behind enemy lines. You will need to tear apart my sinews, my foes, to wrest away what I bear over my heart! He hid his mother in a secret cupboard in his room, where she could sparkle with her other jewelry in the dark. As he said, "Sleep now, Mamãe" and closed the door, she was glittering at the other glass pieces and polished stones, all of them together like lost ships speaking with heliographs.

Helio had never known the halos to misdirect him, but surely he was not meant to think too much about a woman almost thirty years younger than he was. He felt sorry that she lived in a shack half-swallowed by a lip of ground, and if it was true, as Caliopia had said, that Clara's ability to read and write or to identify numbers was destroyed, then her future might be troubled, but he could not venture what to do about it. He was aware above all that Clara was about the age that Felicia had been at her death, and about the age their daughter would now be, and he was angry at his eyes for leading him to a double ghost. He wanted more than that now; he deserved newness—or was he fated to repeat the monumental set pieces of his life, the points of awful pause, like one of those purgatorial souls in the circles between life and death who must endlessly reperform all grand acts of joy and sorrow until they are burned clean? It made him shudder. Maybe dotting those pictures of his hand day after day meant he was already there! The thought that he might belong to this kinship of the lost souls in the vapor—the debtors and those with unfinished business, the lovers and criminals, the noneaters and incorrupt bodies refusing to disintegrate and loosen their grip on the earth—intensified his suspicion that he had been in the host of the living dead for a good while.

Once again, he was spinning a huge fanciful tapestry out of a few sparse threads! When would he learn to curb this tendency? When he dropped in at Clara's each Friday, (it was only decent, he told himself, that on his day at the Lodi clinic he should stop by and check on her health), he schemed about livening her up. More of his pesky embroidery! But could she replace her old jeans and T-shirts with colors? Colors, of course. To offset the smooth yellow and copper roundness in her face, peeling slightly, like an onion. To offset those eyes of malachite. And her hair that stood in an array like baroque grillwork— there was about her something profoundly metallic, strong but not necessarily resilient.

"You are doing beautifully, I trust?" he would ask.

"I am, yes," she always replied pleasantly, though without inviting him in.

Sage-green, cool marbling, dazzling steel and high wires. What am I thinking? he was thinking. Bless me, what am I doing? Blues, satellites, shades of birds on a lake. You lived in the vapor as a noneater. You know about having so much grief that one wants to disappear. He did not dare pronounce— because he scarcely knew himself—what had put an anemone in his chest. Its tube feet were fluttering, waving like streamers welcoming home a hero, but he knew that with the slightest touch an anemone shudders, its color deepens, it retracts. Sometimes, walking through his apiary or in the middle of a dental exam, his hand flew with involuntary urgency to his chest, and he could not say whether it was to protect the anemone from anyone brushing against it and causing it to shrivel or so that he could ride the wild kicking of its legs, his sea-child, his bright lashes.

When his house calls to Clara were finally so unnecessary as to verge on the ridiculous, an ugly incident was unveiled that was, curiously, to bestow upon them a convergent project. One Friday afternoon, Clara burst into the clinic yelling, "Doctor! Hurry! Please!"

"I'm right with you," he said, turning toward her, giving a last tamping down to the filling in the mouth of Jeffrey Riley, Sean's and Ethel's son, but even this infinitesimal delay had her pacing in the waiting room like a caged animal.

"Tell your parents it's milk shakes for lunch today," he told Jeffrey, helping him out of the chair and sending him on his way. "Now then," he said to Clara. "What is this all about?"

She grabbed his hand and led him running across some fields west of the Transfiguration land, past dense thickets and groves. They slowed to a walk and headed several miles into some woods where a cabin sat in darkness under the trees. (He hoped she knew where they were going; he was already lost. A pain opened in his side from the exertion.) She pointed to the large chicken coop set apart from the cabin. "I've been going on long walks, and this is what I found," she said.

They approached the coop slowly. A mangy dog appeared to be cowering inside as the chickens squawked and strutted, stabbing the dog with their beaks when it moved. Only when Helio was close enough to unhinge the door could he see what the creature really was.

"Christ," he said.

"We have to save her," said Clara.

A young girl, her hands shriveled into pinched hooks, picked in the gloppy dirt where she lay, not bothering to fend off the chickens when they aimed for her face. She was unclothed and muddied, too dulled with scratches to pay much attention to Helio and Clara entering the coop. The chickens turned on the intruders in one concerted flurry, rasping feet like rakes across any flesh they could find. Clara, without flinching, grabbed one chicken after another by its neck as her legs were being punctured. Despite the hail of jabbing, she threw them on their backs and stroked their throats long and slowly with her hand. They collapsed as if dreaming.

"What on earth?" said Helio.

"Follow me," she said.

He fell into her rhythm, catching the attackers one after another, flinging them down, and stroking their undersides. By the time Clara and he reached the girl, stunned chickens—eyes closed, wings and damp legs spread—covered the ground, their bellies tilted starkly to heaven.

A bird stirred from its coma, and Clara caught it and drew

a line on the ground with her foot. The chicken fainted when she pushed its head to the line's center.

"That's another way to do it," she said, explaining that whenever a chicken was forced to stare at some infinity—at the sky or a line that meant eternity—it collapsed in awe. Since chickens cannot fly, God had to give them another way of touching Him.

"You know a lot about trances," said Helio.

At first the chicken-girl did not want to leave her home, but she was too weak to stand up and resist. They were afraid that straightening her legs might snap them. Helio almost wept to see how tightly bones could knit together, turning bodies into clothespins. She reminded him of something he had first thought in medical school, so alarming that it made him tender toward strangers: We are only a tarp stretched over a skeleton.

"You can't just hide, or you'll turn into mud," Clara said, though the girl could not register this.

Helio carried the girl out of the coop. Clara leaned against him as they stood with the injured captive. Their exposed skin glistened with beads of blood. The arrow tips of the firs shot high enough to skewer the patches of twilight color overhead, like pins impaling butterflies.

He felt the stinging of a light breeze. Here he was, far from home, the winner of a battle—now what? It was so unfamiliar, this business of winging upon the moment. He recognized that this was no static victory; the work of deliverance had just begun. The night would roll in and swallow the butterflies overhead, though they were held fast for now, and he and Clara were being asked to do no less than commence the study of resurrections.

Helio left the chicken-girl with Clara in the guest house and returned to the cabin to investigate and telephone the police. He found an old woman, purplish and shaped like an eggplant, the vegetable that is the most like a model of trapped gravity. Her eyes were caked like a sick horse's. A pot of oatmeal was simmering itself into a rock on the stove. Without moving her head from where she sat at a Formica table, she rolled her eyes up to meet his.

"Have you taken my granddaughter?" she asked.

"Are you ill?" He recognized about the place the smell of fear, a thickness that coats objects to anchor them in their place, and it turned his stomach.

She laughed. A few darkened teeth protruded from her lower gums like driftwood caught in a sandbar. "Let me show you something," she said, tilting her bulk enough to reach under a pile of newspapers and unbury a framed picture. "A little swan—don't tell me she's not."

It was the chicken-girl, in a party dress and bows, a six- or seven-year-old angel, smiling at the camera. "Seven years ago I got her when her parents died, and I knew she would be better off with the chickens. I'm right, I tell you, right right right." She clasped the picture to herself.

"You need a doctor," said Helio. He had to leave before the heaviness in the room crushed him.

"I've been taking care of both of us just fine," said the woman fiercely, "before you came along! Now you've taken my poor Marina!" She put her head on the dirty table and sobbed. "You're going to ruin her! My darling Marina!"

Helio shut the door behind him. She no doubt deserved whatever the authorities had in store, but he had a touch of old-country attitudes in his distrust of institutions—even hospitals were jails—and he could not bring himself to call anyone just yet. She had survived this long without his interference, and now that the girl was safe, it might be better to leave the grandmother in her blighted peace, at least for a while.

A pretty girl of about thirteen or fourteen was hiding beneath the layers of dirt and the crosshatching of scratches and scars. Clara placed her in a metal tub outside and anointed her with streams. Helio watched the cloudiness evaporate from Marina's eyes. When Clara lifted her up and turned to him with her, it was Clara who was so radiant from the bathing that he felt she held the whole salvaged earth draped across her arms and was passing it to him. She was a fireman carrying the child out of the flames, and he was the one who had been anxiously waiting. He dabbed disinfectant on Marina's painful sores. Out of her dark matted hair they cut knots that looked like snarling furry animals, all fighting for possession of her head. Helio bought new clothes for Clara and her. Clara touched her up with lipstick and a kohl pencil. Marina gleamed beneath her wounds. Her sad history was dissolving.

"Can you speak?" asked Clara.

Marina looked at her, tilting her head.

"She's forgotten," said Helio. "She's probably been silent for the last seven years."

Clara told him that she understood.

He told her about the afternoon of eating the honeycomb after realizing that his father had bequeathed to him not terror but the dark notes of music. (Maybe soon he would tell her everything about his family.) "The sugar in me that day spoke very loudly," he said, "about adventures, I believe."

"If you've listened to sugar, then you know me, and I know you," said Clara. She gave him a description of sugar-speaking. She was wearing a dress he had bought for her, simple and belted, with short sleeves, consisting of panels of the primary colors that were purple, green, and orange where they overlapped. Her voice, warm and eager, revived another one of her memories. Long ago in the islands, to get through the homilies during Mass, she and Eugénio had taken turns brushing the insides of each other's wrists back and forth with their fingertips, something so light and secret over their veins that adults had never noticed how it induced a hypnosis. She and Helio were sitting on either side of Marina, and Clara showed him how to soothe the undersides of Marina's cleaned wrists and arms, over the rawness and abrasions, as they had calmed the bellies of the chickens. With humans, though, it was not only the receiver of this medicine but the giver who cascaded into a mild delirium. The three of them floated on a life raft.

"Don't worry," said Helio, "we're going to bring her back into the world." He imagined himself drifting toward the holy stone statues of Asia, whose roughness is rubbed smooth in patches shiny as black polish where pilgrims have repeatedly touched in petition.

Because the wait between Fridays was too much to ask—was irresponsible, given the work of regeneration that Clara and he had undertaken—and because he feared that Marina's grandmother might come out of the woods to snatch the girl back, Helio decided to move to Lodi. He was surprised at how little this resolve tried his emotions; it occurred to him that something had finished in him long ago, and he was finally acting on it. He packed with urgency. A deadness was eating away at him and would paralyze him forever if he did not hurry to where he might be safe. He thought of the life raft with Marina and Clara, and although he equated the notion of fresh starts with delusion, he did believe that sometimes a person was called somewhere new when he could no longer tap into the continual newness of the place where he was.

California land had gone from crowded and expensive to choking and out of the question, but there was still room to be had if one stayed far enough from the coast, and his incentive was keen. He sold his property in Stockton and bought a house a short walk east of the Transfiguration winery. There was enough land for his beehives. Doctor Anderson, the owner of the clinic, promised him several extra days of work every week for a year. After that, when Doctor Anderson retired, Helio would have a chance to take over entirely. It was risky—he might have to expand the apiary and sell more honey to meet his expenses—but he wore a clean gloss over his concerns, his face expansive as his new bay window with its distant view of the winery. He did not immediately unpack all of his boxes. Instead of chastising his untidiness, he felt himself to be a stowaway on a ship bearing cartons of goods over the waves of land. He was headed for different countries, and it did not matter how much the night tossed him. He walked in his new rooms, stopping to admire things as ordinary and fresh as walls and floors. Where they were smooth was alluring, and so was their pebbling.

CLARA WAS DELIGHTED with Marina's company. She set up an adjacent cot for her, lining it with leaded aprons from Helio's office and hosing them down in the yard when Marina soiled them. Clara did not mind this, nor Marina's problems with words, because it was a pleasure to wake up every morning with someone beside her. Marina was still red-streaked as crabmeat from years of being tucked away in the henhouse, but with every awakening, smiling at Clara, bundled in her quilt, she was growing more limpid, as if she were a queen of the waters peering through some ragged coral that branched over her face and body. Clara was dying to say, as she touched Marina's face, testing the loosening of the scabs that remained a partial mask: Step out completely from behind it, why don't you? Why didn't you escape from your nightmare before this?

On mornings when Marina awoke frightened, uncertain where she was, Clara held a square of chicken wire over Marina's line of vision, figuring that she was accustomed to seeing the outer world broken into hexagonal panes. It was all improvisation, this getting to know someone. She bought edible bracelets from Dermott's Five & Dime; laughing like teenagers, they bit the round banana-flavored candies off the strings for breakfast.

Whenever Helio arrived to apply almond oil to Marina's elbows and knees, stretching her limbs and helping her remember how to stand, Clara observed how carefully he soothed Marina's skin, never in a rush; how he oiled her hands to uncurl them, drawing the fingers outward, his coaxing low and steady. He was never frustrated on days when Marina showed little progress. That alone changed Clara's inner metronome, which was set at rendering everything as a minute waltz. She figured her patience had died with her failure to regain her land, but with Helio she could feel it slowly returning. On the day that Marina finally rose, raising her arms upward, Clara was so excited that she slung her own arm around Helio's waist and received his arm around her shoulders, as though they were simultaneously afraid that the room could not sustain more than one whole person and they would topple unless they braced themselves. She glanced up, but finding him looking at her too she looked away, her arm sliding off his waist.

"Marina!" she said. "You're on your feet!"

Clara held that it was not enough for Marina to recapture a physicality; she had to be restored to what lived outside herself. In the neighboring gardens, toward Glória's and João's house, the fuchsias hung swollen like ripe fruit—the dancing-girl's skirts carmine, cherry, damask—and Helio taught Clara and Marina how to grasp the long stamen running up into their core and with a single sure yank pull it out, the drop of watery honey glistening at its tip.

They performed their morning exercises out with the violet bristles protruding from the artichokes, there in the dark-claret light. Helio's lavender soap was a male-flowering scent as he led them in touching their shoulders, waists, knees, and finally bending down to the ground.

"Inhale with us, Marina," he said.

In—let it fill you—*out.*

Clara led Marina in speeding up the exercises, laughing when Helio became breathless.

"Look what you're doing to an old man!" he gasped.

Because of her son, Clara had learned some axioms of the heart:

Old tired blood of night and sleep starts out purple.

It goes through the heart to wash itself red.

The morning sky is red and purple to remind us that we walk in the air of burst hearts.

Because she could not yet explain this to Marina, she tried with Helio, giving him the history of her land and her little boy.

Caliopia had told him about most of this, but coming from Clara directly it was renewed. Shyness prevented him from pointing out what he found full within the sadness: By painting her sorrows on the sky, she transformed them into colored lights.

After their exercises they were usually invited to sit on Glória's and João's porch and eat tomato-and-mayonnaise sandwiches before João had to leave for work at the dairy. Clara and Helio sat on either side of Marina, talking to each other over her head, checking on her every few moments. Marina posed herself sunward to dry her injuries. Glória cupped her hand over the exact place João's spirit hand would be resting, and sometimes she sat on her crossed legs to put them to sleep because she wanted ghost limbs too. She served pitchers of water flavored with cut peaches and sugar. The wedges looked like prawns with their fibrous legs dangling, the red legs that had clung to the peach stone's rutted face. What an ageless secret, thought Clara, that anything could become an aquarium! She drank a great deal of the peach-water, and in terrible heat she would splash some on her skin so that it glistened with sugar.

It was the first time she already missed people she still had, and her first inkling that true joy creates not memories but physical particles. These Lodi mornings created particles that were the color of the blue that rests in the seat of flames. These were being stored in her as embers that would rise out of her when she died, to burrow in someone else, because they had nothing to do with dust.

Bringing Marina back to life proceeded swiftly, especially with Helio now residing in Lodi. She was an eager pupil, and showing her how to dress herself, use the toilet, and wash a dish did not pose many problems; the years of withdrawal had only temporarily robbed what she had learned as a child. Clara liked teaching her mundane feats because it remade them into small graces, and as she assisted Marina in sweeping the floor, she could watch the task expand into a ceremony, the edges of the action spreading outward in a mist and the center of it turning crystalline. Marina, Marina! Clara practically sang. Who is leading whom? You're making me guess that until we own the jewel imbedded within every act, we are not permitted to know courage, love, or any of the larger wonders.

Helping Marina speak and relearn the names of things were longer rituals. Clara was glad; she hated staying indoors now. She wanted to walk in the air as she had with her father, never tiring of rediscovering hydrangea-walls. She and Helio planned short excursions away from the guest house and into the immediate area, with Marina's arms linked on one side by him and on the other by her. They said aloud what everything was, starting with the tangible:

"*Brier roses:* perfumed, pink. Careful how you hold it, love. The thorns are a dozen little hurts.

"*Cat:* here, kitty kitty! It brushed your legs and then disappeared, Marina.

"Grafting," said Helio, running her hand over the duck's feathers he had blended into a willow (unsuccessfully) to try to create buoyant weeping.

"Feathers. Bark. Willow. Grafting," said Clara.

"Aurr," said Marina.

"Thata girl," said Helio.

"Feathers. Grafting," repeated Clara, afraid of her own forgetting. If reading, writing, and numbers could be taken from her, then her former muteness might return at any time.

"Chalk," said Helio, taking some from his shirt pocket along with a palm-sized slate.

"Chalk," said Clara.

"Virr," said Marina.

Helio wrote *chalk* on the slate and held it in front of her. "Chalk," he said.

"Cha," said Marina.

Clara took the slate from Helio and studied it, frowning. It looked like white twigs on blackness. "This says *chalk?*" she asked.

"I'm sorry," said Helio, taking it from her and hastily putting it back into his pocket. "I forgot. We can stick to talking."

"Bee!" he exclaimed as one flew past.

"Bee," said Clara.

"Yii," said Marina.

"Vineyard," said Clara, pointing Marina toward the hillsides.

"Tell her about it," said Helio.

"It is still mine. It will always be mine. I lie down and wish away the priests who run it, because if I cannot have it, then I will stop anyone who pretends it is his."

"But how long can you keep that up?" he asked softly.

"Forever," she said. "Please take out your little chalkboard and write that for me. I would like to know what it looks like."

On the slate, Helio wrote *forever* and handed it to her.

She could detect only a swirling mass of amoebas, curves, and points.

"I give up," she said.

"No, no," said Helio, "you can do it." He ran his finger through the maelstrom of white scratches, saying, "For- e- ver."

"Sorry, it's a big mess," said Clara.

They held the slate in front of Marina.

"Ahh," she said. "Ahh."

"I could read very well after I learned to speak," said Clara.

"I believe you," said Helio, and they took up Marina's arms again and continued strolling. "I can do more than that, actually. I can attest to what happened to you because I know it myself," he said.

"I lost knowing how after—everything. My baby—" offered Clara.

"Yes, that's how it happens," said Helio. "We have to lose a part of ourselves, or else who or what is missing was never fully inside us. When my family died, I stopped having the power of my eyes." He entertained her with a story about his whale-eyes but was too timid to add that first a glimmering and then a halo had brought him to where he was today. But he did say that he had faith that sometimes lost parts could be rejuvenated.

When they figured that Marina recognized objects—though she murmured only vague sounds—they addressed the personal messages attached to things:

"*Lace,*" said Clara. "This at my throat, from my neighbor in Agualva, Maria Josefa. She made daisies and profiles in star-bursts of threads. Lace is what the whole world is. Sometimes we drop into the open sections in the lace."

"Lace," said Helio.

She told him about the blind spots in the landscape and how to enter them. He vaguely recalled Caliopia trying to clarify this on the day he had entered the halo.

"And tell us more about Maria Josefa," he said.

She described fish-scale art.

"Well! You should start again," he said.

Clara smiled. Pointing to her collar again, she repeated, "Lace."

"Sss," said Marina.

"Lace," said Helio.

"*Corn,*" said Helio. "We've come to another of my grafts. I mixed some ears with pages out of books to make vegetable squares that would be a child's letter blocks. They don't quite work."

"No, they work. I took my baby to see these," Clara whispered. "He passed his whole infancy with them."

"Tell me more," he said.

She told him about Father Eiras and the full life of her child. She mentioned that Glória had picked a bouquet for her son that represented every stage of existence except what came after death. That had found them at a loss.

"I'll look for it in the plant world," promised Helio.

They tried Portuguese words on Marina, naming unseen things in the hope that invoking the invisible might unfasten the spirits in her:

Estremecer—to frighten, to shake or tremble, but also to love tenderly.

Arrebatamento—furor and rage, but also rapture and transport.

Rascar—to scratch, but also to woo.

Saudade—it is an untranslatable word. It is nostalgia. It is melancholy. It is a joy. It is a joy that is held to until it ages into yellowed joy. (Cheese stays milk, despite the setting in of mold.) It is an ancient affliction. It is a modern affliction. It is more than longing, more than yearning. For the past, for glory. For someone, something. It is the declaration: *Your absence has become the greatest presence in my life. Although you are so much in me that I carry you around, this is a pale fulfillment compared with the you that might be before me. Come to me!*

At the uttering of *saudade*, Marina stopped walking. She disentangled her arms from them, and her hands opened, as if expecting all that she longed for to fall from the sky. Instead of catching aimless desire, though, she felt the weighing of the words of Helio and Clara, which were floating freely in the air and landing on her upturned palms. The words were whole and real, gifts that her guides were sending out.

"Forever," said Marina.

Clara and Helio stopped and looked at each other, startled. "Say it again! Again!" they shouted.

"Bee," said Marina.

"Okay! Yes! Yes!"

Marina pointed to her eyes. "Eye," she said.

"Good!" said Helio. "You're alive!"

"Forever," said Marina, beaming. Her scabs looked like leaves ready to fall.

"Welcome back," said Clara, squeezing Marina's hand.

"Call me if she speaks a full sentence tonight," asked Helio.

"I can't," said Clara. "You keep forgetting! I can't read telephone numbers or the dial."

"Then will you remember? For me?" he said. "Remember everything."

"That I'm good at," she said.

At home he could not rest. Clara had seen the sky as a burst heart: Maybe she could not relearn letters and numbers, but she could think in colors. Sometimes he was so slow! He pawed through his closet for a large pasteboard and worked on it with acrylic paints.

He showed up later that night at the guest house, with the pasteboard and box of paints tucked under his arm, as Clara and Marina were preparing for bed. "May I?" he asked.

"Come in," said Clara. "What's going on?"

He took a brush from his paint box and blotted colors from ten different tubes over the numbers on her telephone dial. He dabbed whatever were the appropriate seven shades of paint in a flat beaded necklace near every illustration he had already made on the pasteboard to turn everyone's phone number into a series of colors. Now she could speak to people on the phone by fingering them chromatically.

Oyster white pumpkin ocher sea blue ocher ocher primavera green was Glória's and João's number, next to a picture of a one-armed man.

Caliopia (a woman surrounded by chickens in hats) was silver silver oyster white ocher ocher pumpkin chartreuse.

Marina, wearing one of Clara's robes, ran her hand down the edge of the pasteboard, fascinated with it. "Look," she said, pointing to his rendering of himself with glasses and a mustache. Clara laughed at the bowler hat he had given himself.

"I've always wanted one of those," he said. "Too bad they're out of style." He patted Marina on the back; soon she would be reacting and speaking endlessly.

He was primavera green oyster white sea blue sea blue sea blue banana yellow silver.

Silver sea blue charcoal gray pumpkin pumpkin banana yellow chartreuse was the dental clinic (a broad smile displaying one gold tooth among the white ones).

The hospital, dairy, and police were translated into colors. "The winery?" asked Clara.

"Forget it," he said. "You'd keep calling over there and hanging up." They both giggled. Marina joined in.

He hung the pasteboard near her telephone and kissed them good night again. When he arrived home, his phone was ringing.

"Thank you," came Clara's voice, filling his ear, filling the room where he was alone. "I'm glad you've moved here to help me save Marina."

"It's you and me," he agreed, "to the rescue." He dreamed that night he was an oyster in the blue, chewing light green kelp that would in time be a pearl.

CLARA WAS BASKING in Marina's lesson about caring for someone else. It was Helio's idea to guide her in braiding Clara's hair. With Clara seated in a chair in front of them in the yard, Helio stood behind Marina and manipulated her fingers to shape three rough skeins. "Now they all go together," he said. "Always the outside ones over the center." His hands kept Marina's in cadence when they became thick, and Clara, calmed by the gentle tugging, listened to the chimes within herself. Helio had mentioned that people are mostly water, and she pictured having thimblefuls in her toes, shot glasses of water in her wrists and ankles, champagne flutes of it in her arms and legs, tumblers in her belly and head, set in tintinnabular motion from the braiding, ringing with the tones of their various full-nesses, a tap-tapping out of her water music by the two conduc-tors above her. Her eyes were shut. She was able to feel the pathway of her music, could follow it as it coursed out of her head like electricity and upward into the wound helixes of the fingers, and from there it was easy to travel through Helio's arms and behind his eyes. They contained water too, tapable; like everything human, they were possessed of their own chiming, and she switched to listening to him as he and Marina secured the braid with a rubber band, the end a paintbrush's bristling tip pointing downward between her shoulder blades.

She opened her eyes and saw Helio stepping as a guard in front of Marina and her. The old woman was marching toward them, leaning on a walking stick, a bold flower print stretched over her expanse. She stopped close enough for Clara to detect an acrid oil bubbling up through the grandmother's pores.

"Stay right there," said Helio. "How did you know where to find us?"

"I know where to find what's *mine*." She held out her arms.

"Poor lamb! You're going to throw her to the hounds. I can see it coming!"

"Come back here again and I really will call the police," said Helio.

"You'll see! You'll see how the world takes bites out of her! Chickens hurt less!" said the woman. "Marina!"

"Go away," said Clara, shielding the girl behind her.

The grandmother looked from Helio to Clara. "Please," she said.

"Go away," said Helio.

Crying softly, her head hanging, she retraced her path from the woods. Clara shook the whimpering Marina by the shoulders, saying, "You can't go back! Don't be so stupid!"

It was unlikely that the woman would manage another haunting of them soon, but Clara was furious at this reminder that disruptions could flash in at any time. She remembered nailing the mildewing towels over Father O'Brien's windows, sealing rot with rot. Hemming ugliness in with ugliness so that it would seethe in its own corral and not go near them—that was needed again. Without telling Helio, she left Marina with Glória and took the long trail into the woods, carrying a conch shell to put on the grandmother's porch. Who can resist placing it against an ear to hear the water echoing? She would fill her with tides and drown her.

At the drugstore, Clara bought wax-candy skeletons. Children bite off the skulls, drink the cherry-water inside, and chew the wax until it disappears. She strung the skeletons across the old woman's doorway and hid behind trees until she heard her bellowing.

Clara punctured every inch of the hose near the cabin to make it spout water like a gunned whale.

Marina's skin was almost completely healed. The casing of scabs was crumbling away like dried clay from a sculpture, revealing bright new flesh beneath. The cuts to repair the damage in her hair were blending into shining layers. Her eyes were shimmering and wide. Clara was impressed with Marina's fingers, tapered like homemade candles.

The flower was poised to crack from the bulb, and Clara would tolerate nothing in its way.

She hid behind the grandmother's house, waiting for her to step to the clearing where she tended her garden of stubby roots. Clara opened the unlocked door and then ushered the chickens into the empty house. Let her live in a coop, wallowing in feathers and dirt, and see what it was like! She hid hard-boiled eggs and left behind a picture of them as a warning: Find the jolly Easter eggs! Tear up the place before they decay.

THEY HAD ALWAYS appreciated Marina's loveliness, but when the last of her casing shed, taking with it the remaining evidence of the damages of her former life, Helio and Clara were awestruck. Marina blossomed into an astonishing beauty. She exuded, large-eyed and leonine-haired, an abundance that would only amplify as she grew older. She was still very young, but it was clear that more luxuriance was waiting to unfurl, full-bodied. For now, though, the abundance was simply tender, gelatinous. Helio was afraid she would dissolve in the sun. They were at the stage of introducing her to a bigger sphere of people, things, and tasks, but he hesitated. If anything happened to her, the slightest dismay, it would be as unbearable as catching someone pushing on a baby's soft spot. His every paternal filament was knitting into a cordoning rope to keep her from being exposed to the dangers of others.

To teach her how to scare away trouble, he and Clara collected tin cans and removed the lids. Marina watched as they hammered a nail hole into each of them. They dragged their collection in a trash bag through the rows of corn outside the guest house, tying the pierced lids with twine to stakes. (All Lodians got their scarecrows from cans; no one used straw men anymore.) The breezes lifted the buzz saws, teeth glinting, at the crows. This is how we ward off evil, thought Helio. See? Install something that shines like a sword.

Suddenly, the disks were silver stars, fluttering on leashes, and Marina reached for one.

"No!" shouted Helio, but she had already clasped a disk and was shrieking as blood trickled from her hand. He swept her up and ran to the house, with Clara behind him, and the cut metal they had seeded stirred in their wake.

"We forgot they're pretty and that makes them dangerous,"

said Clara as Helio bandaged Marina's fingers. "We're sorry. Do you understand?"

Marina moaned at her wrapped hand. "Yes," she replied meekly.

Clara maintained that Marina should be immediately taken on her excursion to the supermarket, as planned, because she needed to toughen up in the face of ordinary tumult.

Helio considered the merciless glare, loud containers, and narrow aisles. "Too much all at once," he said.

"She can't just stay here."

"Yes she can. If you still want to take her out," said Helio, "you'll do it without me."

"Fine," said Clara. "A little accident and you go running. We'll go by ourselves."

"Fine," he said. He returned home, regretting his words with Clara, regretting the rebirth of Marina. How long had it been since he had wanted to talk to his father? He would ask, How *does* some frightening speck eat its way into even the sweetest things, Father? Why is evil allowed to mix with what is precious? Will you forgive me for calling you crazy? You were an able scientist. How do good intentions go awry so fast that they can draw blood?

Sometimes it was beyond endurance, the separateness of everyone's life.

Helio TRIED NOT to think about Clara and Marina preparing for their outing to the supermarket. He assured himself that he was absolutely right about Marina not being ready for that confusion, but if Clara was going to be insistent, there was not much he could do. At the dental clinic, he found young Fernando Botelho waiting. Helio recognized him from the trout feed; he had spent much of it towing his mother around by the hand.

Fernando was near tears as he extracted a glass-beaded necklace from inside his shirt and handed it to Helio. The clasp was broken and a few links were strained open. "My father did this," he said.

"Is this your mother's?" said Helio. "We'll make it good as new." He hunted through his dental tools for a miniature pair of pliers. As he performed the repairs, with Fernando silently gazing on, he remembered a rumor about the boy's mother having a brutal husband. Perhaps the necklace had been damaged in a quarrel.

"Is your mother all right, Fernando?" he asked.

The boy took the necklace and nodded.

"Wait here," said Helio. "I'm going to your house to check."

He left Fernando sitting smiling in a patch of sunlight with the necklace in front of him, glittering. The Botelho home was empty, but when Helio returned to the office, the boy's mother was standing outdoors beside her son. She wore a cast on her arm and a brace around her neck.

She must have passed me on the road and I missed her, he thought. Her mottling of bruises horrified him: What drove humanity to knock fineness cold? Was it because beauty declared that exultation was possible and people were obsessed with denying that any transformations might be required of them?

"Doctor," she said, extending her hand. "Thanks for everything."

"I haven't done anything, actually. Are you——? Is it safe?" He was curious but did not want to pry.

"I'm not safe," she said, and her graceful chin trembled over the brace. "I wear a new dress, I get hit. I go back to finish school, the books get slapped from my hands." She tilted her face up like a sunflower to drink in the greatest amount of heat, showing Helio why resplendence cannot hide: It yearns light-ward, gigantically true.

"You have to go where you can hold your head up," said Helio, "no matter what might happen."

"We've talked about going to live with an aunt in San Diego," offered Fernando.

"That's where you're going. I'm taking you to the bus station and buying you tickets."

"I can't," said Fernando's mother, staring at the ground. Her cast was like a tusk that had swallowed her arm.

"You are not going back to that house," said Helio. "I'm going to give you some money, and I'll have your things sent later. There's no point in being afraid."

On the way to the station, he did his best to assuage her fears, but he could only console her so far. If she stayed in her private hell, she would have no disappointments. The old woman was right: Beauty kept low with the chickens might suffer less than if it were released into the world, where it carried with it a virtually inevitable crisis of hope: If it failed, if it were not loved, what other heights were possible?

But proceed it had to, upward, outward.

As he walked them to the ticket counter, Fernando crossed

his hands over his chest and whispered, "Doctor, she'll be safe because I keep her enchanted here."

A harboring heart: That was what could be given at the sight of exquisiteness that was going bravely on, looking so much toward heaven that it was in danger of stepping off cliffs. He sent Fernando and his mother to the balmy but unknown south and hurried to the Lodi Food Queen Market. There might still be time to catch Clara and Marina.

THEY ENTERED THROUGH the magic portals together and got lost searching for the spices. (My great-great-great-great-grandfather who sailed to India is laughing, thought Clara.) Marina blinked under the lights and clung to Clara's sleeve. A woman stopped pushing her cart long enough to run an admiring hand through Marina's bushel of hair, and a man paused to stare at her rich plum mouth.

"Ignore them," said Clara. Should they buy celery tied with wet bands—bales of cloth? Or sacks of butterscotch—gold? Silver foil? Clara liked how everything was lined up in the supermarket, corner to corner, the pyramids exact; there was nothing lacking, and she could pick out anything she wanted. Marina tore away, running to blur the greens and browns into a stream of camouflage colors to hide herself. She knocked over a jar of blackberry jam.

"Sorry that man jostled you," said Clara, steering her away from the broken glass. She had to pry Marina's fingers off a canister of fat. "What, are you going to smear yourself with this stuff? You'll still be pretty, Marina."

A man growing white pennants of surrender at his temples put his hand on Marina's arm. "May I help?"

She screeched, and the man scurried off.

"*Marina*," said Clara. "You're out in the open, that's all. And don't you know that most people like that man with the white temples wear signs of defeat? They're curious about you because you've thrown yours off." Marina's knuckles were bleaching like Swiss chard's stems from gripping the cart. Was she overwhelmed by the choices, the array? Couldn't she decide how to satisfy her hungers? Maybe the darting glances of strangers felt like the pecking of chickens. People have the means to turn us into sieves, with our water slowly trickling out.

Marina cowered on the floor and shoppers gathered to gaze at her. She was an angel alarmed.

"She's breathtaking," said one.

"What is she afraid of?" asked another, pressing her face close to Clara's.

Clara avoided them and knelt next to Marina. "Have we come this far just for you to give up?" she said. "I'm having trouble doing this alone, can't you see? Will you help me out?"

They hugged each other, swallowed inside the ring of onlookers. As the curious stares pinned them to the floor, Clara, tightening her arm around Marina, thought it should be a simple matter to stand and go about her business of choosing what to eat, but the outstretched hands seemed accusatory rather than kind. She wished that she could transport herself through mere thought, sailing invisibly over the trees.

She recognized Helio's hand coming for them, thrusting through the crowd. Because she was so relieved, it was like reaching for her own.

MARINA AND CLARA lay on their cots, recovering from their perilous trip. The hues of the packages under the fluorescent lights still flashed on their retinas. Helio had gone to fetch tranquilizers; Clara would need one too. To comfort herself, she took out the handkerchief that contained the single grain of sugar her father had given her, his last message, and was horrified to open the cloth and find nothing. Marina was in a fitful sleep and Clara swooned beside her, retreating to a familiar state. Within her black spot she wished away Father Prendeville, Father Maximillian's replacement, envisioning the priest packing to leave, but when she tried to swing up out of the lace, she tripped and landed farther down, inside her casket, where she was dead from a combustion of the ravages of the unused love inside her. Caliopia was leading the mourners, lining the casket's satin edges with shells that had ridges like the backs of pigs and lips pink as sows' vulvas, porcine-porcelain smooth.

"Come out of there, you squirrel," said a voice. She grasped a vine that dropped next to her and was hoisted back to the surface. Tio Vitor!

"Vitor! Where have you been?" She cried it in her heart instead of aloud so as not to disturb Marina. Vines protruded from his skin, sprouting grape clusters and offshoots that trailed behind him like chains.

"Battling on, dear," he said wearily, sinking onto the edge of her cot. Though his vines were weighted, he was almost completely nebulous.

"We're losing, aren't we?" she said. "You're disappearing!"

"Not I, Clarazinha. Guerilla warfare is tough and slow, that's all." He brushed back the hair of the sleeping Marina.

"I shouldn't have taken her out," said Clara.

He extracted his mammoth handkerchief and trapped an anguished sob in it.

"Shh! You'll wake her!"

"Salt water kills plants. I'm trying to get these goddamn growths off my carcass."

They giggled. Clara idly braided some of his tendrils. "Why are you upset?" she asked.

"I'm worried about you. You used to be a wizard at reading sugar, and today you can't guess the meaning of a simple missing grain. No, don't ask me," he said, holding up his hand. "You'll have to figure that one out yourself. And where did you get the idea that you could make Marina perfectly elegant and nothing would ever make her distraught again? Trouble and time won't stay in their pens, where they belong. Terribly unpleasant."

"I ruined her."

"For God's sake!" Tio Vitor snapped his fingers and summoned forth a table, with champagne and chopped lilies already poured into flutes.

"Drink this," he said, "and stop making yourself ill, dear. Listen. Isn't it better for something to be wonderful for a while rather than not at all? Mind, she's in for a good deal of trouble because of you, but I'm afraid that's just the penalty for being alive. She's going to be fine, but as for you! Sitting in this hellhole of a box!"

"Sorry."

"Don't apologize so much, Pickles. Drink your champagne."

She tried to hold his hand under the table, but it was like clutching a stalk wrapped in fog.

"You found a treasure under something that was incredibly filthy," he said. "Do it again. And now so will she, because you cared for her."

"And I do for you," she said, seeing that it was within her powers to help someone return from the dead.

The mist of his face blushed a deep rose. They leaned into a kiss, and then he was gone.

Helio arrived with the news of what was to happen next. The authorities were arranging for the old woman to enter the care of a niece who was a nurse in Provincetown, and Marina could go to live with some cousins in Fall River, Massachusetts. He hoped Clara would see the wisdom in letting Marina belong to her own family now. The cousins were excited, since they had not known Marina was alive, and she would thrive on their attention.

Clara headed alone into the woods. The grandmother was sitting dumbly at her table as the smell of putrefying eggs choked the house. Clara drove the chickens back into the coop, but feathers covered the floor. She kicked them up like spiny dust clouds as she searched for the Easter eggs.

She hurled the ten eggs into the undergrowth—let this layer of Eggs be mastered—and gave the old woman a touch taught by Conceição: thumbs running up under the eyebrows, along the bone, out into the hairline. This sweeping over the eyelids always loosened the knotted places, and she did it until the woman seemed at peace.

Clara planted rhododendrons for her where light broke through the crevices between the trees. At a distance the round clusters would be like the heads of infants, soft-pated and unabashed, and close up each flower would be composed of small trumpets. "You'll be in Provincetown," Clara told her, "but you'll know you left these where you once lived."

The old woman sat lost in her thoughts. Even if the flowers could not survive their mix with darkness, Marina's grand-mother might at least sense that in the few hours remaining before they came for her, she was beside what would be new germinations, Chinese-white and crimson and shades of tea-rose. Clara soothed the old woman's eyes once more. One needed to say it gently, but to say it because it was true: Did you so fear loss that you would have killed what you loved? Should a person be condemned to live alone, waiting for death, just to avoid the terrors of the outside? Isn't it better like this—to plant tones pink and trumpeting, even for a few hours, even though they might die?

MARINA WAS STURDIER the next day. "I'm fine, thank you," she said, hugging Helio and Clara farewell, accepting extra blankets to tuck around herself during the journey. After she and her grandmother were taken east, Clara brought a basket of fresh eggs to Helio's house. He needed some consolation too, and noticing that drew her out of her own troubles. She sepa-rated the eggs in his kitchen, holding the cracked shells high to let the long mucous strings of the whites drip into a bowl. She tipped the yolks into another bowl with such care not to burst their membranes that he started to touch the back of her hair, where it flowered over the cranial bulge, just for a moment, with one finger, but he withdrew his hand. She had come to him gracefully, despite seeing in the supermarket how the world might treat unfettered grace. She had come to him with happiness, knowing that strangers might attempt to drive it downward—then he would also be courageous. He helped her beat the egg whites into castles with sugar and salt and shaped the meringues on brown paper, and while the *suspiros* baked, they made dreams, boiling the milk and mixing in flour, sugar, and eggs. Her hair fell toward the spitting oil in a frying pan.

"Don't burn yourself, Clara," he said, holding her hair as she fried the *sonhos* they had cracked together out of the eggs. He clutched her hair tightly, but to keep from hurting her, he moved as she moved, in a shadow dance behind her. When he felt foolish, he took a green twist off a bag of vegetables and tied her ponytail with it.

They rolled the dreams in spice and sugar, and because they could not wait any longer, they burned themselves. Later when they were alone they could both touch their tongues to the roofs of their mouths and taste their dreams again. The scalding from the sighs that had streamed down them like hot clouds would also remain, because moments that do not echo are not holy.

Having fed each other, they were able to walk out of the land of paralysis. Having learned from each other already what everything was, the names possessed by what surrounded them, they could proceed. Clara was beside herself: If joy creates particles, enough of it can construct a person, vivid and unnostalgic.

Therefore they were thinking of each other and not of the dead.

Helio offered Clara his arm.

She took it, and in the neighboring gardens they stopped to marvel at what the other exclaimed upon.

They were skilled at falling into darkness, but if they caught each other, their arms and legs braced against the walls of the chasm, they might have a time of blessed suspension.

"Shall I show you where rhododendrons are going to sprout in the woods?" asked Clara.

"Yes," he said, and they headed past the trees for the dark spots out of which buried colors would rise.

SIX

Sex happens the way a pearl is formed. It begins with a grain that itches in the soft lining until the entire animal buckles around it. With enough slathering, it will relax into a gem, there in the privacy of the shell.

Remove the pearl.

Suspend it on a necklace, wear it, turn your thoughts to flowering.

Plant in the air (if you are in love) orchids: lavender, cerulean, ecru, with magenta arteries—paintings on high to contrast the parched ground—orchids of every freckling, with floral trumpets and tongues.

THE WHOLE NATURAL kingdom turned rabid that season in Lodi. Pumpkins swelled into giants, hill fires drove raccoons into the valley—this utterly deranged the hens—and the winds carried an ether of fennel, peat, and bruised fruit. The grapes thrived in the Transfiguration vineyards, but Father Prendeville left the winery and the parish, claiming that the heat was shimmering in strips like venetian blinds that were impossible for him to see through, and the subsequent priest resigned within a matter of days, also citing the air.

Clara found the heat quite peaceful. While lazing in bed, she was busy figuring that from Helio's sternum to his navel would be about one strained hand-stretch. She spread her hand on her own front, thinking, His middle is now placed here. I have captured the size of him. Her forefinger and thumb might measure him nose tip to chin, and his calf would be maybe four of her hand's widths, side by side. She imagined spanning parts of him, and as the night breeze lifted her bedclothes she put him together, touching his lengths all over herself. *He is here, and here and here.*

Suddenly she was unbearably restless, tired of not facing what she had become. People admired her as a brilliant inventor, with her trances and her stubbornness, and it saved her from looking coldly at the truth: She was a hider—an expert at it! She hid in the guest house; she hid inside her skin; she built men in secret and hung them on herself. Going to a new place with a new person—that would be love, the opposite of hiding. Although love was itself often hidden, it left evidence behind. She believed that any spot where people made love created white lines around the scene, the way police chalk up where bodies fall to eternity. If love were made in many positions, the dark would be filled with bone-white gleams, outlines crowding together to make a foundation. Love resulted in particles of light so densely packed that they became white and piled higher into beams. The cries uttered by lovers rose up as white sounds and attached themselves to the beams, finishing a palace of white light to mark where love was and so is kept as a shrine. Surfaces generated other surfaces to create additional wings, the love continuing to build after the lovers moved on.

Clara went outside in her nightdress to see whether she could find the city of love perched over Lodi; she had always been too caged to notice it before. She saw a towering cathedral over Glória's and João's house, and white huts spotted the hillsides. A sprawl of palaces stretched in the distance, but over the guest house there was nothing but the clear dark sky. She walked eastward, toward Helio's house, then stopped. Without Marina there was no one standing between them. She was as timid as Helio was about seeing each other without a reason.

An excuse soon rode in on the air: A horticultural war began. When vegetables riot, who can trace each battle to its source? Was it one of the Sete Cús brothers who threw the first sack of zucchini onto Viriato's porch and then ran? Squash big as dogs' heads, lemons gashed open from the pressure of inner watery yellow triangles, corn kernels leaking milk—the hothouse land was aching. When Filomena received rhubarb from Caliopia, she drank wine to calm herself. It would be an offense to refuse the gift and an offense not to repay it at once, along with something extra so no one could suggest that she did not richly answer her debts. She brought Caliopia walnuts and marigolds, thinking that Luís II could chew the flowers. Caliopia thanked her profusely and fell heavily into a chair when Filomena left. What was dirty rhubarb compared to flowers! To even the balance, she brought Filomena some jam. Filomena almost cried. Homemade goods! She would have to invite Caliopia for a dinner party. Why couldn't they leave each other in peace?

Glória and João fed their canaries a paste of donated peppers and tomatoes, and the songs of the birds came out piquant. Viriato was suspected of being the donor, and they brought him so many strawberries that he and his wife had to spend a quarrelsome weekend boiling preserves.

Repayments would hit a giant pitch before everyone shook hands and agreed to return to his own exile, but Clara and Helio seized gladly upon this war. She found a bucket of honeycomb outside her door, with rivulets running over the brim. To repay him, she carried cuttings of rosemary and seeds for black-eyed Susans to his house to start a roof garden—a legacy from being born in a small country where people planted their roofs to own more land and as a sign of the melancholy trust that one day a siege must come. Helio bought flats of basil, thyme, and petunias for her projects, and they hauled sacks of dirt up the ladder to strew on his house. Greens, yellows, and pastels soon became visible on the red roof, and from a distance Clara could see her mark like a quilt she had tossed outward from her bed. Most afternoons, when Helio returned from his patients, she was already at work, waving to invite him to ascend into the garden. A sunflower leaned against the chimney and herbs were drying on old honeycomb frames. The sun baked the hose when Clara stretched it up to the roof, and the water came out warm enough for tea. She filled a jar with water and crumbled in dried mint. Once while drinking her tea, the heat made them unwind backward, side by side, to take in the light.

She had heard that men can get the sun inside so awfully that they must have a cool cloth pressed to them. The sunbursts on the cloths must then be wrung out. She filled a pail with water, removed his glasses, and smoothed a damp towel over his forehead. She twisted the heat out of the towel: When the sun is captured out of a man, it will make water boil. Leaning over to see her own reflection in the pail, she thought, Look! Look at the simmering break up my face.

He left her on the roof and went into the house, where her feet were heavy above him, and he gazed up underneath her, into her shower of ceiling dust. It was not just her hands on his face now, but all of her. He knew she had pulled her skirts high into her lap and was crouched over him to pat the earth firm around some seedlings.

The kitchen floor had her traces. Her fingerprints smudged the cupboards and imprints were faint on the towels. Everything thereafter was the finding of her veronicas: After a tough gardening day, she often left him a full charcoal of her face. A footprint was halfway up a wall—her shoe-tying habit? A carelessness that came from living in a wooden house? He loved the hourglass of dust it arrested for him. He checked his gardening hat for signs of the back of the head he had wanted to smooth the day they had made the sighs. One of her hairs fell out and landed as a perfect circle on the floor.

He went out in the hope of finding the plant that would complete her son's bouquet, something that captured the time of spirits—the beyond. He found nothing worthy of offering to her and returned home. He stopped midpath as he approached his yard and stared. When he returned from an aimless walk, it was clear from faraway that his house had become a woman. Her eyes were the two front windows; the door was her mouth; the herb shock was her hair. The sunflower was the sprig in her garish hat and the hose snaked up her forehead as a bulging vein. She had altered his house into this agape lady; she was around him now, and he would live inside her.

ONE DAY HE emerged from his house to see her teetering near the roof's edge, her arms outstretched and a leg kicked out. Her head and limbs made a five-pointed star. He ran to catch her as she plunged backward. They crashed into the mud and lay together quaking with fear and relief. The earth was wet from her garden dripping over the side, and her spine weighed down the center of him. He wrapped his arm around his fallen star and looked through his splattered glasses. It was like peering through one of the dotted works of his hand.

"Do you know how to make angels in the snow?" she asked. "Doesn't it start with people falling back like this?"

"Yes, it does," he said, settling his chin on top of her head.

They knew snow only from pictures and had to content themselves with making mud angels. While she lay faceup on top of him, he flapped his arms like wings. He opened his legs wide and them snapped them closed to make the angel's ruffled skirt.

She laughed and, although he held her clear of the mud, she moved her arms and legs with him. They fluttered as if flying, and then they got up to see the angel they had pressed together into the earth.

THE BEES HAD no reason to attack Helio. He had not stepped into their flight paths or disturbed the hives. Often in warm weather he neglected to wear protective coveralls and veil, because bees were gentle and the occasional sting felt no worse than a brush with nettles. The bees picked one of his exposed days to go crazy. A great lasso of them knotted around him and drove in their daggers.

Clara heard his screams as she worked on the roof. By the time she reached him, he was inside a black cloud, rolling on the ground to crush the stinging bees like a man caught on fire. "Get out of here!" he said, but she would not leave him. The bees turned on her too, and the strength he needed to carry her to safety got him to his feet. He ran until he could collapse with her in the shell of their mud angel. Water was running off the roof to fill it. He kissed her welts. "You silly woman," he said, "sometimes people die from this."

He ran water into the angel and dabbed fresh mud on Clara's wounds. After peeling off his shirt to shake out the dead bees, she scooped mud onto his chest and discovered that plastering his welts made her forget her own distress. Whenever she stopped, her stinging returned. He must have felt the same, because he could not stop dabbing her arms. She shucked her dress so he could touch down all her pain, and they sank into their pool to kiss and to stroke each other with mud until from a height it would seem they had disappeared without a trace into the center of the angel.

She did the most remarkable thing he had ever known. The cry of coming is also a moan of breaking apart, and every woman he had loved always turned her head aside to release the lonely cry into the dark, at most to adhere it with closed eyes against him. That was everyone's instinct, everyone's fearful lungs and stunted nerves, and his too. Not Clara's: She kept her mouth clamped on his as she emptied herself fully into him, and she never broke from her eyes entering his. Straight into the legend of the whale-eyes, into the realm of him. The mud churned and covered them like a blanket. His lungs inflated with the jubilance she breathed into him. He followed her by roaring this mingling of his air and hers back into her, and as his eyelashes blinked in lockstep with hers, he thought, It is Clara—Clara, not the embrace of ghosts.

Some of his wounds reopened, as if to stay as the founts they had been when this moment began. When he took her into the house and she slept cleaned in his arms, he felt how wrong he had been about his recent years being motionless. They had been moving relentlessly toward this moment, to securing her presence, and now that he had it, now that it was a resting place, the journey would be toward making it remain, remain beautiful, this lighted moment.

Helio stared down into a tub of honeycomb with its rigid alveoli, at the sextagonal cells white and broken-chambered. It was like the leading of many tiny stained-glass windows containing segmented pictures made mellifluous from the sun, shades of auburn, straw, russet, pecan, almond, saffron, sienna, copper, terra-cotta—with some pockets illuminated into colors like annatto, the dye for butter, or the odd jewel of lobster-red, or of chestnut, topaz, coconut, mandarin, hazel, or madder-purple.

Clara squeezed the stained-glass picture until honey spurted from the hidden compartments. Helio plunged in his hands to tenderize the comb with her until it was an ambergris that they shaped into dolphins, donkeys, cats, cows, hoglike monsters, and doll people, and they coursed them like boats through the honey. He smashed some animals into a wax heart and swam it over to her; she took it, chewed it into a cud, and leaned forward in a kiss to pass the ground-up heart into him. Before it dissolved they tongued their heart back and forth as honey dripped in strings, bridge and harp, from the span of their arms and joined hands. They fed each other more animals while undressing, and when she settled impaled in his lap, he said, "Let's not move."

The only sounds were their jaws gently grinding horses and cattle and birds. The sun turned the honey on them into crystals that glistened, but neither of them opened their eyes. The wax inventions dissolved in their mouths, the granules on them billowed down. Still they did not move, and Clara thought, A green vine of you is stretching through my center out to the arms that enfold the you in me back around you.

Do not move. Never move.

WHEN HE TAUGHT her that the touch and smell organs are close together on bee antennae, she demanded to know more. In a book from his library, he pointed out illustrations of the trigla fish, whose fins develop certain rays like fingers, with organs of both touch and taste, and of butterflies that can taste with the tips of their legs. She loved the revelations of such fine mix-ups and was impatient to enter the many worlds right beyond her reach.

She loved him for inhabiting and giving to her one such world of amazing secrets.

Helio let her hear colors. While lying in a hammock with him inside her, his heated words were all of a kindle, crimson, and the lulling ones turned marine aqua, so that she heard not the words but the colors of them, emanating from him and connecting to her in an arc. It scared her and she clamped down on him the way barnyard animals do when they fight to get away but stay joined. She panicked, and while struggling to get him out of her, they twisted the hammock around and were suspended, locked together, in a sealed net cocoon.

Some days they kissed like pike fingerlings, the fish that touch lips before one consumes the other whole. He also wanted to be an anglerfish: The male fuses to the female by letting his mouth atrophy against her underside. He is joined with her forever, and what he receives through her nourishes him for the rest of his life.

"What are these?" he asked one night, his fingertips tracing the white streaks of her internal winding-sheet still faintly visible on her skin.

"I wished them there because I wanted to die," she said. "But that's gone now."

"For good," she said.

To color in any signs of death on her, he diluted the juice of blackberries and dabbed it over the injured pale patches, matching his painting with the splayed rose over her heart (where Glória's hand had stopped the charge of the winding-sheet) and the animal-birthmark jumping from her side.

Clara tasted his salt by licking his neck, and she measured his erection so she would have it again when she was alone: more than her hand's widest stretch. Sometimes when he disappeared in her, she cried his name, since this was how she imagined love: It could be a dissolving mirror to mirror, but it could also be a jolt of swallowing someone alive. In the lake outside town, the moon came down to join them in the water, and in its illuminated round center, she encountered more of love's odd, unforeseeable glories: She came from arching against his rough belly, and he would thrust her skyward, and, suspended, she knew she was fated to search for this feeling forever. She kissed his eyelids. Over the water they were building a basilica of white light, its walls rising sheer—and she was being lifted to touch the ceiling of it.

Another time, she touched his voice. He spoke her name and it appeared in her palm, as if he had handed to her who she was since loving him: a prism, with its full complement of rainbow. We probably die, she concluded, when all our senses merge into one, or when a person stays trapped inside us. She put candles near the hammock they had made into a cocoon, because it occurred to her that we must honor with fire the places where love almost kills us.

THE MORNING THAT Clara moved in with him, putting her life in the guest house behind her, Helio's watch stopped and died. He was so excited as he helped her carry her things across the fields—her clothing, shoes, the sugar doves, and her pasteboard of chromatic phone numbers—that his stomach secreted an acid that made his hour and minute hands slow to a crawl and then expire. He stomped on the watch to make sure it was dead: Let this be the day on which time was arrested. Every day would stand still, a suspended heartbeat.

Into the abeyance of time he wanted to heap everything that Clara had lost, and he began by helping her return to fish-scale art. Barrels of dried scales were shipped specially to the house from the docks of Oakland and San Francisco, and she did what she was born to do: Place clear panes with dyed panes, round upon round, piecing together scenes.

Instead of gluing the disks into flowers as she and Maria Josefa had done, Clara's compositions were of *morte-macaca*, because she wanted to guard the tranquillity of her new life and new home. If she worked on monkey-death pictures, the creatures of the night could not say, "Is this Clara Cruz we see, without her usual nightmares? Is Helio no longer alone? We must remind them that people can die as absurdly as gibbering monkeys." To work properly, the death depicted had to be an instance of yammering nonsense, so that the creatures would say in fright, "Look at the troubles near Clara and Helio! Let's go—we have no work to do here!" Only a bizarre way of dying counted as a monkey-death, something that suggested the screech of angry animals. Dying of old age was not a monkey-death, but being torched by firecrackers was.

With Helio's encouragement she opened a *morte-macaca* business to offer everyone protection against harmful outside forces, the way frightening masks will keep away demons. João was one of her first customers. He commissioned a scene of his Tio António, who had gone to seek his fortune in Brazil:

> One day in the Belém countryside, António saw a billboard of a woman holding a colossal cup of coffee full of waves and little sailboats to remind Brazilians to drink oceans. The woman was winking and, dusty and tired, he accepted the invitation to sleep beneath her. The billboard collapsed and broke his neck. His head pierced the tides in the cardboard cup. He was the uncle who died with his head bobbing in a coffee sea.

Filomena Mendes needed to exorcise a grim story:

> Her nieces Maria José and Angela Coelho, ten-year-olds, were helping the women make soup in the church kitchen, but they were bored with washing kale. Maria José bet Angela a foot rub that she could not hold her fist for three seconds in the hot oil on the stove. They waited until no grown-ups were looking. Angela won but died of shock twelve hours later. Maria José became mute for fear of drawing someone else into a monkey-death.

Clara had special affection for the muteness of the surviving girl and rendered her stricken eyes with emerald scales.

"Thank you," said Filomena, grateful for the safeguard of the scale-picture because she felt so vulnerable living alone. (Robert never stayed throughout the night.)

"I hope it helps," said Clara. She was jubilant: Helio was a genius. Working with the disks made her feel perfectly at home, more than she had ever felt in the guest house.

The *morte-macaca* she designed to hang in their bedroom was a commemoration of one of Helio's whaling cousins, Eduardo Pachão:

During a sea voyage, Eduardo's crew fastened a whale's jaw and the attached spine to the stern. Eduardo climbed inside the skeleton to go surfing. He wanted to be Jonah, but with a better view. Gripping the bones over his head, he rode with a glad holler until the rocking ship swiveled the cage and trapped him inside. Before he could be rescued, a whalebone harpooned him. The men worked frantically, but the sharks tore Eduardo into nothing but a skeleton himself. He was left as a wind chime inside the empty animal.

At night they lay beneath this gossamer canopy, and its gargoyle effects kept away anything that might intrude upon them. Helio thought her work was a little grotesque, but as a doctor he perceived the wisdom in letting her dictate how she would guard against future unrest.

She liked to sleep with her head on his chest and her hand encircling his penis.

"Look at the wind chime you made out of a man," he once said drowsily.

"From the scales you gave me," she replied.

"Pink dreams," said Helio.

"Yes, *sonhos na cor-de-rosa*, sweetheart," said Clara.

B<small>EIGE RED GREEN-FLOWERS</small> were flour, tomatoes, and broccoli. Purple-rectangles yellow green-sticks blue were cartons of milk, corn, string beans, and blueberries. Red-T yellow-sticks pink-wavy-rivers were steak, spaghetti, and wine. Helio not only learned to decipher Clara's shopping lists, he made his own in colors and shapes. When she told him about her father, José Francisco Cruz, a Grand Banks fisherman who had discovered that colors hide in all things, including the darkest night, Helio resolved to tumble into the world of colors with her. He would pour every variation of this law that he could find directly into their bloodstreams!

To recapture her lost ability with reading, he chose twenty-six tints for the alphabet and set about copying his books for her to fathom as oil paintings. Every letter was a staccato splashing, and a page was a tessellation of tiny blocks.

"Clara, what do you think?" he asked, holding a chapter in front of her.

She absorbed each line, pausing in shock when the colors were lurid or to go ashen when they were livid.

"What is this from?" she asked.

"A mystery novel," he said, "but you're the detective. What do you see?"

She studied the pages and pointed to certain color combinations that had enough of a frequency that they could be registered in one glance: *and* was gold smoke oyster-white and *the* was black straw lobster-red. But instead of separate daubs, they merged into miniature palettes, whole and storied, no longer three strokes, but a triune.

"Well, fine," said Clara, "but why don't you make words into their own color-shapes instead of spelling them out?"

In new translations he changed *and* into a gold hook and *the* into a black one. Other familiar words were soon reborn and the artwork changed from blots and squares into flourishes. *Run* turned into an apple green wave; *peace* into a half-salmon, half–canary yellow pillar; *die* into a round stippled patch with ragged eggshell white dots when the death was violent and smooth dots when characters died in their sleep. She cheated by peeking at the endings to count the number of eggshell sprinkles and brace herself for a sad finish. Before long she was digesting entire pages of dashes and curves. She had no interest in comparing her color-books to his originals to see whether she could acquire again the alphabet that looked like fishhooks on a white beach. Speaking was tuneful; why did speech have to lie drained on paper? She admired the basic color-letters because they were the concentrations that happened when plain language was forced into bloom. But because alphabet-words as well as color-words yielded decoctions, she and Helio often discussed without any problems a book's tone and essence, subtle shadings, obscured motifs, and passages of lightness or pitch.

One morning Helio took the stack of dotted pictures of his hand that he had completed since she had moved in and he riffled it with his thumb. Although it had been only a few weeks, the flow of the hands should have shown at least minor signs of aging, but none were apparent. He was amazed. During their color-times, all the natural laws, any forward impetus that did not pertain to creating pictures or reading shades, were in utter pause.

Clara added magenta, pink, lime, and melon color-dots to one of the hands. "Since you've given me colors, I'll give some to you. Now I'm in your hands."

Thereafter, his hands left the realm of the real even farther behind, and spiraling out of his dotted fingers were houses, and Clara's face, whimsical, in points of the shades he desired.

SINCE THE DEMISE of his trout farm, Viriato das Chagas's trust in the living had been growing steadily dimmer. His wife, Carmen, assiduously divided her time with quilting bees, canning projects, and bowling, and he wondered whether her frenzy might not be a cover for an affair. It would serve him right. They were both drowning in this tepid bath of a marriage.

His daughter, Cristina, was sitting on the divan in the study, painting her toenails. Choking back the urge to rip the cotton from between her toes and bark at her to get a job, he extracted a book of Fernando Pessoa's poems from the shelf and began to read aloud the "Maritime Ode."

"Daddy," she interrupted, "what are you doing?"

The women in his life always regarded him as if he were insane.

"I thought you might enjoy hearing one of my favorite poems." He returned to his recitation.

"Really, Daddy, how long is it?"

He slammed the book shut. "Never mind," he said. "It's only as long as longing."

She looked at him quizzically and returned to blowing on her toenails.

Viriato clutched the poems as he escaped through the adjacent hallway, and as often happened when he felt lost, he put his hand on the walls to steady himself. He had left the Azores on an ocean liner as a small boy, and now whenever he was in a corridor with doors on either side of it, he relived the sensation of searching for his berth, stumbling as the waters rolled beneath him while he tried the locks of every cabin. Sweating profusely, he grabbed a table in the hall, trying not to drop the book. He would not give Cristina the satisfaction of thinking she was saving him from a heart attack.

He staggered toward the house of Doctor Helio Gabriel Soares, uncertain what he would say to him or to Clara when he got there. But he needed to look at them. Two nights before he had watched them leave the movie theater, their arms around each other, Clara laughing as Helio imitated the robotic speech of the muscle-bound hero, Clara pushing his glasses back up his nose for him. Viriato thought it must be heaven to be so much in love that one might explode from it.

Clara supplied the answer of what he would request. She was holding pages filled in as intricately as a Persian carpet when she opened the door. "It's Walt Whitman," she said brightly, gesturing with the stack.

Helio appeared in jeans and a denim shirt streaked with paint, wiping a brush on a rag. The smell of turpentine snapped Viriato out of his dizziness.

"Viriato? Coffee?" asked Helio. "Come in."

Viriato held out the book of Pessoa's poems like a messenger who had to make his delivery before he collapsed. "I would love to see the 'Maritime Ode,'" he said, his voice shaking. "You can keep it, but I have to know what it looks like painted."

Helio spent several days on the "Maritime Ode," and while he worked, Clara reread her old favorites—Aquinas was arabesques, and her fingers grazed the splatters of the *Moby-Dick* passages like fish coursing in channels. Viriato almost cried when he held the finished work: Pessoa translated into color ended up, with its reds, bursts, and valves, shaped as a living vessel.

"My God," said Viriato. "I said it could stay yours, but I'd like to have it myself."

"Fine with me," said Helio. "Clara?"

The men turned to see the sun through the window embellishing her shoulder-length brown hair with flickerings of scarlet. After caressing one of the new pages with her hand, she paused to sniff it. Then she ripped a border off it and chewed a page of Pessoa, savoring the ship of the poem and its wild pumping.

That was right, just right, thought Viriato. Pessoa had written the mournful heart that Viriato could not claim for himself, because it belonged inside them all.

Helio saw that if she could feel, smell, and taste her books, then hearing colors was the next step in truly belonging to the harmony of shades. What worked with stories could also work with sheet music, and he transposed some sonatinas into rainbow fillets and bands of dots, with white gaps as rest marks.

He bought a used baby grand piano for Clara. She was beside herself to be living in a house with a musical instrument—the kind that smiled and showed its teeth! This was yet another world he was giving her. Some mornings in amazement she wandered delicately through the rooms, as if padding through the chambers of a heart.

He mixed hybrids from the twenty-six oils he used for book translations to give every one of the eighty-eight piano keys its own blend. The size of the blotches on his music-paintings told her the time value of the corresponding keys; a grace note was a whisker. Chords were hue-triads. She slowly figured out the gradations and the melodic phrasings: A silver, emerald, tan arpeggio might roll into rapid azure to dun to mustard dots in the treble octaves, with color washes haloing the soft notes and black pitchforks stabbing the accents. Sometimes, in her eagerness to move through the music, she got careless with the phrasing and had to remind herself to slow down, not to rush through the colors. It was better to consecrate every moment as if it were forever. She worked so diligently at the piano that she forgot to go into her swoons to get rid of the Transfiguration priests—the land had fallen away from her. She gladly practiced endless hours to fill the house with anthems.

Helio made love to her against the body of the grand and while she rested on the bench, but that seemed somehow indivisible from the color-playing. So did things away from the piano:

cooking dinner and bathing with him and working on her fish-scale projects.

Caliopia Silva came by to pick up the *morte-macaca* scene of her Tio Carlos:

> Carlos had intercepted a letter addressed to his wife and hid it in a rock fissure. He suspected her of having an affair and wanted the depths of the Azorean earth, not a mere teakettle, to steam open her shame. When he slid his hand into the crevice, vapor erupted and murdered him. His hand percolated into the recesses of the rock and he was suctioned in up to his shoulder.
>
> When villagers freed the dead man, his fingers and arm retained the shape of a damp, contorted root system, and a plasmic gravy of skin had fused over the incriminating letter. The truth about his wife's lover was sealed inside him. It was said that his days ended not from the steam but from having betrayal seep into his hand, and that Carlos was unforgiving enough to die just so he could take the letter bodily to his grave.

"His hand looks better than my plumbing," said Caliopia.

"In your house or in your body?" asked Clara.

"*Your* plumbing is probably in great repair these days," said Caliopia.

The two women burst out laughing. Clara still thought of Caliopia as her godmother in matters of bodies, lace, and mourning.

"Helio painted me a page of the blues," said Clara. "Like to hear it?"

Caliopia nodded, and upon having herself filled with the colors of sorrow as the sounds poured out of the keys, she grieved so loudly that Helio came running in from the yard, where he had been grafting. Tears were streaming down his face. What is it? he wanted to bleat. You're making sadness poignant!

They moved the piano near a window that faced the road so that others could bathe in the sounds of colors. Helio transposed music feverishly for Clara. Passersby who heard their coloratura fluttered with confusion: Who are the hungry ones? They? We? Why? Why am I weeping?

Sometimes instead of having dinner, Lodians stared at glass ornaments and marbles in jars of sparkling water. The whole town was shouting: To eat! What is that alone! Dazzle me I dazzle!

Clara color-wrote a poem and he translated it into fishhook letters:

My Life with a Beekeeper

Bees are daisy yellow and go fishing in flowers that are china blue-white. My beekeeper brought buckets of honey to court me. I think he hoped the sugar would rot my teeth so I would also go to his dentist's chair. Bees bother the udders of cows, which are erections hanging from breasts, swelling and dripping. ("This is the sex part," she said, reading over his shoulder.) Because of him, numbers are now mine as pictures: 2222 is four swans floating; 11 is an empty railroad track (where I once lay); 4444 is upside-down ballet dancers; 8 is either infinity on its head or the beekeeper handling a fishing line, because it would get tangled, or the beekeeper and me making love and getting twisted in the hammock. ("Infinity," said Helio, "and the hammock.") He makes me hear water running in colors underground (not the words of these colors but the blasting of their feel in the earth): maroon (the shade of sailors at rest, like my father, José Francisco), flax yellow, slate gray, cream, olive, apricot, beige, honey, shamrock green, and gold gold gold gold

gold gold gold gold (the remainder of her poetry ran off the edges gold).

He conceived "For the Blank Pages in Cows" to pay homage to casein, which was the curd first separated from the whey of an acid-bathed milk and then washed and dried. One use of casein was as a paper coating to improve the grip of pigments. Milk could therefore shimmer in the fresh leaves of a book and help it hold colors. The final lines of his poem, in fishhooks:

> Hell and horror disperse and bursts of hope
> rise as cows give us a breastful of
> white paper to love

A further breakdown in plain alphabet describing the colors (sadly inexact and wanting, Helio admitted, as with all translations):

(Helio-shape, blue, untangling a fishing line) (gold hook) (fava beans, in red) (smoke red sky blue!*) (gold hook) (treble clef of smooth gray stars locked with a fire-orange bass clef) (red arrow) (a clay-red tuba on a mother-of-pearl pillar on a diamond-embossed 22—the number twenty-two, or, to follow Clara's idea, a brace of swans, floating) (white dot ringed in cinnabar) (purple whisker) (queen's crown, lemon-shaded) (scarlet heart) (Clara's face, in emerald) (ocher square) (*breastful* = *breast*—a whale's tail fluke, in chartreuse, + *full*—Clara's hand in washes of orchid) (red arrow) (white square) (grace note ??!! ^ ^ grace note, in aqua glitter) (XX, in lavender) (Clara's face in gray, the color of Proteus's eyes)

He adored combing her hair. He soaked brushes in sinks of honey and water and dried them like sweet thistles near the beehives. She was careless about her partings, and he liked to straighten the tender line on the right side of her scalp, making each hair fall neatly into place. He brushed upward beneath the main waterfall of hair, with the grain, the rows in the wake of the teeth perfect as a harvested field. "Yes—don't stop," she murmured, and he felt victorious: It was impossible to think of anything else to do or anywhere else to go, and that was his idea of enthrallment. He imagined that if one were this much in love, then dying was not a lights-on, lights-off affair but a transition through intensities of color. One plunged initially through the combing waves of a deeply red sea (the color of the highlights in her hair), through crests brash as a rooster's tongue-red comb, then past the ctenophores with their whip legs and comb-jelly heads flailing one's body to scarlet. Next would come the swordfish schools that reduced one further to a mass of vinelike sinews, seeded pellets, and a claret stream. The briny water would cause more diffusion and lightening: One would turn coral-colored, sink toward rose, and then be thinned into a translucence like the blind fish, pretty as glass, that hide in caves, their innards retaining a pinprick of salmon-tint for a heart. So it is not heartless and ugly in the darkest haunts of the red ocean! When one who started as redness is finally on the verge of becoming clear light, there is no need to crash to the floor. It is possible to find lobsters scuttling, with their sights aloft in a soft meat sponge at the tip of a fragile eyestalk. All of one's scattered palenesses can drift to rest on these eyes and harness the host lobsters into a fleet. After his death, while anticipating hers, Helio would command his fleet to wait to catch Clara. He wanted all the pieces of her, as they faded from brilliant red to shiningly clear, to rest on his. He would say, I have heard there are waterfalls—some are little cascades, some big cataracts— that exist *within* the ocean. Uncanny, isn't it, that they are not wiped out by the vaster water? That they live at all, when they should be overwhelmed and dead? I believe these inner-ocean waterfalls will stand out like a fall of your hair. Let's go! We'll find them and divine the secret of being outpourings that refuse to be swallowed up, and if we can not solve the riddle of the falls, then we will at least ride them, surf them—hold fast to me—my fleet will comb through them with you, for the pleasure of it.

He kissed the smoothness of her hair. He feared nothing.

ONE DAY WHILE Clara was rereading the paintings of "For the Blank Pages in Cows," the tinctures of the words came alive. The hues in front of her eyes began lilting, the coral and brassy tones erupted, a dialogue between the milker and the cows slurred into euphonics, and she heard the shades calling to her in rhapsodies. Colors could not only guide her to producing sounds on an instrument; they had sound themselves! It meant that words could be reborn as colors but also as actual music. Her heart was pounding. With the piano already arranged for tinted sheet music, chromatic language slid easily into place. She matched Helio's work to the keys, and tolling in the house were the intonations of the shades of milk hitting a metal bucket, of cows snorting, and of straw being crunched.

"Clara?" he said, emerging from the study. "It sounds like all outdoors in here."

"It is!" she said. "It's inside with us! I can play books directly on the piano!"

Their library awoke clamoring. Compound color-words were easily expressed as chords; letter-by-letter dabs as a march of quarter notes; the turquoise circle that spelled *birth* became a whole note on the turquoise high C. Pillars were glissandi from the salmon key to the canary, and it was uncanny how many dyes of the formerly black keys, the signal to play accidentals, speckled a story's major conflicts and how many minor-chord tinges overwhelmed the subplot. Sections with characters refraining from action invariably showed repeat patternings in yellow, and medleys overran the crowd scenes.

To convert words directly now into painted music, Helio used the octaves from Italian sonnets to compose simple primers, confined within one scale and with repeated blue, yellow, and red rhymes. When he gained confidence, he translated short selections from large works, from Virgil, Dante, Melville, José Maria Eça de Queiroz, and Luíz Vaz de Camões, into musical spectrums on octavo-sized paper. It was slow labor for them both, but when she mastered these canons, and also their original works about the bees and cows, she touched the furthest plenary hunger of the universe: to fuse painting and language divinely with music—their Father and Lord, and with them the consubstantiated Trinity.

Could a book be presented to an orchestra and, upon hearing how it was played, might artists ply their brushes so that anyone seeing only the canvases could recite the words of the original book?

Helio thought that the people who could achieve this turned into swans who are suspended in pure wonder as they sing an exquisite air in their last mortal moment. Though facing death, swans dare their most transcendent song, and their fortitude makes them the most idolized of the birds. When he wrote a painting in tribute to swans and Clara converted it to music, the caged birds throughout town chewed their iron bars, desperate to fly toward the rejoicing, and the people of Lodi begged Clara for a concert.

Helio set up rings of chairs near the piano and opened bottles of wine. Clara wore a white silk shift and greeted the guests at the door.

"What a pretty dress!" exclaimed Glória.

"And there are roses in her skin now," said João, kissing Clara on both sides of her face.

"I've heard glorious things coming from this house," added a Sete Cús brother.

"Please come in," said Clara, feeling for the first time that she was in a house made hers.

Filomena brought some Chardonnay.

There was a scraping of chairs as they took their places. Helio stood in the back. Though he would have preferred the front row, any room that had Clara in it was a cure for *saudade:* Her presence was the entirety of what he could want.

She stood before them and bowed. "And for my composer," she said, gesturing to him.

There was general applause.

To praise João's missing limb, she prefaced the evening with Pessoa's "Bodiless Arm Brandishing a Sword," with its abrupt breaks and notes wide apart for the line "God is a huge Interval." The poem's *D*s and *E*s dappled the piano score oyster white and lobster red, with eight *the*s as black pincers. João's flesh and ghost hand clapped together at the conclusion. The dairy workers in the audience keenly applauded "For the Blank Pages in Cows," arranged with casein-based tempera paints and tempered with rods, chains, and spirals in the stanza about bacteria, which caused one of the Sete Cús, a bit drunk, to tell barnyard jokes, but when the piano rendered the oils of a swan musing, "Do we ask for astonishment before we die, or do we die because we ask?" the room fell into a hush.

Everyone handled the paintings of the closing number, and some guests said that with such symphonic shape these had to be Camões. Helio said, "Yes, none other." Some in the audience began to weep at the mere mention of the great poet's name. Caliopia and Glória dug conch shells out of their handbags and held them to their ears so that the music would strike them salted and double-force from the echo chambers of the sea.

Helio leaned forward and the women with the shells wept as Clara dived into the finale, rich in scales, from the fifth book of *Os Lusíadas,* when the giant Adamastor bellows that still and forever he will love Thetis as no other. Helio watched Clara swim into the opening sea green whale black circle jasmine crescendo and the violet to black ties. Tomorrow he would grind water biscuits with almonds for her favorite dessert Eat-And-Cry-For-More. He would have to do a dotted hand that held a piano in its lines. Had the Soares house finally come out of its darkness? O to hold on to the light of Clara, now that his struggle was over! Her pearl earrings shone as she hit the dominant chords, white stars white stars shaded pillars, and he saw the felt hammers pound the reclining harp in the body of their grand as she released Adamastor's painted roar: "I am the Cape of Storms and Thetis encircles me! To be this near, to see her without enfolding her—behold my chains, behold me in torment."

T O T E A C H H I M how the landscape is completely in lace, Clara drew two swans floating on the left-hand side of the page. She added exclamations to make them astonished. Helio made a contribution by drawing the biological symbol of the New World beneath them. To the right of these he drew a fermata, resting like a lone eye, because he wanted this time of the color-world sustained:

T H E Y C O V E R E D T H E I R left eyes and peered with their right at the swans above the New World while sliding the page back and forth about half a foot from their faces. The mark of the holding disappeared and reemerged, into and out of the blind spot. Though held closely, the holding still slipped into the unknown, but they knew it was not being erased; it was only here and there invisible in their hands. Therefore they would always be holding one another, whether or not they could physically see each other.

Clara explained that at her son's death she had begun a search for flying, singing colors, because that could be used as a formula for a resurrection of bodies. Were they swans yet? She could eye-paint him pink, and he could do the same for her, and they contained the music and language of shades. But how could they set themselves flying? How to make their wings work? They agreed that the key would have everything to do with love, and they lived so suffused with it for the next three years that they fashioned their own flight, because the earth dropped away from them.

SEVEN

Fados, *the songs of fate, wail in the cafés of the Azores and all of Lusitania, including the homes of the Portuguese in California. The lyrics approximate the timbres of grief: disjointed, in the cadence of actual moans and pleadings, and the music weaves them into a net that can catch whatever the listener's soul casts toward it.*

Two lines from a fado:

> **Navegar é preciso,**
> **Viver não é preciso.**

This has two meanings:

> *To navigate is necessary,*
> *To live is not necessary.*

Or:

> *To navigate is precise,*
> *To live is not precise.*

A widow in the town of Lodi, California, wrote a fado:

> **As a child I thought love was for angels,**
> **But fate says that it is the unbroken horse**
> **Dragging us behind its sleek haunches**
> **From the moment we try to ride it**
> **To the day we die.**

GLÓRIA SANTOS SANG to her hunger as she dripped water through used coffee grounds. The coffee came out gray, and the knives and forks in her stomach reared angrily. In times of want, the stomach sprouts its own cutlery, and if nothing appealing comes along, it will begin to devour itself. Every morning the melodies of the canaries buoyed her toward her chores, but today her inner knives and forks tapped in a brisk tempo on her stomach's lining, and this overpowered the song of the birds and they had no choice but to be a chorus to the gnawing inside her. João had been laid off again at the Lodi Sunlit Dairy (with his missing arm, he was often the first to go during lean seasons), and he was out looking for odd jobs. She had a basket of sewing projects collected from neighbors, which was generous considering that the era of plenty was drying up for everyone. When João returned, she grasped his unseen fingers and swung her arm in rhythm with his airy one, dancing away their pangs, flinging back her head when his ghost hand caressed her spine, singing to drown out their hunger.

The more famished they were as the days passed, the louder their singing. The Lodi Portuguese called Glória and João *Os Passarinhos*, the Little Birds, or simply the Rinhos family, and when their house shook with music, friends delivered meals to Saint Monica's Rest Home. The Little Birds refused to accept charity; João packed up the goods and delivered them there anyway, and well-wishers could only elect to save them a trip. Whenever a feast was enjoyed at the rest home, he and Glória felt coddled.

Clara, however, insisted that they accept food from Helio and her. Glória and João had always been gentle caretakers, content to settle in the background, and Clara was pleased for the chance to return the favors they had always given her. Famine was in the air, as if bounty had to be answered with planes of resistance to prevent people from floating wondrously indefinitely. She and Helio were not immune, and they could feel the outside trouble seeping into their three-year-old color world, invading the house through cracks and doorjambs. Doctor Anderson had retired as promised, and Helio was away more to deal with the clinic. Its overhead had shot up, and his translation of books into musical shades had slowed because he needed to make money. Every day of the current month she awaited her overdue check for ten percent of the winery's sales, and whenever she or Helio demanded to see Father Righetti, he was never in, nor had he answered Helio's letters demanding an explanation.

One afternoon she finally received a Transfiguration envelope and tore it open. There was no check, and as Helio read the letter to her, there was no mistaking the final lines:

> . . . given the financial crises currently besetting the winery, we are sure you will agree that since no formal contract exists between this establishment and you, there is no binding obligation to continue what has been hitherto a gracious endowment on your behalf.

Father Righetti's signature ate up the rest of the page.

Clara took to wandering at night, slipping out of bed as Helio slept to check on the white palaces of love outside. A pagoda was erected over Helio's house, with a white crane above it with a girder in its beak. (This was a city of birds rather than machines.) The crane was constantly there with a new beam so that their roof would never have to be completed, but Clara surveyed their pagoda with dismay. Bite marks gouged out entire walls, which threatened to topple the whole tower. Other distant palaces of white light were also in tawdry shape. The very air was hungry, and she worried at these signs of impending ruin.

FILOMENA, HEARING AGAIN from Robert Paganelli that he would not leave his wife, succumbed to the generalized want that was on the breezes. Naked at her sink she sanded her body with a salt paste to slough off the dead cells and encourage pink ones. There had to be a means of removing Robert from her skin. Although they were in love and he stared at her in public, this beacon refracted off his wife, Teresa, before hitting Filomena full force. She said good-bye to him yet another time and ate and drank with fury—bourbon that drained her hair oils, Russian dressing, caraway cheese, bittersweet chocolate, Heavenly Hash ice cream, and beer, until she feared that the menu was spelling itself out on the clean slate of her epidermis. She was supposed to be writing about Azoreans in the islands and in California for the Luso-Historical Society, but without Robert her notes became nothing but canonical hours, turning her days into Gregorian chants—ritual plainsongs unharmonized, unaccompanied:

1. *Matins and Lauds.* Sing Matins at midnight and Lauds right before daybreak, or chant them both in the predawn, when darkness and light are inseparable. Night becomes day; the day joins night.

Filomena studies how Portugal sent prisoners and livestock to till the unsettled Azorean land, and then the *donatários* and missionaries arrived to yoke the men and the broken ground. Crime and holiness lay together until they were much the same.

She awakens with Robert dissolved once more within the approaching day.

2. *Prime.* Filomena's dawn host is a round white aspirin. To her bleary eyes the pill's trademark stamp might be the wheat fronds imprinted on the transubstantiated wafers she received when very young. She believed in her prime that she could ingest

body, fields, wine, bread, and promises that would radiate beyond night.

3. Tierce. The third canonical hour, but also a cask with less capacity than a hogshead's. She drinks her first bourbon of the day and writes about the Lodi *matanças*, with their slaughtering of pigs: Gummy pork bladders, with red and blue veins sketchy as those in a dollar bill's fiber, were blown into balloons and given to children to bat, and wine bottles of blood were stored in houses for thickening soups and making *morcela* sausage. A tierce is also a sequence of three cards in the same suit. Hour of sacrifices and games! Of furious squeals, and drinking. Until spasms of hate for Robert cease, she knows she is not done with him.

4. Sext. The clock's hands join at noon, vanishing into each other, arrested in an arrow pointed heavenward. Time stops only when one thing lies completely possessed by another. Filomena sips, writes nothing.

5. Nones. Christ died in the ninth hour. Betrayal was not Judas's gravest sin, because holiness came from his infidelity. But Judas despaired, and that is the only sin God does not forgive.

Filomena struggles against the slackening day to document the old California Portuguese Hanging Judas festivals, when they tied a ragged effigy to a tree and later threw it into a bonfire. Many drunk celebrants began romances with Judas heat on their faces.

None of these festivals remain, although a person wearing ugly or disheveled clothing is still called a Hanging Judas. None of the former participants really care. Filomena looks for more ice. There is none. None remember that despair and not the loss of a divine man was the evil that lingered.

6. Vespers. Hour of the Angelus, Filomena's head lolling like the clapper of a ringing bell, the day approaching its grave. Field-workers stop, everyone stops—stop, mark this moment of the angels flying over nature, over a day's words vermiculated so badly that she sees only wavy lines. Squirrely whirly. With anger she falls upon a selection from Cicero's *Ad Familiārēs* as a heading for her opus's Domestic chapter: *Quid aliae fēminae faciunt? Vōs vidēte. Id dēsīderō vōs dīligenter etiam atque etiam vōbīscum et cum amīcīs vestrīs cōnsīderāre.* What are the other women doing? See to it. I want you diligently to consider this again and again with your-selves and your friends.

7. *Compline.* Bed spinning. Only nine at night, but she is a doryman alone in the wormwood waters. She cries, "I am a monk illuminating history! Restless with my canons! My poor head!" She crams a handful of bedsheet inside herself because she cannot stand being so untethered.

Teresa Paganelli accepted the invitation for tea. In the begin-ning, Filomena wanted merely to touch Robert by handling the person he touched. Teresa had known about her husband's lover and wanted to see more closely whatever her husband had seen, and so see him. For a while when she and Filomena made love, they clutched only the wraith between them. This presence, pale and chill as fog at night, gave the ravenous Filomena an idea. She would use them both to clutch moonlight.

She bought Teresa lace pillowcases, fed her minted lamb in bed, and kissed her until within weeks Teresa was her prisoner. Then Filomena refused to see her and hung up during her tearful phone calls. Now in public Robert and Teresa both looked haunted, not with each other but with secret anguish over her. Filomena predicted how this recompense would re-solve itself. Sunlight directly strikes everything, including the moon, but things under a nocturnal influence must settle for whatever cooled and shadowy beams the moon deflects. It is a region of indirectness. Although still alone, she had doubled the aimless desire sent her way, reasoning, A sad fate, but better to live in moonlight than no light at all, especially now that time is speeding forward and sorrow is attacking whatever moves over the land.

CLARA HAD NEVER visited Eureka and had not seen Father Teo Eiras in over ten years, but if she lacked the courage to go face-to-face with him again, then she was wrong to think that love had strengthened her. Wasn't that its purpose—to prepare her to confront any given number of people and events? Helio could not convince her that Father Eiras's sway over the land was long dismantled, because to her the priest would always be responsible. Despite Helio's protests, she insisted upon going alone.

The bus ride to Eureka was arduous, and some townspeople gave her the wrong directions to the rectory. She was exhausted when at last she climbed its creaking steps and knocked. The white paint on the walls was peeling off in strips as large as blank sheets of paper. It was a plain house on a stilted foundation, inviting in a moldy way, like a boy's tree house. As Clara collected herself, an old housekeeper, whose hair stood up in tight white flowerlets like a cauliflower's, opened the door and asked hoarsely, "Come to pay your respects?"

She hesitated. "Yes," she replied, her initial plan already dashed. She had imagined barreling into the room and asserting her demands, but her body was stiff from the journey and the speech faltered in her throat. The front room was crammed not with religious statues but with knickknacks—ceramic eggs, blue medicine bottles, shells in water-filled dishes encrusted with beige salt silt—that made the room appear confined but busy. Homemade paper roses were dusty on random unsteady tables, and a meager scent of camphor assailed her.

"He's in bed. To tell you the truth, I think he's perfectly fine," said the housekeeper. "Sometimes he gets it in his head that he's the invalid king."

Her nerves were tensed, as they would automatically be in a

hospital, but not because she was about to confront the father of her child. In her mind he had diminished into a vague form, like the caped man on the bottles of Sandeman port, and she had so thoroughly scraped him off all of her senses that even the mild aversion that arose as she stepped into his bedroom surprised her. She looked evenly at Father Teo Eiras, who seemed to balloon downward from his jaw. He was half-hidden in blankets, with a sheen of sweat: a gourd in a frost.

"I'm here to ask you a favor," she said. Again her plan crumbled; she had rehearsed declaring what he had to do, but instead she was giving him a chance to think he was aiding her.

He propped himself farther up. All he apparently needed was stationed within reach—magazines, crossword-puzzle books, a decanter of cognac, tissues, a box of dried fruits.

"Will you hand me my glasses?" He did not call Clara by name. He could have picked them up himself, but she would oblige him with this minor compliance. After studiously cleaning them, he put them on and immediately glanced away from her.

"We have something to discuss," said Clara. His failure to look at her—like the old days of not seeing who she was—made her stronger.

"Have your talk in the fresh air," interrupted the housekeeper. "Get out of bed and go for a walk with this nice young lady."

As they passed the eucalyptus that smelled like unwashed bodies and the warm fire colors of the citrus, apricot, and cherry groves surrounding the rectory's property, she explained that her checks from the winery had stopped. If he drew up a contract stating that he had promised her ten percent each month, and if he backdated it, it might restore her income. Minute as it was, she refrained from adding.

"Do you really think I have that kind of power?" he asked.

It was her turn to glance away, and they dodged the squashed fruit on the ground. "I see it falls and rots before you can get your hands on all of it," she said.

He bent to pick up an apricot for her. "Here, this should be good if you eat around the bruises," he said. "I'll tell you what. Our deal can be quite simple—"

"Deal?" She stopped.

"Can't we decide what's right for both of us? Now that the child is in heaven, what do we have to fight about? If you forgive me for everything I've done to you, I'll do as you say and you'll have your contract." He turned his yellowed face to her and held out the apricot.

She did not take it. "That's a dishonest—"

"So is a fake contract."

She stepped backward on watery legs.

"You ask me for a phony document that will earn you a profit, while I do not ask for a single dollar, and in return I request only some peace of mind. Something that will cost you nothing," he continued.

She did not know which sickened her more—having him mention "the child" or that his features were unaccountably melting like a mewling schoolboy's.

"You're joking," she said, and he turned to head back to the rectory.

The bees around the smashed fruit made her lonely for Helio and his advice, but she had to show that she did not need him every living second. If she absolved Father Eiras, who would know? Helio would see that she had won precisely what she had traveled after and she would have the paper to slap on Father Righetti's desk.

"Wait!" she called out.

He did not alter his steps, and she had to run to him. "Okay!" she shouted. He was not smiling when she reached him; he seemed burning with fever. That he sincerely needed to extract this out of her made her instantly regret what she was about to do.

"Go ahead." His words were round and cool as coins.

"I forgive you."

"For everything?"

"Yes."

He waited.

"I forgive you for everything," she said.

On the bus going home, she clutched the paper tightly. To think that he had such a mild faith that a few offhand words from her could restore him, that one could hand over forgiveness as easily as handing a man his glasses! Worse, she had to trust him, since she could not read what he had written. She pressed her sides to contain her nausea on the jarring ride. Her head ached with the revelation that her fish-scale business was based on a false premise: How misguided to assume that only an outrageous death qualified as a *morte-macaca*. All was a monkey-life, and therefore to all would come a monkey-death. Her fish-scale self-portrait should show her jumping out of her skin, with Father Eiras flailing her empty hull as if beating a rug. She was dying to leave her history, her body, her home—everything. (In the new kingdom she had devised for her son, people would not have to be themselves alone their whole lives. They could fly beneath the shelter of another identity in a faraway place.)

She was stuck in a sphere of older men, and she was terrible at reading the future. Probably because what was ahead was disturbing: She was twenty-eight. In ten years she would still be young, but Helio would be sixty-five. These were the facts, whether or not she planned to face them. She loved him, but perhaps that was giving her the backbone she needed to think ahead, to realize that although the world of shades was gorgeous, it was not the only arena available.

He greeted her arrival with new paintings for the piano, and he looked at the document she handed him and confirmed that Father Eiras had indeed written up the contract as requested. When she did not seem relieved, he suggested that she play the colors. She startled him as she hugged the pages of musical language between them. He alone saved her from being a failure—all that he did was designed to make her an artist and a conquerer! She could not admit that her embrace was from the guilt of what she had thought about him, and the sadness of knowing it would prey on her mind again.

SHE HAD NEVER broken from the faith that the land would be hers someday, but when Father Righetti and the other winery managers discarded the flimsy contract from Father Eiras with hardly an apology, she felt further from her wellspring than ever. In a last attempt to claim it, she carved out a sizable tomb within one of the hillocks in the vineyard, tunneling a limited amount each day and hiding her work with loose branches. The most difficult detail was arranging rocks and dirt on the top of the incline, underneath which she planted a rope that dangled its free end within reach inside the tomb. The debris had to hold steady until she tugged the rope, coaxing an avalanche to seal the entrance. She shivered as she stood before it, but that was good. If she felt no fear, then her final screams would not pierce the roots and rise as far as possible through the vines and into the fruit. Her vehemence had to penetrate every grape to end up within every bottle of wine that would ever be sold from the Transfiguration property. She would interrupt dinners for decades to come. Guests would listen to her yelling in their glasses and would pour her down the sink, and those who drank her would double over with a bellyful of moans. Private drinkers would crawl into bed terrified (covered with *terra*, indeed, as she would be herself)!

She crawled into her sepulcher and lay on her back. Her head was toward the entrance, about an arm's length away, so that she could seize the rope during her last flicker. It was important to have her last cries infiltrate the grapes directly, to ensure that the angry living parts of her would mingle in the fields, continuing to grow in the soil, protesting for as long as the grapes reproduced. When they confined her to a casket, the sound waves of her shrieks would harden the carbon of her bones into diamonds that could drill through the sides of the box and travel through the ground to rejoin the siege. She hoped Father Righetti would find her body and that Helio would be spared. Leaving him this way was horrible, but he would try to talk sense into her, and sense was far beside the point. If she did not become what was hers, her life with him was already dead.

She dropped into a gap in the dark lace around her and landed inside a dim, high-ceilinged auditorium. Mud soldiers surrounded a podium where a mud judge stood with a lobster for a gavel. Two cuckoo birds perched on either side of him—nasty pirates who invaded other birds' homes. Cuckoos are thought to become fertile merely from watching a potential victim working on a nest.

"Step forward," said the judge. He wore a flowing webbed robe spun continuously larger by black widow spiders with red-hourglass abdomens. The spiders dangled like tassels as he gestured toward her. "Have you enjoyed your visit with us thus far?"

"Not especially," said Clara. "Have you seen my parents? And how is Tio Vitor, and my baby?"

The cuckoos squawked with mirth and the mud men suffered cracks and other casualties from laughter. The judge pounded the lobster until it splintered, and the court had to wait while he picked out and ate the meat. A mud general dashed forward with a skull filled with melted butter.

After tossing the shells over his shoulder, the black widows jiggling as he moved, the judge was given another gavel.

"I demand to see my loved ones," said Clara, "and to know why I am here."

"Those inquiries are interesting but are beyond our jurisdiction. Please escort Senhora Cruz into the next room," he thundered.

The cuckoos, drooling, plucked Clara up by her shoulders and flew her toward the door marked EXIT. It occurred to her that maybe the cuckoos were so excited by her plight that they were ovulating. She squeezed her captors until one of them dropped an egg into her hand, and she smashed it over the doorway, right as they were about to carry her through, to spell EXITO. It was a telling curio that in her first language the word meaning "success" was so similar to "the way out" in her second language. She clung to the doorframe as the o dripped egg into her eyes and the cuckoos tugged.

The door dropped away, and as she prepared to pull the rope and finish descending into blankness, Tio Vitor pulled her from the tomb.

"Did you get your love of melodrama from your ax-wielding mother?" His foggy eyes and mouth were like condensation inside a prison cell of vines, barely detectable. "Or are you just selfish?"

"I don't know what to do anymore."

"Ah, well then, self-burial is a fine choice."

Her lip quavered.

"Here, here, none of that." He brushed the dirt off her skin. "I don't think you're crazy. A bit high-strung, though." He paused. "That was supposed to make you laugh."

"Sorry."

"What did I tell you about apologizing so much? Frankly, your idea is superb, and I'm annoyed that I didn't come up with it first. I want my lungs to vibrate inside every glass of their wine." He slipped inside the tomb and called back, "Love me, and say good-bye."

Before she could stop him, the rocks were tumbling, barring the opening, and as she tried to dig him out, the ground rumbled so mightily that it threw her several yards. She heard his screams ripping through the tips of leaves and cracking open vines, renting stakes and rising seismically along the slopes.

When Helio later asked if she had felt the earthquake that afternoon, she made no reply. It was the beginning of keeping life-and-death secrets from him, and she seemed so distant that an unpleasant truth shocked him: Love in their color-world had made her gorgeous and far-ranging. Other men noticed her, and she was noticing them. Maybe he was an old fool and it was better to send her on her way, but he was not that gallant. He could not bear losing her. But when her mind snapped back from its wandering and she approached him, she was so clearly returning from some fantasy that had excluded him that he pushed her aside.

REPORTS CIRCULATED THAT the new casks of Transfiguration wine were turning to vinegar. Customers at tastings were spitting it across the room, and hospitals were treating drinkers who were exhibiting the symptoms of food poisoning. Father Righetti resigned. The outcry grew at a time when the subsequent harvests were being destroyed with blight, and the Church was relieved to sell the fields and the winery buildings to a company that planned to build an entertainment ranch on the property.

Helio could see what it did to her. Instead of the land coming closer, it was more than ever being dug away. He understood what losing one's grounding did—it was a rug pulled out from beneath the feet—but he had no idea how to keep her from stumbling. She was likely to confuse her discontent with this with how she felt about him, because that was what driven people did. They ran from their loved ones when surroundings got the better of them. He offered to move elsewhere so she would not have to see her land converted into a fake ranch, but part of the problem was that her entire adult life had been spent where others had installed her, and a bad case of wanderlust had been long in the making.

She did not say no when he asked her to marry him, but the fact that she had to think about it told him what he most feared: He could be many things to her, but he could not be less old, except as love could refashion him, and he could not be other men. Did she think of him as a parent? He had not stopped to think that she had been alone for so long before him that looking for a father first made complete sense. It did not mean that she loved him less—this was a small consolation—but it meant that if he had helped her grow up, there would come, as it did to all offspring, the inevitable days of discontent and disengagement.

One night when he awoke and she was not beside him, he searched everywhere until he found her huddled on the ground in the garden neighboring the old guest house.

"Clara?"

"This is where we carried my baby and his blood drops hit the dirt. Viriato said that the dots spelled *A . . . men*, but I've never been able to see it," she said.

He had not yet located the flowers that he could give to her as the hereafter, to finish the bouquet that she and Glória had begun to hold every phase of life. Helio had vowed to find them for her, and yet here they were, with the ghost of her son invoked, and he had to fight his sense of helplessness.

He lifted her from her hiding place. The wings on her ankles carried her legs up around his waist, and they waltzed in the dark. There was too much he could not replace or find for her, and he kept her head on his shoulder so that she could not look at him and tell that he was cracking inside like unoiled leather. He knew even before she did that she was going to leave him. How was it that people could never remain where they were once they had scaled to the most beautiful things in the world? With the invariability of physics, in this time and all times, they had to slide down the other side of the mountain. Tonight, though, the dance near the invisible *A . . . men* was theirs, and nothing would disturb their steps in the cold.

D ESPITE VITOR'S PENETRATION of the grapes, the
land had not been won, and in the process his spirit had
extinguished itself, proving once again that Clara could scheme
magnificently but that the outcomes were never as she planned.
What did Helio know about this sense of fruitlessness? she
fumed. Whatever he did turned out reasonably close to what he
had anticipated. Even the grafts that did not work—those were
experiments, and he was therefore not set up to be disappointed.

It was bad enough that he failed to understand her frustra-
tions, but he was also becoming absurdly watchful, as if even the
possibility of scheming, one of her claims to notoriety, was to
be denied her. Sometimes he followed her to the market and
then pretended he was on his own errand. He tried to urge her
to come to the office with him. Ever since he had spotted her
in town talking—was that a crime?—to Chris Mayer, the
twenty-nine-year-old rancher who had come for temporary
work on the Bettencourt place, he would hardly let her out of
his sight. It was starting to drive her wild.

"A few innocent words," she said.

"There are no such things," he said, "as innocent words."

Imagine!

Chris roved from job to job and explained to Clara that
covering a vast territory was the key to finding many fortunes,
and it underscored a difference between the old and the
young—the young never believed they had arrived where they
were meant to be, and the old concealed where they had dreamt
of being. There was nothing worse than being old and wondering where one might have gone, he vigorously explained to her.

New land. Her own. That might be the answer. If only she could
meet Helio ten years from now, after she had lived, with him ten
years younger than he was now.

Could she make many areas hers by leaving shrines? Candles were already near the hammock-cocoon where she had almost died of love. On the site where Chris told her about searching for newness, she constructed a ring of brick shards. She begged Helio to fuck her harder so that their sweat left a rash of gooseflesh on her thighs. The next day she wore a shrine of inflamed skin—proof that they had loved.

Helio showed her the dancing bees. To tell the others about a source of nectar, an explorer bee did a tail-wagging dance that gave the compass points of the new location. He and Clara witnessed an excited hive learning where a treasure trove was, and he said, "Isn't it good that they always tell each other exactly what they've found and how far it is from the sun?"

One day he decided to expand his garden, and he invited any Lodians who wanted to make a little money. João (working slowly, since his ghost arm was withering), a Sete Cús son, and Chris Mayer showed up for the initial hoeing. When they were panting and growing slick, they rested in shade while Clara fetched the ice water she had stowed near some bushes. She rescued a chipmunk that had fallen into the pitcher and warmed him in her hands. The animal trembled and she stuck him between her breasts and folded her hands to secure him there. The night before, Helio had come between her breasts as she held them together. Since she never rinsed off the shrines of love, always keeping them stuck to her as long as she could, her cleft hid a dry scaly patch. The chipmunk stirred it alive and wet as if Helio were coming between her breasts again. She breathed in the reborn salt water just as the pulsing creature washed it away.

When Helio called, she spun around with the animal in her blouse and saw all the men waiting for her. He stood in awe: Her heart was pounding clear out of her chest toward them. Chris hurried to her and held his hand below her throat. Helio hugged himself as something leapt into Chris's grasp. She had given a stranger her beating heart.

She wanted to go on a trip by herself, as she had to Eureka, but Helio did not trust her. Maybe nothing had happened between Chris and her, as she shouted at him, but it seemed only a matter of time.

"You can't lock me in a closet!" said Clara. "I just want to get out of piss-awful Lodi for a while."

"You haven't told me why." He poured himself another glass of wine.

"For the same reason that everyone else likes to take a vacation."

"I would be happy to take you anywhere."

She was going to bounce back and forth through the ceiling! She *should* have let Chris kiss her that time he tried. "That's not the point."

"Then what is? Clara, dear, it's perfectly normal that after three years together, one person or the other gets a little agitated, and you've had some difficult times lately with the winery—"

"O stop it! Just quit it! You're always so damn reasonable!"

"One of us needs to be." He sank into a chair and ran his hand over his scalp and then checked himself before she could think he was worrying about his thinning hair.

Clara went to sit beside him. *Because I want to go alone:* That was what he wanted her to say, but she could not. He would hear it as *without you,* which amounted to the same thing, she supposed, but it sounded much crueler than she intended. She had a desire to be on her own, just for a bit, but not to hurt him—what a mess. She sounded like such a child. *Because I need to find what else might be out there.* Even to herself, she could not push to the imperative just beyond that: *Or to find who else might be out there.*

"Only for a while," she repeated.

"No," he said, but that night he slipped a page from the Song of Solomon in colors into the flat zippered compartment of her suitcase, a gift of himself, since there never was any stopping her.

THE LAKESIDE WAS marked with green stringy fennel cud, chewed and then spat out by swimmers who had cleaned their mouths with its licorice. On the slopes lay tangles of ferns, bamboo, spongy rot, foxtails, and the Indian soap plants that boys liked to pull out of the crumbling banks and peel and dampen and say to a girl, "Got something on your hands? Watch me. Whatever it is, I can wash it off."

When Clara introduced him to her shrines, Helio used them as a trail to find her. The day he followed her to the lake and saw her sitting and laughing with Chris Mayer and another man, he grasped the scruff of hair at Chris's neck, shoved his face into the water, lifted him for air, and dunked him again while Clara hit her fists on Helio's back and wailed at him to let Chris go. The other man pulled Helio off. After slapping away the water bugs skittering over Chris's head, she shoved Helio and ran.

He drank wine on the porch while waiting for her to return home. When she marched wordlessly past him, he grabbed her arm. "Where have you been?"

She threw off his arm. "Nowhere! Anywhere but here!"

He drained his glass. "Were you with Chris?"

"Jesus!" she exploded. "Jesus fucking Christ! I made him bring a friend along to the lake, just because I knew you'd be spying on me, and—now this is a laugh!—I didn't want you to think anything stupid, but of course instead of that you just act stupid."

He took off his glasses and rubbed his face. "Clara——" he began.

"I like talking to him. Okay? Big deal."

"You can talk to me."

"No, I can't." She slammed through the front door, calling back, "I really need a vacation from you. A very long vacation."

He followed her into the house. "You can't."

She was upstairs. "My suitcase is already packed," she announced.

When he tried to take it from her, she sidled around him and hurried down the stairs.

"At least wait until morning," he said.

"No. I'd rather sleep in the station."

He caught her as she was lugging her suitcase through the kitchen, and he grabbed her hair, threw her down, and then he was lost, without any idea of what to do with her kicking and screaming except to lie on her with his own dead weight. She strained upward and his shoulder, heavy over her mouth, muffled the yelling. He remembered the rope in the bottom cupboard and hardly winced when she bit his arm as he hauled her, pinned like a small sea animal glued beneath a crab, along the floor. It took a while to fumble for the rope and entwine it around his arm, because he had to stop constantly and brace her back down with his elbows and forearms. He knotted her hair around his fist so the linoleum would not rip at it and hurt her as he dragged her like an inchworm to the dining table—hump rising in the middle with her stomach pulled upward in cadence, head straining forward, bodies flattening, hump rising again.

He held her down and reached onto the table for his fishing knife to slice the rope in half, and he tied her wrists to one table leg and her ankles to another. She struggled against the restraints, rattling the table, and as she knocked her head against the floor, a shower of salt rained over the side. "Please let me go," she whimpered.

When he stood and saw her lying like a calf ready for branding, chafing her hands bloody in her fight to get away, he severed the rope binding her wrists with a single knife blow. Her dripping nose spread a glisten on her face as if snails had shimmied across it.

"I'll let you go, Clara," he said, pulling her upright and

holding her wrists against his cheeks. "First let me put cold water on these." He ran water over a towel in the sink and then bowed his head under the stream to wash away the wine churning inside him.

He had turned his back only for a minute.

"Don't, Clara! Don't do it, don't do it, I'll let you go! I'll let you go! I'm sorry, I'm sorry, sorry! I'll do it—I'll cut you free!"

She had taken the knife and raised it with quivering hands over the rope tying her ankles. Her leg muscles had twitched. As he dived to save her, she stabbed through not the rope but the membrane above her left heel, between her ankle and hamstring. She shrieked as Helio pulled out the knife and cut her loose. He bandaged her foot and tucked her into the bed in the guest room. By morning she had vanished.

Every night since then, supine in bed, waiting for her return, he heard their screams, hers alone, his alone, then swarming together over him. He found dried blood in a pore in the wooden table: evidence of what he had done. His eyes magnified it, thinning it from red to an infinity of cells, stretching like a gigantic fish scale until she was as large as the world before him, and completely light. All that remained of her. He plunged his fishing knife straight into his right foot.

THE GRAFTER, DOCTOR Helio Gabriel Soares, grafts in order to make the world in a new image and likeness and to effect fusions between families. He sculpts talismans that, as they grow upward, might contain clues toward computing what Clara had dreamed would be a resurrection of bodies. He grafts because it can increase the amount of tint and oxygen in the world; it manifests a yearning that life may begin afresh; it encourages unfolding toward the sun; it heals the ailing.

There is an element of panic in the career of the grafter. In the weeks when it became apparent that Clara would not return, he grafted a quince cutting to a pear tree; passionflowers to parsley (to invent a redemptive herb—unsuccessful); lemon buds wet with saliva to lubricate entry into almond rootstocks; roses to roses; pumpkins to water lilies dyed red (the color of her hair, the color of his mortal sin) (to devise love with a hard shell, to protect from grief those beloved of the grafter—unsuccessful).

Clara! If only you would come back to see how the garden is made new. You could be a vine—anchored here, but wandering at will, to stretch outward wherever you wish.

Sometimes the grafter pricks a finger to pump blood into clefts in the fig trees. He wants to beget fruit shaped as fists, with the thumb between the index and middle fingers, so those who are dear to him can eat amulets against curses. (He hopes the *figas* will sprout by the time Clara returns.)

The grafter grafts her leftover fish scales—clearnesses and colors—to the dot-drawings of his hands so that light and darkness may combine, the core elements that create a human being. At night he grafts his plea for forgiveness onto the air so that it will be carried to her. He asks her forgiveness for driving everywhere looking for her, for alerting the town, for badgering

Chris Mayer, who knew (said that he knew) nothing. The grafter labors however it occurs to him, because he cannot bear that he made his love weep. He spins his magic by slicing flaps or tongues in plant cambium, the tissue that will develop into both wood and rind. He binds interlocking parts until the wounds show signs of a permanent hold. Some such conjunctions include saddle, splice, cleft, bud, or side grafts, which describe the forms of the tongues and the lappings together. Buds known as eyes may also be inserted into the cut receptacle of a stock plant.

Helio later discovers that in fact Chris Mayer had gone off with Clara for a weekend, and that she had left him too.

There are various flare-points and problems of compatibility in forging a lasting union: Cambial locks involving different ages and sizes require a great deal of care, but there is no reason to think that a more mature plant will necessarily loosen its grip on a younger scion. Years might pass before a graft breaks, without a reasonable explanation. Tissue anchored to other tissue may be damaged by internal stress, predators, or inclement weather, and by stimulations caused by the grafting itself, other plants in the area, hormonal changes, or how well the wounds healed at the joining. Introducing a third scion can exert enough tension to destroy a once unshakable graft. What headaches!

The grafter nourishes his grafts with mist, with anxious expectations, with affection. He feels the thirst and sorrow of his grafts. One sword in his heart is the knowledge that his grafting is unlikely to fuse cells in a chimera—a genetic mutation that creates an original species. (That would be a trophy to give her!) He is confined to conjoining plants that already exist; vegetable laws restrict his art. He cannot grow cucumbers already pickled or cross asparagus with grapes to make javelins of wine.

In spite of these sorrows, the grafter continues for many reasons:

Ad majorem Dei gloriam.

Para cantar um hino sacro, um cântico à vida.

To behold the mystery in living forms as they bloom like different languages.

To give his whale-eyes a height rather than always a depth in which to rest.

For the love of seeing a higher exaltation unspear from a solitary root.

For the hope of watching offshoots thrive once they have departed the main plant.

For the faith that from his anguish, glory will one day ignite: Pears mated with sardines will yield sweet fish in the trees; fava beans with oysters will bear green pearls in cottony pods. (At long last a use for those horrible beans! A means of converting them from scourges to gemstones!)

The grafter grafts because he realizes that he is much older than the missing woman he loves and that he will undoubtedly die first. Now that she has left her own story, he will bequeath his grafts to Clara with this valediction: Anything that bursts from my handiwork—it is yours. I made what I could, and then passed on.

Let my epitaph be:
Behold my works.
All I have left are my memories of you.

Hᴇ ɢʟɪᴅᴇᴅ ᴛʜʀᴏᴜɢʜ Twain Harte, Paintersville, Drytown, Garden Acres, Atwater, Diamond Springs, Terminous, Placerville, and sometimes as far as Marysville or Paradise, searching for a roof garden, for any sign. He would implore her to forgive him. Even if she refused to come home, he wanted to stare at her long enough to imprint her on his retinas. The searing would grow brighter until eventually she would turn into a constellation and he would say, as stargazers do, Now I know you by your shining fragments, distant but fixed, and by your celestial name.

Three weeks after finding no trace of her, he turned to her shrines, lighting the candles by the hammock. He burned more lights at the mud angel, at the spot from which he had first seen his house become a woman, and near the garden where Clara's son had spilled out his A . . . men.

On a summit near his apiary, as his whale-eyes surveyed the red flares that marked Clara's haunts, he realized his mistake. She was not restricted to those places; she was in the combs of the hives, the wax that sealed grafts, in the scent of thyme, in the breezes over the drained pond, in that navy-and-scarlet molten pool that he and everyone else carries on the inner lids, even with the eyes tightly shut. He set fire to the path connecting the fields, where she had first brought him trays for a roof garden, because that was a shrine, and he torched the shed to honor where they had made love in the afternoons. The trees were easy tinder and the dry grass ignited. The bees poured from their hives in an angry tiger-colored swarm. Cinders fell like black snow, and when the sulphur hurt his lungs, he turned to flee, but the flames had circled around and trapped him. Plants were dying in their own incense as everything collapsed into one huge shrine as far as his whale-eyes could see. When the fire caught him, it became a blue halo so hot that for a flash he could not feel it on his skin, and he thought, Of course I must burn too, because she is not so much everywhere as she is within me.

When the star that has the key to the abyss falls to earth, the locusts will come out of the smoke, as if from a large furnace, to attack men; but this time thousands of bees formed a protective canopy over his melted flesh instead, making a fierce but musical firmament.

He screeched in the special baths, bloodying the water before blacking out. Even the air hurt. They wrapped him like a mummy and changed the gauze when it was suppurating. The doctors told him, "Men who have lived on fire are never the same. Their skin color and texture change so much from day to day that they are literally different people who do not always recognize themselves each morning in the mirror. You know, don't you, that something has happened that has made you no longer yourself?"

Which trumpet blast is it, he wondered, when one-third of the water will turn to blood, one-third of the sea-creatures will die, and one-third of the ships will be wrecked? Which blast is it when only the living and the dead will remain as all the water turns to blood? When fire gapes to receive us? Purgatory is then supposed to be abolished.

But on the day when every person ever born will be poised at the rim of these carnal waters and the fire, I'll insist that God let me find Clara to cushion her fall, and in thanksgiving, instead of following heart's desire and clutching her to me, I'll use my last strength to hold her above the danger. If you turn to face me, Clara, please give me a sign that you forgive me. Then you will ascend as seraphim do. I'll beg that some Purgatory be saved for me; I'll gladly be a creature in the vapor, because I wish to remain a soul forever unfinished, with mortal memory of mortal touch. There I will have you, and there, as I sink, I will be spared the unspeakable blandness of heaven.

✳   ✳   ✳

ON THE ONE-MONTH anniversary of the night she left, and of the sole brutal act of his life, horror at himself made him take to his bed. His house had survived, but a moat of ash surrounded it. Filomena Mendes moved in to nurse him, and it was a good arrangement for them both. Because she had to care for someone else, she drank little. They tried making love, but it often hurt too much, so they settled for a peaceful coexistence, sleeping together sometimes past noon.

CLARA, ALONE IN a Phoenix motel room, splashed water on herself to wash away the dream of Helio lying on a table with a fountain of blood spurting from his chest. The doctor in the dream had refused to help and abandoned her when she yowled that everything was pumping out of Helio. She lay full-length on him to stop the bleeding, but it continued seeping between them until they were sinking into a pond. He tried to push her up and away from him so she could breathe, but she insisted upon making blood angels together and would not let him go. She awoke kissing him as the pond covered them.

That morning she had discovered the sheet of a painted song that he had tucked into her suitcase. Odd how much time could pass without knowing what she had been all the while carrying around. She wanted to go home. She could not dial a regular phone, but she had the number on a piece of paper. She woke the motel's manager up at one in the morning to have him dial it for her. It was midnight California time. She hung up when the voice of Filomena answered her ringing. Clara enlisted the manager's aid every night for a week; Filomena's voice always came across the line, increasingly irate.

Had she really expected to be gone for weeks, without being in touch, and that he would wait for her? She met a man named Douglas at a campsite near Tucson, and he seemed nice. When he asked her to travel with him, she figured that crossing the whole country was what she was meant to do. Her money was about to run out and few jobs were available to her. If they settled a while near a beach, she told Douglas, she could do fish-scale pictures to earn her way. She tried Helio once a week as she moved farther eastward, and still there was Filomena. He had taken up with someone else, but then so had she. That she had brought this on herself was no comfort, and soon she quit calling.

FILOMENA CARED FOR Helio until she decided she could no longer stay in the same town as Robert. She picked Chicago as her city of escape simply because she had never been there. She lived by herself in a hotel while looking for a new life. Occasionally she called Helio, and he did not mind that it was less because she missed him and more because she was lonely. He was grateful she had stayed long enough to nurse him back to health, although the therapy on his skin grafts would continue. He encouraged her: Chicago had plenty of historical societies and she could work for any of them.

"Anything else you need?" he asked.

"Will you beat up Robert for me?"

He laughed. "Sure. But if he hits me back, my skin will break open like a papaya's."

"What are you today?"

"Today I'm purple, with red squares and brown lines."

"Good-bye."

"Good-bye."

In her hotel room, she filled glasses with whiskey, in diminuendo order, from a full tumbler to a drop-sized dose, and then she drank her whiskey-xylophone. One scale and she forgot about Lodi, two scales and she would forget the man of the night before, but she could not forget Robert. The juice drained from her hair, she destroyed her stomach, her bones fizzled, her lymph became absolute water, and her head collapsed into a bread sponge. As she lay down, a stone might have sunk through her face and continued out the back of her head.

When drinking made her almost wholly liquid, she went to live in water, which is colorless and clear, but so much blue hides in it that the blue streaks of Robert inside her would surely have a home. Water's blue is majestic, but the blue of unrequited

264

passion is frostbitten-blue. Nevertheless they blend together. She swam weightless, without kidneys, breasts, or palate in the hotel's pool and practiced gliding along the bottom, barely visible to those above. Once she stayed in for such a prolonged minute that the lifeguard dived in to save her. The chlorine bleached her; the xylophones sapped her of vitamins. Her heart and mind did not show, because most of them had flown away to Robert. A few parts of them flew to Helio. If her gills kept inhaling the crystal pool, she would finally be as transparent as water in a glass, and her remaining blue streaks would combine with the rippling of the pool.

Each day standing at the edge, she prayed: Very soon I'll drop into the water and finish melting in. The other swimmers on that day might note a brief sparkle, bright and well-submerged. I am only a firefly, after all, a nervous insect, flaring, whirring; let me burst before I'm swallowed; I'll be a light down below, and then at last I'll be gone.

LODIANS NOTICED A bad feathering of the cream in their coffee: During the Sunlit Dairy's decline, the white moths of death were curdling the output. Instead of a fruity or barnyard savor, the butter tasted of rocks and refused to clarify. Milkers coaxed the cows, taking them off the automatic machines and working them with one hand pressing the teats upward and then pulling them downward, and the other hand steadying the yeasty milk-moons of the udders. In this way the men mimicked calves, but unknown frights were still holding up the milk.

Helio Soares invented a Latin medical term to diagnose their condition: *animal animalis*, "animal of air." Language itself illustrated that flesh and spirit have the same root. He hypothesized that the psyches of cows contained a collective imprint of a slaughterer's sledgehammer hitting their skulls. Now and then it raced out of ancestral memory: the pregnant moment after being struck, in which a cow pauses on its feet, completely dead and still completely alive, an *animal animalis.* Many people and animals might, in their last throes, sense an inexorable slipping toward death, might weather a stunned moment at its approach, but this is when they remain as yet outside death. The cow, in a supreme act, shows in its eyes not that it knows it is about to die but that *right then,* standing there for a transcendent moment after the blow, *it is* thoroughly dead. Helio thought that the Lodian cows were suspended in a premonition of their own possible futures as victims of *animal animalis* and were therefore living and deceased at the same time.

Helio was himself, he freely acknowledged, an *animal animalis* when life without Clara entered its eighth month.

A variation of *animal animalis* affected the Sete Cús brothers and the other workers when the dairy closed: They were stunned but had to move and find new jobs.

266

Glória and João became animals of air by selling the house of the Little Birds and retiring to a trailer park near Sacramento.

Caliopia, already saddened from burying Luís III, became ghostly from mourning the loss of her friends.

V IRIATO DAS CHAGAS refused to vacate the tub until a method of altering his life came to him. The water was so hot that it was inflaming his skin. Very Roman, he thought, ignoring his wife's and daughter's pounding on the bathroom door. Alphabet letters barraged him as he looked inward—he had definitely been a mail carrier and a reader of other people's postcards for too long. After the letters settled out of view, he glimpsed one of his heteronyms, the light-beings that the poet Fernando Pessoa believed existed in everyone, with their own names, histories, and physical attributes. He had first detected heteronyms over ten years before inside the son of Clara Cruz. He himself was not merely Viriato, but:

Colonel Jaime Freitas, steely and tall. Jamie led workers against their bosses until no one in California had to work anymore, whereupon he retired to a mansion, where his savvy was brought to bear quelling the quarrels of the women who argued for the chance to sleep with him.

He also saw **salted cashews.** Had sitting in warm water made him slip into the wrong tube inside himself? He had come across one of his snack addictions.

He would open a heteronym business in his study! Now that everyone was leaving Lodi and the ones remaining were fading, he would amplify everyone with spirits to repopulate the town!

Caliopia, almost eighty, called on him because her sight and her hearing were worsening and she wanted to ask her internal beings to guide her. Viriato waited until he could see two heteronyms spiraling in the aura around her. She was also:

Ana de Amparo Serpa, an iron-haired, wild-animal trainer, famous for her advice on attacks: If an angry dog rushes for you, bare your neck and offer your jugular. Stare hard into the dog's eyes. It will be frightened by your courage. Salvation may come from thrusting our most vulnerable parts straight at danger. The boldness of delicacy will sometimes shame the rabid into retreat, but if we die we die without fear. Bravery makes our eyes glisten after death, and fear gives them a matte finish.

Ana de Amparo never uses chairs or chains against lions and tigers. Her jugular is the only whip she owns. When putting her head into the mouths of beasts, she thinks, If I die now, it will be while diving headlong into a regal cave. Your palate, master, is a lovely vault of bone. It is not utterly black in here. Your uvula glimmers, a lantern at the mouth of the mine shaft.

A gray whale, born sleek and black but torn into gray patches from sloughing off barnacles and limpets. Untamed animal! Strong enough to use its tail and fluke lobes as shields to hoist a man upward, as if he were the fleshy rod of flowers in the spathe of a lily.

"I'm an animal trainer *and* an animal? Thank you!" Caliopia's hands flew to her crepelike cheeks.

"I'm only introducing you to what's yours," said Viriato modestly.

Helio Soares, leaning on a walking stick, also availed himself of Viriato's services.

"I'm sorry you lost so much of your skin last year, but you're looking much better, Helio," said Viriato, helping him seat himself in a chair.

"When I checked in the mirror today, I was beige, with green circles. Yesterday I was peach with tan marks," he replied.

Inside Helio, Viriato found two branches of the same creature. Both were a song to Clara:

A starfish, in program music:

I keep growing new arms. I cling all limbs and a mouth to my favorite creature and, lifting her off the ocean floor, we wander toward the ache of passion in pearls. Moans consume the shell beds: The oysters can beget gems that are the luster and shape of trapped and polished light: blue-gloss and imperfect. We watch as the ardor of the oysters creates swirling music and designs, for *barroco*, an irregular pearl, is the jewel from which the baroque takes its name. The pearl beds purl long murmurings that bubble into lacelike purls of air that interlace as they ascend to break on the ocean's surface. The purling sounds within the air purls are released. The man on the shore breathes these sighs of pearls as a reminder that baroqueness originates in the sea. He exhales the ornate air; it reenters the waves; it rolls back and forth and back; on he goes, with insides vigorously laced.

A starfish, in absolute music:

barroco barroco barroco barroco barroco the purling sound
ascending into lace purls, purls lace into ascending sound
purling the purling sound ascending into lace purls lace
into ascending sound purling pearls purling pearl's *barroco*

Helio gave Viriato another ten dollars. "Please give me Clara's heteronyms too. I'll take care of them for her."

"I don't think I can—"

"You can do it," said Helio, and an incarnadine flush colored his neck. "Because as I'm sure you know, she is completely inside me. Read them out of the Clara I'm carrying around."

Viriato found two heteronyms within Helio's *saudade* for Clara:

Jorge Dinis Xavier Prado, 12, sand-colored hair, blue-pool eyes. He discovers that figs hide their flowers moist inside, and when halved the raw fruit says, I am an anemone finally set free.

I burst in rays inward instead of outward. My sweetness will spread on your tongue.

At the seaside, Jorge finds figs waiting open in tide pools. When he probes the figs, they blush. Touched, their tentacles close tightly and shudder around his fingers. He sees it is possible for men to make love with water life, and he leans forward, his back to the sun, and whispers, "No need to let go, my shadow will hide us."

Xica Linda Pereira, 18, pretty smile, mud-lake eyes, a sixteenth-century cook's assistant in the Palácio Real in Sintra, Portugal. She uses parsley bouquets dipped in white wine as an aspergillum over oxen skins to prevent blistering when the animals revolve on spits in the kitchen chimneys that divide the sky. Savoring the hot tallow rain, watching suet seep from the meals of fussy nobles and royalty, Xica chants "Rhapsodies to Fat" in both rhyme and reason:

> Wall-splashing ping of unction extreme,
> Ooze of sardine, halibut, bream.
> Blubber-fried roe, peppers well oiled,
> Jelly from hoofs, eel's gut uncoiled.
> Bacon-From-Heaven—an almond cake—
> Sausage with kid roast, lard-basted hake.
>
> Butter a cockscomb, watch it sizzle.
> Feed the King the oxen's pizzle.
>
> From the spit sings splitting meat,
> Mouth crackling wide, grease-drooling in heat.
> Flesh howls and sputters a warning cry—
> "Hungers soar and flames lick high,
> But eating slakes mock-turtle fire,
> While truer craving lies deep in desire."

For all the rich feasts served this court for its pleasure
Are beside my love's courting the less-fatted treasure.

And under the roasting oxen, Xica marvels:
Human nerves are mostly oils.
We love with our nerves.
Love renders us a banquet of drippings, salves, saturates,
banquet of creams. I once loved a dear man fatly.
Fat calls smoothly even when I am alone. I miss him. I read
his name in the kitchen's dusty grease stains the way people read
clouds.

"Come, my dears," Helio said to Jorge and Xica, and he
walked out with them on his arms, with everything male and
female that was dreamed out of the dream of Clara. They would
search for fatted meals. Together with the starfish, they would
live in the bastion that is defined by *cleave*—a grand but unsettling word that is at once its own opposites:
To pierce, sever, divide by a blow;
To cling, adhere, ever to hold fast.

BOOK III

EIGHT

The island of São Jorge is long and narrow, a lightning bolt in the sea. When the pet cats of a family there died, the mother said to her son, "It's upsetting, but it means that Death passed over the house with its habit of taking the smallest things first. The sheep will be safe, and we'll still have our living."

But the sheep died that afternoon, and the woman consoled her husband by saying, "It's sad, but the sheep sacrificed themselves for our sake. Death would not be vicious enough to backtrack so soon, but just to be safe, let's replace the animals."

That instant, however, the child cried out, choking, and died in his mother's arms. Devastated as the father was, he knew he had to go to the marketplace at once and buy new livestock to protect his wife—she was tougher than he was, and he would have gladly died on her behalf, but he did not trust Death to appreciate her superior powers. She was riveted over the child, and saturnine rings encircled her eyes. "There is no need for you to go," she said, "because I can feel myself already dying of grief." With that she submitted.

The father was so overcome that his ribs curved inward like scimitars and his respiration almost ceased, but instead of being allowed to follow his family, his mind and body continued to function. Each hour was a stone tied to him, but these weights were insufficient to drown him in his despair. He did not restock the barnyard and scarcely moved from bed so that Death would find him more easily.

Months went by and, bored with staying in bed, he began to move about listlessly, when who should slide down the chimney but the enormous fountain pen that he recognized at once as Death. A gauge on its side showed it had an eight-liter capacity. Presumably as it wrote, the 8 at its height—the number of both completion and regeneration—would be tilted into a googol.

"You're a pen?" sneered the father.

"Tsk, tsk," said Death. "How absurd to think I always wear a dark hood. What one chooses to write with me may be good or bad, frightening or not, depending on how my fluid is spent."

"What took you so long? I thought you knew the road to my house better than that."

The pen was not affected by this sarcasm. "I've been busy. Are you aware of all the circles that exist between life and death? There are those who do not eat or sleep, those whose bodies do not disintegrate; there are the artists, the ventriloquists, the poor and starving, the spirits with unfinished business, and those whose minds are in another world, for instance. I like to prod them with my point and bathe them with my ink."

"I'd love to chat," said the father, "but why don't you do what you've come here to accomplish? Don't spare me—I'm ready for worse than what you put my family through."

"Don't worry, I saved a sizable torture for you," said the pen. "You have remained stalwart, and my way of defeating you will be that you must go on living. It is a slow death I've fitted you for, to belong to the circle of those who know whom they love but must live without."

Helio donned a hat to protect himself from the sun and, as he did every Friday in the five years of Clara's absence, he took up his walking stick for the journey to the post office to mail his weekly letter. On the way, he paused to inspect the grafts that were progressing nicely out of the fields of ash surrounding the house. Clara would be pleased. He was particularly proud of successfully grafting a photograph of her to some roses. On the stems, the green of her eyes had produced emerald glass teardrops in place of thorns. They caught the sun perfectly. He eagerly anticipated the day she might see them.

Today he was pink and purple, with yellow rays (where old skin grafts were acting up), and very festive. He was going to be a multicolored man attending the Lodi Fair, an event he thoroughly enjoyed. Now that he had entered his sixties, it was important to get out as much as possible.

At the post office, he lifted his hat courteously to the young man behind the counter and inquired, "You've heard, I hope, that the fair is in town?"

"No," said the young man briskly, stamping the postmark on Helio's letter. "No time anyway."

"Surely there is always time for the fair," said Helio, clutching the lion's head of his walking stick. "One should always be on the lookout for wonders."

"Don't you have anything smaller than this ten-dollar bill?"

"I believe I may have the proper change." Helio paid his postage, and when he doffed his hat again, the young man shrugged. Helio profoundly missed Viriato, who had moved to Los Angeles the previous year to open his heteronym business in a place where he would be more likely to earn a steady living from it. As a greeting, Viriato used to bellow out the colors Helio was on a given day, and after posting his letter they sometimes shared a bit of whiskey until Viriato's boss interfered.

Helio's favorite booth at the Lodi Fair was always the one with the thaumatropes. People were invited to paint or sketch designs on both sides of a disk that was then revolved fast in a machine, so swiftly that the image on the first side lingered in a spectral flash as the image on the second side instantly twirled around to meet it. The two designs grafted into one picture that hung in midair. Faces could be superimposed on other faces, or a ship on one side of a disk could be put into a bottle on the other side. The display was to demonstrate the endurance of vision and the way that the eye clung to its afterimages. The machine proved that ghosts persisted, even after something was hidden from view, waiting for another impression to join with it.

"Hey! You in the hat! Wanna try?" asked the barker.

"You have read my mind," said Helio. The man no doubt recognized him from the previous years. Helio propped his walking stick against a wall—with its lion's head outward to scare away thieves.

He colored a disk with Clara's swans and exclamations over his New World on one side, then turned over the disk to put a fermata on the other side. The man operating the machine let him do as many as he liked. By repositioning the fermata each time on its separate side, Helio was shown:

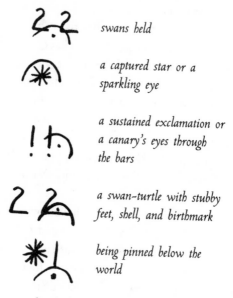

swans held

a captured star or a sparkling eye

a sustained exclamation or a canary's eyes through the bars

a swan–turtle with stubby feet, shell, and birthmark

being pinned below the world

Onlookers applauded, and a larger audience gathered. A patch on Helio's hand changed in happiness from bruise-colored to rose.

"My good man! Your disks are so bright, they're ideal for this next glorious marvel. Brand new to the fair just this year!" purred the barker, slapping another metal contraption.

"I am all yours," said Helio, surrendering his disks. Their vividness lent itself to another visual truth: Colors, either alone or in combination, blur into white or clearness when spun rapidly. He was unaware of this until the barker threw a switch and the disks sped faster than the first machine, fast enough for everything to leap away, and the whole design—the astonished swans, the New World, and the holding—passed into lightness.

At first terror clutched him at seeing how quickly his designs could disappear before his eyes, but then he realized that of course everything was still there, whether visible or invisible. It told him what he had, in his solitude, sensed deep down but had not known how to diagnose: These last years had never been a blankness! Here was scientific confirmation! He had been whirling Clara so fast in an embrace inside himself that what appeared to be a vacancy in his life was actually her colors, and his, and the shades of the globe surrounding them, blurred into light as he spun with her in his heart. Together they made a white swan.

He departed the fair, thinking, This discovery about our spinning would be grander, Clara, if you were finding it with me.

CLARA RETURNED TO the Azores for the first time since her childhood, ostensibly to learn some new fish-scale techniques to apply to her business in Miami, but she and her husband, Michael, both knew it was to contemplate a separation once again. Douglas had lasted as far as the end of the country before vanishing, and she had married Michael after a string of men, for no better reason than that she was weary and he was decent. Partly this trip was just a continuation eastward, but mostly it was so that she could worry, without telling Michael, about the possibility that she might be pregnant.

Terceira was smaller than she remembered, but she knew that was to be expected, and although she had Portuguese words inside herself, she had never spoken the language. She was a stranger coming home after twenty years, but there were pleasant surprises. She had forgotten how delicate the houses were in the village of Agualva, whitewashed and trim. The Serpa Pastelaria remained open, run by people she did not recognize. The hydrangea-walls rolled in a mighty purple crisscross over the hills. She visited her old house and the residents invited her in. There was the mantel, where the queen conch had rested! The shell was gone, but Clara ran her fingers over the holes where her mother had nailed the kitchen curtains, hoping their tautness would pick up her father's singing.

She knocked at Maria Josefa's door and it gaped, revealing a tiny white-haired woman who peered at her through heavy glasses. Then her hand flew to her mouth and she pulled Clara toward the kitchen. She almost overturned the sugar bowl in her excitement as she sprinkled grains on her head. ("Come kiss me.")

Clara hugged her. Maria Josefa could not speak English and Clara could not speak much Portuguese, but they could communicate with sugar. Maria Josefa poured them both glasses of port and offered a tin of wine biscuits. She said in sugar that she was a widow and her children were grown and gone. Eugénio lived in Toronto.

America-shape, patted out by Maria Josefa. ("How was the New World?")

Smooth and rough patches, by Clara. ("There is almost too much to tell . . .") Fish-shape. (". . . but I haven't lost what you taught me with scales.")

Flower-shape + thread, by Maria Josefa.

Sugar clutched in fist, interrupted Clara. ("I'm really here for the Feast of Our Lady of the Pears. Is today the day we make the flower carpet?")

A mound of sugar with a thumbprint in the center, by Maria Josefa. ("You'll stay here, of course . . .") Eye-shape. (". . . and I have something to show you.")

She led Clara to the back room, in which there was a bed, an old upright piano, and cartons with what had to be several hundred letters. Clara sensed what they were with a clarity that made her lungs beat like wings. She ran back to the sugar-eyes and covered them with her hands. ("I can't read.")

Maria Josefa removed Clara's hands from the eyes. ("I'll read them for you.")

They were from Helio, every one of them postmarked on a Friday, the day of the week when they had met eight years before. Maria Josefa opened one and frowned: They were written in color. Clara pointed to her heart to indicate that she was a color-thinker. Maria Josefa rose, kissed her, and left her with the flood of Helio in the room. Most of the letters implored her forgiveness, some were chatty with Lodi's gossip, and a few repeated his hope that she might someday receive these, since Maria Josefa's house was the only address he could attach to her. She color-read about the lighting of her shrines that had led to the fire, and about the roses grafted to her picture.

"I thought we had all possible loves," one letter concluded. "I loved (and love) you father to daughter, and man to woman, but why had I never considered loving you son to mother? My Clara." She took to her bed, gesturing to Maria Josefa that she needed to rest before the festival. How desperate she had been to run away to new people and places, and yet here she was, back at her origin, defeated in her dream of fleeing her history. It was never a battle she should have—*could* have—undertaken. No one had talked to her in color for years, and it struck her that love's purpose was not merely the imparting of courage; it was not some blessing of the ships that propelled one on an aimless voyage; love was its own arrival as well as its own end, as surely as her past was immutable. It was a past that belonged to her, *was* her—the truth of that could never change. Right now the history that she carried seemed as important a part of her future as the unknown events still ahead. She ran her hand over the bed's wooden headboard. What did she look like grafted to a rose? Did she really have the power to induce emerald tears? He knew so many things about her that she did not know herself.

She awoke to the sounds of the Feast of Our Lady of the Pears. Flags were flying in front yards—Portuguese, Brazilian, French, Canadian, and American—to announce where the grown children of the houses had emigrated. Everyone was hammering together cross frames and stencils for the flower carpet. The wooden alveoli were then filled with dyed sawdust and diced petals. The stencil was lifted, repositioned, and re-filled, creating one continuous belt that connected with the segments of the carpet made by the neighbors on both sides. Some designs were very plain and others intricate, with many convolutions and inner boxes, spokes, and latticework. The carpet wound through the streets and met at the crossroads, unfurling blue ladders, yellow gyres, and parallelograms of minced azaleas, hydrangeas, and lilies of the Nile. There were squarish pears and stylized daisies made from neon-pink, green, and violet sawdust.

Clara helped Maria Josefa nail together a wooden man. They dumped different jams into every corral of the stick figure. He had jade-lime eyes, lemon arm- and leg-cells, and a mouth and triangle of red preserves inside his chest, but the sun soon dissolved him into disjointed soups and then crystallized him into sugar. Clara tried to help her swat away the flies that hummed as they blotted out the man, sticking to him until he was nothing but a teeming blackness. Covered with a sheet, the trapped flies jabbed upward, making the man alive in tremors and jolts as he shook his fists against live burial, demanding, How can this be how I end—a rug of insects, puddles under cloth!

(O, Tio Vitor, sacrificed inside the land!)

For her link of the carpet, Clara pieced together rough wooden diamonds to make Helio's whale-eyes. Mocha-colored balsa shavings for irises, lavender sawdust for halos around the eye sockets, coriander for eyelashes, shredded lilies for the whites of the eyes. She centered pictures of herself upside down in the squid ink–darkened dust of the pupils.

When she noticed an elderly man with bloated hands, she squealed, "Henrique!" and jumped over the flower carpet to run to him.

"Baby!" he shouted.

His hands were heavy as pillows as he hugged her and patted her back. They could speak English, because Henrique had been a dairyman for a few years in Connecticut, but he had milked so many cows there hoping to save enough money to buy a vacation house in the islands that his udder-hands each had doubled in size and he could no longer work. "But why have you returned to this boring little place?" he asked.

"To say hello to you, silly."

"I can't believe that I'm hearing you talk." He escorted her in the promenade of villagers circling the streets as they pretended to inspect the flower carpet while inspecting one another. When he asked her about Father Eiras, she said that he had lost the land but that she had not regained it either. She omitted any mention of having had his child.

"That sorry bastard. Your father used to make me laugh, the way he complained about him freeloading at your house. And you see, your father was right."

She pointed to some hydrangea-walls and said, "Why don't we walk over there, and you can tell me everything you know about my father and mother."

He offered one of his teatlike fingers so they could hold hands. She listened intently until he began telling something he referred to as the tale of the big cow riot. She grew drowsy in the cottony air that reminded her of the goat-bar, and inside her eyelids she retained Helio's lavender and mocha gaze. When she and Henrique returned to the village, the festival's procession was ready to start. Young girls in white and deacons carrying biers of Our Lady, Saint Anthony, and Saint Joseph or swinging thuribles of myrrh trampled the carpet. Women followed them with brooms, because in recent years spectators had become hysterical, once the celebrants passed, to see their tapestry so soon in a shambles, and they needed to remove it quickly. But the shape and colors of the whale-eyes, even after being swept away, remained soaked into the ground. Maria Josefa scrubbed the eye-stains, but she could not undo them, any more than she had been able to wash away shadows almost two decades before. Everyone was flabbergasted at the permanence of the eyes.

Clara enlisted Maria Josefa's aid in painting the keys of the piano in her room different tints, using the dyes available from coloring the flower carpet's sawdust. Maria Josefa admitted that this was strange, but she was delighted that Clara had come up with a way of covering the dirty cracks on the keys.

"Now then," said Clara, settling herself on the bench. "A concert." She played some of Helio's color-letters, stringing them together into one swelling, until the walls of the room drooped away like ripe petals and she was floating high above the islands, seeing everything. She was speaking back to him in music what he spoke to her in shades.

"God," said Maria Josefa, sighing. "You are cutting open my heart. Paint the piano anything you want. Paint my whole house."

When Clara stopped and looked at the envelope, at her name in fishhook alphabet letters, the shock hit like the sound of shattering glass: She could read her name, written in his hand! She could recognize the address, with its numbers! Nor was color-reading lost to her in compensation. When she embraced Maria Josefa, the old woman thought it was from the joy of the music, but for Clara it was from the joy of everything found.

Outside, the whale-eyes remained vibrant on the ground. She touched them good-bye; she was going to visit the big island of São Miguel, her mother's birthplace. She journeyed to the Vale das Furnas, where a devil writhes in a famous patch under the surface, his brimstone exhalations turning the ground into cracked, dried lips. His gimlet tears bore upward into geysers. Craters of boiling mud and sulfuric steam thicken the air. Children are warned to stay away from the hot springs in this valley (one a year is claimed by the scalding spray), but visitors are generally not afraid of this devil. She joined some tourists sprinkling coarse salt over pots of cabbage, red peppers, garlic, carrots, turnips, onions, black sausage, hens' breasts, and chunks of pork leg. They covered the stew with cabbage leaves, tied the lid securely to the pot, placed it in a burlap sack, trussed the neck with twine, and lowered it into one of the natural furnaces to cook for several hours. They told her that in her grandmother's day, a dead, plucked, and cleaned chicken would be stuffed with pork and vegetables and lowered without a pot into the steam.

Mineral pools of ham stock–colored water lay on the other side of the evil valley, and clear water ran from between the rocks. Clara drank a handful. Here was relief, a refreshing drink on the other side of a land of sorrow. She could see her reflection in her handful as she brought it to her lips, although much of it trickled away from her.

Not far away were the Terra Nostra gardens, where tropical plants flourished and eight gazebos were scattered. Clara entered one. It was said that everything uttered in a gazebo could be heard in the far-flung others, and her breathing mingled as part of the octet's:

Clara heard the great-granddaughter of a Weaver of Angels, someone to whom unwanted newborns used to be given. They were drowned, suffocated, or exposed to the cold after a make-shift baptism by the Weaver so that they would die as pure innocents, woven into a band of cherubim before the world could turn them evil. "Forgive my ancestor the Weaver of Angels! I cannot sleep at night because you babies beat your wings against my head! Forgive her, and leave me alone!" called the woman.

Through a fog around the second gazebo emerged the croon-ing of a sufferer of *Sebastianismo*, the faith that King Sebastião, who fell during the battle of Alcácer Quibir and whose body some claimed was never found, would return one day in the mist and lead the Portuguese to an enchanted age. "I am here, Your Majesty!" said the Sebastionist mournfully. "I await you!"

Clara heard, from the third gazebo, the spirit of a nun who had diverted her longings onto vanity-dolls. These were the puppets or cotton creatures whose purpose was to absorb the follies and vain desires of their owners. When the nun coveted a new pair of earrings, she gave them to her dolls instead. She painted new dresses on their bodies when she yearned to attend a fancy dance. When she craved a man, she covered the dolls with flowers blooming wide on their thighs. "Dolls!" sang the nun. "You're fired! You did a terrible job of sapping desire out of me!"

Tio Vitor, clear of vines, drinking his champagne, was lounging in the fourth. "Glory be, kitten," he drawled. "We meet again. See? And you thought you were rid of me."

A bird flew from the fifth gazebo. "Mamãe," said its wing. "It is I!" It was her son's hand, dashing upward, its bones identical to those in the wing, to clutch the light.

Her father, José Francisco Cruz, shouted from the sixth, "Clara, that water you drank between the valleys of heaven and hell was your Soup of Sorrow. It is your sadness that you must first pass through an infernal landscape to find it; it is your joy that you know it when it is in your hands, but even then much of it slips through your fingers."

"Papai, I've guessed about the single sugar grain you gave me that disappeared from the handkerchief where I kept it. You were saying, 'I am gone but not-gone. Maybe I am dead and missing—what am I but a single crystal?—but look more closely! I have permeated the whole fabric I left behind.'"

"Simple, eh?" He grinned. "And the sugar rock wrapped in paper that you presented to me: 'Do not worry about the blank pages of your future. Sweet mountains are hiding inside them.' You know, my angel, that's been your problem. You push onward so hard that love and beauty drop away. Let them be a platform on which you stop, high over time. From there you will be able to see forward and backward, into the past and the future, but you will stay suspended in the present. That will find you the whole world, in a way that collecting names and places cannot."

"I know, Papai."

When she heard her mother calling from the seventh gazebo,

she wordlessly headed there—ran. She was finally going to hold her mother's outstretched hand. "Mamãe," she said, and her mother's eyes closed with relief. Her hands trembled toward her daughter. At last she would be able to relax in paradise.

BACK AT MARIA Josefa's house in Agualva on the island of Terceira, there was a note saying that she was with relatives on the island of Faial and that Clara should make herself at home. When she saw the whale-eyes still burned into the ground, waiting for her, she took out a piece of paper and paused with a pen in the air. She settled its point onto the paper, pushed it sideways and up and down, her heart beating hard enough to accelerate the rhythm of her hand. Writing in fishhook letters had returned to her, although her script was shaky. She wrote:

> Rua Mãe de Deus
> 22
> Angra do Heroísmo
> Terceira, Açores
> Summer 1998

Hello sweetheart,
I hope this reaches you. As you can tell, I'm in the Azores. An even bigger surprise is that I am writing this myself! When I played your color-letters on the piano, it all came back to me. I am terribly sorry to hear about your injuries and very glad to hear that you are better now. I wish I had known. What's new with me? Well, I make a living with my fish-scale work in Miami (thank you for getting me to do it again). At the moment my husband and I are separated and I don't know where that is going. (I'm just trying to bring you honestly up to date and hope that doesn't hurt your feelings.)

The color-letters are wonderful. They make me cry.

How many times did you ask me to forgive you? I'm the one who needs you to forgive me. Can you, please? I imagined there were many worlds for me to discover, and when I was younger I thought that whatever was beyond me had to be a better place somehow. But I don't always think things through. I realize it is possible to have the entire world with someone, the world that makes the idea of "other worlds" seem like fragments. It was not *a* world but *the* world when we made words and colors sing, and when I had you. Does it help to know that you have never left me?

Love & Saudades,
Your Clara

Under her alphabet name, she signed the color-name he had given her: a pearl wave, framed with gold.

Her relief was so tremendous after mailing the letter that she dived into the ocean. While stroking through the water, she exclaimed to herself, I used to think, after my boy died, that I was swimming in the bile of evil frogs when I was swallowed in the green waves, but I was an idiot! I have been alive inside my child's blinking green eyes! The sea is his aqueous humor! The frogs were yelling at me, and are still chanting: "Green! Everywhere! You are bathing in him, and because you kept him in your womb, he is lighting your way in thanks!"

For she had never lost what she had carried close to her heart.

LODI WAS NEARING the close of its annual three-day Dot-Drawing Festival, during which the thousands of pointillist hands that Helio had produced daily over the years were lined through the fields near his house, pinned to an army of billboards erected for the purpose, with numbered cards indicating the correct sequence. The festival was held every August 26, with an increase of 365 drawings each successive time, and a side exhibit featured a few of Clara's *morte-macaca* fish-scale pictures, donated by their owners.

Visitors were running through the fields to set the hands in motion and watch Helio age. He himself, awkward at these events but also pleased, ladled out punch—a decent compromise, he felt, between hiding and milling about. Caliopia helped. They were allies at these events. Her dimming eyesight could register only the hands dotted in color during the height of the Clara phase, and she needed an escort over the uneven terrain to get to them. She knew that she provided him with an excuse to stand unabashedly contemplating this display of the color-hands, and that was fine with her. Ever since he had given her a puppy to be Luís IV, she was fond of granting him small gifts.

"Ready for your stroll?" he asked, trying to sound casual.

"No, not yet," she teased.

"I think some kids are smudging a week of my late fifties. We have to go tackle them."

"A rumble! How lovely."

They walked slowly, neither of them regretting that they could not run fast enough to blur the hands into a moving stream. They both understood that they were going to study the portion that was itself the most alive because it was from the days of active love rather than the remembered love for Clara that would remain until and including his final day. Helio's own hand (blue and brown today) could not resist touching the dots that Clara herself had added to the pictures. The crowds jostled him and Caliopia as she squinted to take in the speckling of hues that opened his palms into rivers. Helio did not mind that he no longer was doing his best work; it made the color-segment stand out more as a jewel in the center of his days.

"What if you'd dotted pictures of your face instead?" asked Caliopia.

"No," said Helio. Rows of his empty grasping stretched over the land. "This way I've left the record of wanting to hold something."

Caliopia patted his arm. "You have indeed."

The workers were collecting the pictures in order, since it was the festival's last day, and the finale, for those who lacked the stamina to run or who wished to revel in the process again, was about to start. Some teenagers, drinking beer and yelling, hurried to grab a spot near the stage and almost knocked Helio and Caliopia over. Many participants were wearing the souvenir glasses that superimposed on everything seen through them the flecks of muscae volitantes, the attack of flylike dots on his eyes that had inspired this project long ago, after reading his father's notebook.

"Another successful year," said Caliopia.

He never knew how to respond to such a pronouncement. His days had fallen into a sufficiently pleasant rhythm, yes, and the festival was increasingly popular, but was that success? Maybe. He believed that the best a lone man could do was to mark with ceremonies whenever he did something that told life it could not perpetually dash onward, leaving him behind. That was more like it: Success was whatever lodged a protest against life's bad habit of moving ruthlessly along. Not that time obeyed such a wish; the millennium would not fail to arrive in two years.

He lingered on the outskirts of the crowd with Caliopia,

amidst murmurs of "That's the artist!" and "Strange looking!" and "Yeah. He's strange looking because he got caught on fire."

"Sss, sss, sss," said Caliopia to hush them.

"Ladies and gentlemen!" shouted the master of ceremonies. "Behold!" Attendants stepped forward one by one, riffling successive stacks that each contained one year, and Helio's young hand shrunk old once more. Everyone was charmed, although a few gasps transfixed the audience when the hand passed through its era of being torn by flames. During the concluding applause, the workers busily restacked the pictures in reverse order.

"Here we go!" said Caliopia. "My favorite part."

"Mine too," agreed Helio.

"Ladies and gentlemen!" the master of ceremonies boomed over the fields. "Don't blink; don't move! The highlight of the show is about to commence!"

Helio's years were riffled backward and he dissolved from old to young. He watched his hand leap from being gravebound to being tumescent, plump, and cheery with water. Bravos were unleashed at this mockery of death and everyone bid farewell to the hands that would be resealed in a vault until the next August 26, when the artist would live, dive into his own demise, and live again.

"Go on," whispered Caliopia, feigning exasperation. Part of their ritual was that he would escape before he could be called onto the stage, and she would cover for him.

"You're sure?"

"Get out of here before they haul me up there too. And don't insult an old lady. I can get home myself."

At first when he saw the airmail letter in his mailbox, he assumed that one of his own had been returned to him. He took it out and held it, staring. Today's hand would have to be dotted out as shaking! It was the letter he had been awaiting—not merely for the last five years, but for his entire life. The 22 in the return address jumped out at him. She had sent swans—two of them, floating! He fled to the neighboring gardens to climb an orange tree, because he needed to read it up in the air. He ascended with the letter in his mouth (a pirate with a sword between his teeth, storming the rigging!) and settled against a bough. Strangers covered the land in the distance, but he was alone with Clara.

He wept as he read the letter slowly, for the first of what he already envisioned being countless times. His whale-eyes magnified the waterfall of his tears into a cascade. His medical training had taught him that by covering an eye, focusing on a waterfall, and then quickly looking at another object such as a rock, the object would stream upward. He stared through his waterfall of tears, then covered an eye and glanced swiftly at the 22.

The swans soared into the blue.

He was flying with her!

She had bestowed upon him a last link in finding a formula for a resurrection of bodies:

1. Do you love someone? Twirl him or her in an embrace until colors blur into lightness, and you will be swans. Cry when your beloved is not there, because your waterfall can also make you transcendent: Until you feel the sorrows of love as well as its joys, you cannot possess love in its entirety.

2. Next, eye-paint your beloved pink, the Azorean color of dreaming. (Or study yourself in a mirror, and be your own pink swan.)

3. Note how the pinkness is music, because as a swan you are singing an aria. Note how you are language, because of the lyrics.

4. You contain shades spun into paintings, and you can sing and fly. You are resurrected as a body of art.

Holding her letter to himself, he would stay for all time right now; he would sing to her, speak with unearthly language, and transmit shades; he would feel this moment to such a degree that she would not be absent; he would postpone his descent forever.

Let this suspension be divine.

A strange gladness possessed the weary Helio: Sun-lobsters with feelers and tails poured through the cutouts formed by the leaves where he sat in the orange tree. The sky swarmed with the world in reverse, with sun-carp, sun-octopi, sun-dolphins, sun-tuna. Air hummed through the cutouts to make a wind song out of the marine life. The long rays bursting forth dabbed sun-lobsters everywhere. Later on he would trace their contours on the leaves to trap some of them. He would gather several of these light-animals—here were the plants that captured the realm of the spirit! The bouquet for Clara and her son was complete! What erupted from his heart for all the living and the dead was:

> *Join me in singing "The Canticle of the Sun-Lobsters."*
> *What we have tear-sown is what shall be reaped with rejoicing.*
> *Luminous soul-singing blooms; enter a season of joy,*

because he was looking down at the garden furrows where Clara's son, her continuance, her legacy, had dripped from his chest. Plants had grown tall around the spots laid bare by blood, outlining in vivid green what everyone thought had disappeared. The tallness of the grasses had hidden it from view. From his lofty perch he saw that the boy's heteronyms lived, spelled out, scored as if by branding irons on the ground. The tears shed by the mourners who had carried him had seared out round musical notes surrounding the proclamation of the blood. The dappling had actually increased tenfold, had been growing without end. No one had seen it before because it required the vantage point of the sky. And so it was and so be it he was uplifted, for the dead patches of salt and heartshedding on the earth had burned clean with accompanying music a living word:

A . . . men

He was so astounded that he received the light within an animal, and the light that was without an animal, as a sun-whale swam into his open mouth and onto his tongue. He could scarcely believe how clearly the child of her heart had been calling out, how insistently those who were missing sowed their bodies and their prayers. Now when climbing the lobster-trees, or picking squash marrow, or digging up potatoes with eyes—before all of it, Helio would think, I'm going out to play with my new hero, who left his signature in the world! He stood in the tree and shouted, "Clara! Love! I doubt I shall ever see you again. But you here abide, with me and with what was born from you! This instant is our eternity."

CLARA, RESTLESS, ALONE in Maria Josefa's house in Agualva, felt summoned to the tinted piano in her room. She matched each piano key's colors as she painted them in unbroken streams spilling over the ledge of the piano, down its wooden case, down the legs, across the floor, and toward her bed. She brushed the eighty-eight ribbons in continuous lines up the bedposts and over the sheets, stopping where Helio lay during dreams in which she was certain he was sleeping beside her. She brought the color streams up to this outline, surrounding a blankness of him with dozens of chromatic umbilical cords tying him to the piano. The memory of his shape deserved to rest within a vortex of the tones he had woven so often into a net of singing, of shades, of poetry. But what good was it if he were not present to share it with her?

He was.

He was calling to her from this open patch on the bed, saying, "I am a lake, because the happiness of being beside you is rendered in particles of water. It is white because the eighty-eight colors you have brought me have fallen into the water and I am spinning them into a luminosity. They come from a piano, so there is also music here."

She answered him, "And there is language too, since I can hear you speaking." The pearl song of his starfish-heteronym sang from the lake:

> Barroco barroco barroco the purling sound
> ascending into lace purls,
> purls lace into ascending sound.
>
> Instead of dying of grief, it is better to live in joy.
> Live saying Pinxit. Scripsit. Sculpsit.

Saying *Floruit:* My soul did, yours did,
and so did our masterworks flourish,
and in being done we created ourselves forever.

She gathered up the paint-soaked bedclothes and held them as if looking down at a child lying across her arms, wondering, I must decide what to do next. Here is the reality of it: Can one go back to a source of majesty once it has been overthrown? If I were to return to Helio, wouldn't the same dilemmas resurface? What about the difference in our ages? If I'm pregnant, should I return to my husband? Will the baby survive? Should I go to Lodi? How would Helio feel about it? Or shall I go forward toward something completely unknown?

And the lake that was draped over her lap, with the colors of its shores smearing her arms, replied: Do not decide anything now; hold me. Do not plan or worry beyond this present instant in which I am with you. In which I am art and music and words with you. Let us sculpt this moment to be everlasting like no other. For here is the seal from which all grace comes: We must create Pietàs in order to live. Flesh that is torn, flesh that is dead or dying, even as it is rotting through your fingers—hold it next to your heart. Find ripe and tender flesh too, and hold it in your arms, because your life depends upon it. Whatever you choose, hold it for as long as you can, and ask for its blessing.